ROWDY

BLACK OPS MMA BOOK 2

D.M. DAVIS

www.dmckdavis.com
Cover Design by D.M. DAVIS
Cover Photo by DepositPhotos
Editing by Tamara Mataya
Proofreading by Mountains Wanted Publishing & Indie Author Services
Formatting by Champagne Book Design

This book is a work of fiction. Names, characters, places, and incidents are either the product of the author's imagination or are used fictitiously.

The octagonal competition mat and fenced-in design are registered trademarks and/or trade dress of Zuffa, LLC.

This story contains mature themes, strong language, and sexual situations. It is intended for adult readers.

ABOUT THE BOOK

D.M. Davis' ROWDY is a messy, meant-for-me, sexy, contemporary romance and Book Two in the Black Ops MMA series.

ROWDY:

You think this is a love story. You're wrong. It's a massacre.

A massacre of who I think I am,
where I come from,
and who I thought I'd have a future with.

One wouldn't have me.
The other couldn't.
Both stole my heart.

You think you know me. You have no idea.

REESE:

He thinks I'm a lion.
I'm really a mouse,
afraid of the demons nipping at my heels.

No one can touch me.
No one except him.
I don't fear his touch.
I crave it.

Darkness is my enemy,
yet his Shadow doesn't scare me.

He's the only dark I'm not afraid of.

When their pasts threaten to topple their future, can the lion and her beast prevail, or will the darkness overtake them?

NOTE TO READER

Dear Reader,

First off, thank you for picking **ROWDY** as your next read. I'm deeply grateful and appreciative, and for that reason I want to advise:

For maximum enjoyment, I suggest the **Black Ops MMA** Series be read in order to fully experience the world and the characters who inhabit it.

Please start with NO MERCY before diving into ROWDY.

XOXO, Dana (D.M. DAVIS)

PLAYLIST

Bruises by Lewis Capaldi

Under the Bridge by Red Hot Chili Peppers

I Should Probably Go To Bed by Dan + Shay

Fall by James Arthur

Simple Man by Lynyrd Skynyrd

Natural by Imagine Dragons

Is it Really Me You're Missing by Nina Nesbitt

Run Run Run by Ashley Hess & Leo Cody

Tear In My Heart by Twenty One Pilots

Grow As We Go by Ben Platt

Speechless by Dan + Shay

Savage Love by Jawsh 685 & Jason Derulo

Maybe by James Arthur

10,000 Hours by Dan + Shay & Justin Bieber

Bodies by Drowning Pool

Running by James Bay

Fire Away by Chris Stapleton

Never Gonna Be Alone by Nickelback

Let Me Love the Lonely by James Arthur

Best Part of Me by Ed Sheeran feat. YEBBA

Rowdy's fight entrance song:

Wolf Totem by The HU feat. Jacoby Shaddix of Papa Roach

DEDICATION

For my sister, who was brave in ways that I am not.

I miss you every day.

1976 – 2019

ROWDY

BLACK OPS MMA BOOK 2

CHAPTER 1

CAMERON "ROWDY" JENKINS

YOU THINK THIS IS A LOVE STORY. YOU'RE wrong. It's a massacre.

A massacre of who I think I am.

Where I come from.

And who I thought—hoped—I'd have a future with.

I set off from Texas to California, seeking my MMA dreams. I'd caught a glimpse of that dream, hitched a ride on the tail of a shooting star. Only it wasn't a star at all. It was an angel.

And she wasn't—*isn't*—mine for the keeping.

She belongs to the devil.

And he has no intention of letting her go.

Like devils do, he took what was his—what had always been his—with no apologies.

And here I am wanting his angel, regretting she's not mine, while at the same time lusting over the devil's sister.

Ironic? Nah, it's my own damn fault. There's nothing ironic about it. I knew Frankie was taken the minute I laid eyes on her. The way she scowled at the sun for having the gall to be sunny and bright when all she wanted was dark and dreary, she was a kindred spirit after my own beat up heart. Only hers was locked up—tight. She denied it. Kinda.

She saw something in me, the same I saw in her: a dark, angry brokenness. A hurt that can only be caused by those you thought would love you, but don't. The ones who should protect you, but chose not to. The ones who go out of their way to stomp on the only good we have in this world—love. Or at least the possibility of it.

For Frankie that was pretty much every guy in her life. Her father. Her asshole ex, Austin. And at the time, Gabriel, the devil himself.

Turns out, he really loved her. He punched through his own issues and came through in the end. Married her.

He makes her so fucking happy, it's painful to watch.

He did that.

I offered, but she turned me down—flat.

She was holding out for the devil who planted his seed in her womb before he broke her heart.

I held her hair while she puked her guts out.

I held her as she cried over *him*.

I wiped her tears, bought stock in Kleenex, and had an endless supply ready at the waiting.

I did that.

She leaned on me.

I let her.

Because I needed her too, her light, her strength, and the simple joy it brought to feel needed. The fact she's sexy as hell doesn't hurt either.

I hadn't felt needed in a long time. Maybe ever. I'd certainly never felt that tightness in my chest when Frankie looked at me. When she smiled. And when she laughed, I swear I heard angels sing.

Corny as fuck.

What I feel for her straddles the line between friendship and the ache to kiss the hell out of her.

What she and Gabriel feel for each other is far beyond friendship. They're soulmates. He's the devil to her angel; though, in the end, he resembles more his namesake, Gabriel the avenging angel, than the devil.

Now, months later in a Vegas hospital waiting room, I'm pacing, uneasy, unsettled, unhinged by the fact Frankie is back there somewhere with her husband, giving birth to their first child.

The one I offered to raise as *my own*, to love better than blood because I *chose* to love him or her. The *one* I was ready to pledge my life to as well as its beautiful mother.

Gabriel is the one holding her hand, not me.

He's the one loving her with all his heart... Not me.

Fuck me and my stupid thoughts for believing I could be what she needed.

I need to punch something—someone. Hard.

Wrangling my wild-ass hair back into a top knot, my eyes land on the striking dark-haired beauty sitting only a few feet away.

Reese, the devil's sister, who I long for in a way that's a little frightening, considering Gabriel would punch my face in if he knew the thoughts that race through my mind at the mere sight or thought of her.

Dirty, dirty thoughts about an effervescent girl who's entirely too innocent for a dark fuck like me.

Are you confused? 'Cause I sure as fuck am.

On one hand my heart longs for Frankie and what we could have—*almost*—had.

On the other, my cock knows who and what it wants, and it's Gabriel's baby sister. Though we're practically the same age, she's a babe in experience compared to me.

She's innocence to my sin.

Light to my dark.

Breath to my void.

One glance and my need to hit something calms, and my heart starts to gallop toward her, aiming for its own angel who looks at me like I could be her savior instead of a crush or a fuck.

I can't.

I'm no angel whisperer.

I'm a fucked-up kid from Texas with my own darkness that will only sully her virginal soul and body.

But still, the aching muscles in my chest and the one in my pants think they've found their homing beacon…their salvation.

I'm so fucking screwed.

A rough grip on my shoulder has me tearing my eyes off Reese to land on Gabriel. His haggard eyes are glazed and barely focused.

"She wants to see you." The gravel in his voice sounds painful, like every word is ripping up the lining of this throat.

No. Fuck, no. I can't see Frankie like this—in labor—having the kid that could have been mine. *Fuck.* "Yeah, okay." I'll do it if she needs me to.

I follow the grim reaper through the maternity ward. The sign up ahead reads *Labor and Delivery.*

Each step feels like I'm leaving skin behind, parts of me falling off, sticking to the linoleum floor with each squeaky step.

I wipe my palms on my jeans, smear the sweat from my upper lip.

Jesus. It's like I'm escorting myself to the gas chamber—voluntarily.

A quick knuckle-rap on the door and Gabriel is pressing through, holding it open for me to follow. As I step forward, he releases it and continues inside, forcing me to catch the door or faceplant into it.

My nails would claw at it if they were long enough. Fuck me till the cows come home, I guess I'm doing this.

On a deep sigh, I step inside.

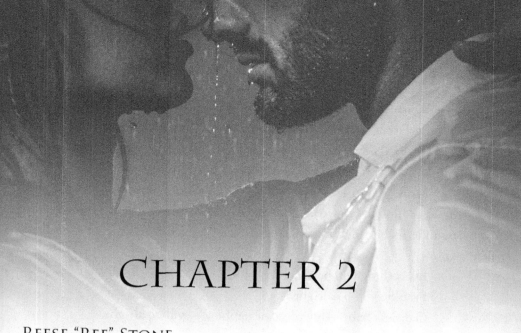

CHAPTER 2

REESE "REE" STONE

THEY SAY IT'S CALMEST BEFORE THE STORM.
It's really dark too, in my experience.
Bad things happen in the dark.
Things you don't want to see... And can never unsee.

It's dark outside, past midnight. I've been here for hours. Sitting. Waiting. Secretly looking at *him*. He barely notices me. On the rare occasion our eyes meet, a flash of something I can't comprehend passes over his face before he steals it back along with his gaze. His blues are so much lighter than my own, pale like a well-worn pair of blue jeans that are soft from washing and fit like nothing else.

He's like nothing—no one—else. I don't fear his closeness. I don't fear the darkness that shrouds him at times.

He's the only dark I'm not afraid of.

Yet, in some ways I am terrified.

I fear the way he makes me feel. The things he makes me want to do. The thoughts that bombard my brain of the wicked things I want him to do to me. What I want to do to him. A shiver runs up my spine. I close my eyes and bite my lip.

No one else does this.

I stay clear of men.

Abuse will do that to you. I'm a quiet wreck most of the time, fearing my father will show up around any corner, behind a closed door, hiding in a dark room. Except when Rowdy is near, which is not nearly enough, the fear dissipates like steam, wafting away.

Mom's hand lands on my bouncing knee. Nervous habit. I get a quick smile but no words. Rarely does she have words for me. But the twinkle in her blue eyes and the dip of her chin tell me all I need to know.

Everything will be alright.

Frankie will be alright.

Gabriel's baby—my niece or nephew—will be alright.

I believe her.

Or at least I believe that *she* believes it.

Mom is a woman of few words. Sometimes when she's cooking, lost in a recipe, she'll chatter away, an unconscious stream of thoughts, her soul reaching out to connect. But if I respond, acknowledge her verbal diarrhea, it'll cease, and the quiet is nearly as consuming as the dark. That's not to say she doesn't speak to me. She does. Mostly nonverbal cues I've learned to read well over the years. A tilt of her head, the slant of a brow, a flash of her eyes, a shrug of a shoulder, a tilt of her lips. The woman is full of things to say. You just have to know how to listen.

My father, the son of Satan himself, made sure my mom forgot how to speak, how to communicate. How to hug her children. How to face the world head-on and say *fuck you*. But we survived my father—thanks to Gabriel. My brother kicked our dad out when he was barely fifteen, but big and strong enough to beat Satan's spawn within an inch of his life for what he tried to do to me—for what he did do to our mother, repeatedly.

Gabriel saved us—saved me.

But still I'm afraid of the dark.

I'm afraid of men.

All except one… Well, and Gabriel, of course.

And maybe…

"Hey, Reese, you doin' okay?" Captain Jimmy Durant eases into the seat beside me after handing my mom a steaming cup of coffee.

My gaze darts to his before finding my fingers.

Damn, Reese, give the man a break. He has purely good intensions.

I slide my eyes back to his kind green ones. "Yeah, I'm good." He wears his fatigue on his face like skin cream, unseen but its effect evident. "You worried?"

Frankie has been in labor for what seems like days, but in truth, it's only been fifteen hours. I think that's kinda normal for first-time moms. Though, I doubt Frankie gives a crap about what's normal. If it feels like days to me, I'm sure it feels like an eternity to her. I'll need to be extra nice to her for not only putting up with my brother but for pushing out his ginormous kid.

Cap leans back, stretching his long legs, crossing his arms and ankles. "Nah, these things take time. Their munchkin will get here when he or she is darned good and ready." He speaks like a seasoned pro, even though he doesn't have any kids of his own.

It's sad. He'd make a good dad. He has enough surrogate kids in his life, so maybe he doesn't feel like he's missing out. But I think it's the kids he could have had that are missing out on having him as a father. I know a thing or two about sucky fathers. Cap would definitely not be one of them.

Yeah, Cap is another man who doesn't scare me. He can be scary at times, especially when he's frustrated and calling my name in that deep, gruff, commanding voice of his when he can't find something on his desk. Usually, it's right where it should be, if he'd remember my new filing system.

I started working for Black Ops MMA pretty soon after Gabriel won his big fight—the one in the ring, not the one to win back Frankie's heart. Cap became busier than ever, forcing him to make the tough call to move his second and newest gym back to Vegas where so much of the action is, and where his first gym is located. Luckily, everyone came with him. Frankie and Gabriel bought a place outside of town not too far from the new Black Ops MMA elite facility. Coach Long, Jonah, Rowdy, and all the other fighters moved too. Cap is like the Pied Piper of fighters. Where he goes, they follow.

The move bringing my brother back to me made me more than happy. I felt settled and a peaceful in a way I hadn't felt since he'd moved away, or, truly, since he'd left for the army. Having my family close and growing is how it should be.

My apartment isn't too far from Gabriel's house or the new gym. Mom's is a little farther out. We may be able to convince her now to sell and buy something closer when she realizes how much time she's gonna want to spend with her new grandbaby.

Cap bumps my shoulder. "Don't worry. That brother of yours won't let anything happen to his woman or child. He'll burn down heaven and hell to keep them safe."

"That he would." A smile warms my lips. He totally would. *Let's hope it doesn't come to that.*

Most of the fighters are here, waiting to see what their king, Gabriel, has. But I'm really only looking for one fighter in particular.

"It's late. Don't worry about coming to work tomorrow—"

"No, I'll be there. You—"

"Take a few days, Reese. Spend it with your family. Be with them."

"Cap," I breathe, surprised at his generosity toward me. I'm not one of his surrogate children. I'm his employee. Maybe it's for Frankie—who he sees like a daughter—and Gabriel, who he'd call son if it wasn't for the fact that he's practically his son-in-law.

If love, not blood, chooses your family, then Cap is Frankie's father.

His focus slips past me to my mom. "I'll make sure she gets home safe." *You don't need to worry about her too,* is what I hear in his promise.

Maybe Mom and I are part of Cap's family, his collection of broken-souled misfits.

I wouldn't mind.

He's a good man. Rough around the edges but smoothed out enough to not get pricked if you get too close.

Pricked. Makes me think of Rowdy, Darkboy, as Frankie calls him. Those two have a unique bond. Gabriel doesn't seem to mind. I, on the other hand, am not sure Rowdy isn't in love with her. I can't blame him. She's amazing. Tough and feisty. Overcoming her own horrific father and ex-boyfriend who treated her like trash.

I want to be her when I grow up.

Maybe if I was, Rowdy would love me instead.

CHAPTER 3

"**D**ON'T JUST STAND THERE, DARKBOY.
Come in," a red-faced Frankie barks from the hospital
bed surrounded by machines.

The sight and smell remind me of the last time she was in the hospital after an emotional confrontation with her ex, Austin. Gabriel had barely shown up in time to save her as she fell down the stairs at Cap's flagship gym.

Austin didn't push her.

It truly had been an accident.

Turned out, Frankie was already pregnant with Gabriel's baby. She just didn't know it. Emotions and dizziness were the culprit.

Moving toward the bed, I shake off the memories of the last hospital visit, her being unconscious and beaten up.

She's fine. She's in labor. She's not hurt. I tell my inner protector to stand down. Not like the man holding her hand would let me throw any testosterone-laden, misplaced ownership in her direction.

We're friends. That's all we'll ever be. I shove my fists in my pockets to keep from reaching for her other hand.

A flash of Reese's face hits me like a two-ton brick in the gut. I'm a messed-up fuck over two women, pulling me in different directions—both a no go.

Gabriel presses a kiss to her forehead. "I'll be right outside." His eyes linger on her, their gazes locked, love pissing all over each other, marking their territory like we all don't know who they belong to.

"I'll be right here working on getting your baby out," she beams at him, corny as fuck.

Kill me now.

His lips twitch, but the budding smile is squashed when his glare swings at me. "Make her cry, I make *you* cry."

"Understood." He's a crazy fuck if he thinks Frankie bursting into tears is not a 200% possibility. "But," I point at the love of his life, "pregnant."

The corners of his eyes crinkle as he chuckles like her hormonal crying is the cutest thing he's ever seen. "Do your best."

With the click of the door, it's just me and the woman I promised my future to. "You doing okay, darlin'? Need anything?"

I swear to God her eyes well up with tears. I feel the impact of Gabriel's pending wrath on my face.

She nods vigorously. "I need this baby out." Tears stream down her reddened cheeks. "Like now." She starts to sob, allowing me to see a little more of her fear than she showed Gabriel.

I move lightning fast, pulling her into my chest as I sit on the side of the bed. "Shh, now. It'll be okay."

This I know. Comforting Frankie is as familiar to me as breathing.

"You got this, Frankie. You're the strongest woman I know." That's no lie. She's been through so much and has come out stronger for each and every trial and tribulation.

While I rub her back, she fists my shirt, squeezing me tighter, like I might slip away. "You're pulling away from me," she manages on a shaky breath.

I can't help but laugh. "Darlin, if I hold you any closer, I'll be inside you."

She slaps my arm, her face buried in my chest, the wet of her tears feeling like home on my shirt. "You know what I mean, Darkboy. You've been pulling away, leaving me in the dust."

I knew that's what she meant but hoped she'd let it slide if I made a joke about fucking her. Best friends, that's what you do, right?

"You've got Gabriel and the baby. You don't need me." *Not like I need you.*

"You think I don't need you? That I don't want you in my life? In my baby's life?" She's hurt.

"You know what I mean."

She pulls back enough to flash her wicked gray eyes. "Just because I turned down your marriage proposal doesn't mean I turned down our friendship. It's because I love you so much, I couldn't do that to you. You deserve to find your *one*. And that's not me, Cameron." Damn, she's given-named me. "And you know it. You think you love me, but you don't." My scowl has her smiling and brushing away her tears. "Okay, you're right. I do love you, but I'm not *in love* with you."

"Yeah, I've got that." Don't need the reminder.

She slaps her thigh in frustration. "Dammit, Rowdy, you're not in love with me either. You love me, sure. But you're not *in love* with me. I don't make your dick hard. I'm not the one you fantasize about."

She's got me there. But I also know she could be that.

I don't say it.

She knows.

We shared a hot kiss once. Made me hard. Made her wet. Left us breathless.

We *could* be…more, but we're not. Never will be.

That little spark we both carry for each other doesn't have enough heat to be more for either of us—not without us both feeding it fuel.

Just because it's not our path doesn't mean I don't think about it. She still has me by the heart, even if she never had me by the balls.

"Just because I love Gabriel doesn't mean I don't love and need you." She grazes my cheek, her fingers burning a path into my hair. "You would've made me a good husband and a great daddy to my baby." She blinks away more tears.

And damn if my eyes don't prick.

"But we both deserve epic. Gabriel is my *epic*. You need to pull your head out of your ass and claim *your* epic love. She's waiting for you."

I shake my head, not trusting my voice or my watery eyes not to run over. Maybe I don't deserve epic.

Her forehead hits my chest. The monitor beeps, and she moans through a contraction. I watch the screen and soothe her through it.

When her pain finally ebbs, I've found my voice, "She's too innocent. I can't dirty her. I can't be—"

"Fuck." Her flat palms slap my chest as she pushes back. "You're right. She is innocent, like all of us were at one point, but she's seen some shit in her life. She's not a child, and she's not sheltered or privileged. She may have baggage, Rowdy, but I've never met a man more capable of handling her past and treating her right more than you." She palms my cheek with such tenderness, tears threaten—again.

Pregnancy hormones must be contagious.

"If you don't think she's worth it," she shrugs, "then okay. Let someone else have her *innocence*, as you called it. Let some other asshole *dirty her*, as you say it will. Which," she pokes my chest, "is total crap. A woman losing her virginity is not her actually *losing* anything or getting *dirty*, you asshat." Frankie lies back, wiping the last of her tears. "You could love her right or let some other guy love her wrong. It's up to you."

Damn, that verbal hit hurt. The thought of some guy touching Reese has me ready to rip out lungs and testicles.

"Isn't it up to her?" I mean it's not like she doesn't have a choice.

"Exactly. It's up to Reese if she gives you her innocence." Frankie's hand finds mine. "But it's up to *you* if she chooses someone else Gabriel will have to kill for doing her wrong because she thinks you're not an option."

I'm not even going to touch the whole *doing her wrong* statement.

I may have to piss on her leg, or lick her cheek, at the very least. You know, *licked it. It's mine* kinda thing.

Base? Yes.

Uncalled for? Nope.

Sorry? Double nope.

The monitor spikes, and Frankie's grip on my hand has me wincing for mercy. "Damn, woman. You want me to get Gabriel?"

She nods. "Wait." She pants through another contraction. "I wanted to ask—" a silent cry cuts her off.

"I'm getting Gabriel and the nurse. Your contractions are coming faster."

When I'm nearly at the door, her call stops me. "Rowdy?"

"Darlin'?" Whatever she needs, it's hers.

"I need you to stay in my life. *Be* in my life."

"I'm not going anywhere, Frankie." I turn, taking a few steps back to her bedside. "I mean it."

On a broken bobble-head nod, she rushes out the words, "I need you to be my baby's godparent."

I freeze.

"You hear me, Cameron 'Rowdy' Jenkins? You will be in my life. In my baby's life. You will teach him, or her, the most precious lessons you have in that Texas-sized heart of yours. You hear me?"

Swallowing around the lump in my throat, I give her the only answer I can. "I hear you, darlin'."

"Good." She kisses my hand and squeezes. "Now get me my man so I can push his megasaurus-sized child out of my shocked and terrified vagina."

"I can't unhear that," I mumble, kissing her cheek, then open the door to find a pacing Gabriel. "She needs you."

She's always needed you.

He barrels past me, rushing to her side. "Angel."

"It's time, Big Man. Call the nurse. Call the doctor. Then hold my hand and tell me you love me as I curse your name and bring our child into this world."

He growls, "Fuck, Angel, you made me hard."

Yeah, that's my cue to leave. I'm nearly run over by the nurses running into the room.

All eyes hit me when I step into the waiting room. I'm not sure if they can see the devastation on my face or the concern in my eyes, but I know one person does when I meet her blue gaze.

My heart jumps, and the pit in my stomach eases. "It won't be long now."

CHAPTER 4

MY THERAPIST SAYS I HAVE PTSD FROM A stint not in the military but from growing up with an explosive father who went from zero to nuclear at the snap of a finger, a drop of a glass, an untimely sneeze. Sometimes I thought a flap of a butterfly wing was all it would take to set him off. Never mind a wrong look, a roll of an eye, or in Gabriel's case, a cross word.

Gabriel is three years older than me, but he could be ten for the difference in life experience. He did his best to protect Mom and me. He sheltered me from the worst of it—or at least he tried. More times than not, he succeeded. When he didn't… Well, yeah, not going there. Let's just say my fear of the dark and loud noises are not the only things I'm afraid of—they're not my only triggers.

But at the moment, the world is rushing in as all the air leaves my body because of a stupid noise. I know it was just a rack that got knocked over, the weights clanging and banging as they collided before landing on the mat.

But my fear is telling me *he* is coming.

Any second now I'll hear the bark of his anger and feel his wrath on my cheek, across my back, the twist of my arm.

Pain is coming. It always does.

My back flat against the gym wall, nauseated and sweating like I'm in a sauna, my eyes screwed shut, I slide until my ass hits the mat and bury my face in my raised knees.

It's okay. It's okay. It's okay, I repeat infinitely.

It takes everything I have in my arsenal not to rock back and forth, or roll to my side and cower in a balled-up, fetal position.

He's not here. It's okay. Breathe.

"Reese?" Jonah's voice breaches the buzzing in my head but fear has stolen my ability to speak.

I whimper at his touch. *Please don't touch me.*

"It's okay, Reese."

"Someone turn down the damn music."

Cowboy?

No, I like the music. I focus on the beat, trying to steady my racing heart.

"What the hell happened?" His anger I recognize, but it's a voice I know belongs to a man who will not harm me. He's not angry at me. "What the fuck did you do?" He's closer.

"Me? I didn't do shit. Found her like this." Jonah returns Rowdy's irritation.

"Reese, baby, it's Rowdy." A light touch to my leg.

"I wouldn't do that. She practically growled when I tried to touch her," Jonah warns.

"Obviously, she didn't want *your* touch. Can you get the guys out of here? Give us a minute?"

With my eyes glued shut, I can't see Rowdy, but I feel him in front of me, crouching, easing closer. "I'm gonna squeeze behind you, Kitten."

Panic has me flinching even though I want him closer. "Rowdy," I manage around a sob, trying to warn him.

He won't like it if he finds Rowdy touching me.

"Shh, baby. I won't hurt you. You know that, don't you?"

I'm not scared of you.

Rowdy eases in behind me, placing me on his lap, cradling me in his arms against his large chest. "I won't let anyone hurt you. I promise. No one. You hear me?"

I hear you.

"Not your father. Not a single person will ever hurt you again."

I sink into him on a deep exhale, like I'm not embarrassed by the state in which he found me, like I'm not devastated and lost in the chaos in my head, the fragility of my nerves, the residual fear my father left me with—reasonable or not.

"Shh, Reese. I got you. I got you. I got you, baby," he soothes with words and gentle touches.

Slowly the panic eases.

The buzzing stops.

The tears dry up.

And still he holds me.

He holds me as my breathing evens out.

He holds me as fatigue sets in.

It feels so…good.

Warm lips skim my brow. "I'm gonna take you home, Kitten."

Settled on the couch under a blanket with the bottled water Jonah handed me as we left, I leave my Kitten to scrounge up some food or order in.

Shit. *My Kitten.*

I don't even know where that came from. She's not *mine* despite what my instincts are telling me, and though she was scared shitless by something that happened at the gym—the sight of which I may never recover from—she's no cowering baby animal. I saw—*see* the fire in her eyes. She's more like a lion who's pretending to be a mouse. Gabriel is one tough motherfucker—I know there's some of that in Reese too. We just gotta help her free it.

Speak of the devil, my phone vibrates with a call from Gabriel.

"Who told you?"

"Fuck, man, can't you ever say *hello* when I call? You know it's common courtesy," he fakes a calm I know he's not feeling.

"Want me to open doors for you too? How far are we taking this politeness?"

"Fuck off, Cam. Tell me how she is."

"She's resting." I open the fridge and smile at the jackpot of food. "Damn, your sister eats well."

He chuckles. "Yeah, she likes to cook—it calms her. She gets that from my mom."

Does he get it from her too? 'Cause he's a damn fine cook.

My mind drifts to all the ways I'd love Reese to feed me.

"How'd you get her home?"

I frown at the phone. "In my car." *Why is that relevant?*

"No, I mean how did you physically get her out of the gym and into your car? I know how she is when she's having an episode. She doesn't like to be touched. He—"

"I carried her." Yeah, I don't need those details he was getting ready to share. Any details need to come from Reese herself. Her choice. Her timing.

"She let you?"

His incredulous tone is pissing me off.

"Yeah. Why so surprised?"

"Because she barely lets me touch her with some coaxing, and she *knows* I'd never hurt her." Still that tone, like I can't possibly be worthy of his sister's trust. After my conversation with Frankie, this is feeling a little too close to *Rowdy's not good enough for Reese.*

"She knows I'd never hurt her." It didn't require coaxing either, just a little reassurance, so she knew it was me and not the man in her head. My blood boils at the thought of her father—or any man—laying an unwanted hand on her. Never again.

"Huh." That's all Gabriel says for a few beats as I search her fridge for the perfect comfort food that'll be easy on her stomach.

"Is there something else?" 'Cause I'd really like to focus on food instead of the fear she had on her face, in her voice, and ravaging every cell of her body.

"I was on my way to my car when I called you. I was sure she needed me. But maybe you're what she needs right now." The astonishment in his voice wouldn't bother me nearly as much if that revelation didn't surprise me too.

There's been something between Reese and me from the first moment I laid eyes on her. Corny as it sounds, it's like the heavens opened up and shone a light on her midnight hair, lighting up her blue eyes that are so much like her brother's but with an added depth of hurt I recognize.

My want of her is strong, but the weight of her innocence is daunting.

She's Frankie's family now—another complication if I go for it and break her heart. I can't mess that up if I intend to remain in her life and the life of my godson, Maddox, and they are too important for me to lose over a woman I shouldn't have anyway. "How are Ox and Frankie doing?"

His voice is pure joy when he responds, "They're good, man. So good. It's amazing to watch the love of your life dote on the other love of your life. I had no idea it could be like this."

"Yeah?" Me neither.

My parents have a good marriage, but I'm the second to youngest and pretty much raised myself with help from my little sister who's only a year younger than me. Perhaps we raised each other. My older brother was definitely no help. But this awe in Gabriel's voice, I have no idea what that feels like. I know what it looks like now that I've seen the three of them together.

Ox is only three weeks old. I pray they can keep the love and glow going. What's that old poem? *Nothing golden can stay...* or some shit like that. A good marriage and being a good parent require work. I hope they have what it takes.

I hope *I* have what it takes if I'm blessed enough to experience it.

"Listen, I should probably mention—"

"Don't," I interrupt. "Don't betray Reese's trust to tell me something she wouldn't want me to know."

"Fuck." His frustration buzzes through the phone. "Call if you need anything."

"Yep."

"And, Rowdy?"

"Yeah?"

"Thanks, man. I mean it. She doesn't trust easy, and men... Well, she doesn't trust at all. It's sayin' something you're the one she does."

That affirmation gives me a little glow of my own. I quickly smother it. "Don't read too much into it."

"Don't negate the rarity of this moment."

"I'm not." Trust me. I feel the weight of it growing with each passing second.

CHAPTER 5

AVOIDING ROWDY HAS BEEN EASIER THAN avoiding Cap or my brother. I stayed home the day after my meltdown. Cap understood and told me to come back to work when I'm ready. He's entirely too lenient. I'm going to have to do something about that before someone takes advantage of that man's savior complex. He's entirely too giving. For a guy so big and gruff who barely utters two-syllable words, he's all heart.

It seems my avoidance game has come to an end as I stare down Cap and Gabriel, who chose to corner me in Cap's office.

And by *corner me*, I simply mean Cap nicely asked me to come into his office after he finished talking to Gabriel about me, no doubt.

The palpable silence is deafening as these bigger-than-life men look at me with puppy dog eyes, terrified I might breakdown in tears… Again.

I can't take it. "Look. I know what happened the other day can't happen again. I'm prepared to resign—"

"No one said it can't happen again—" Cap interrupts, only to be interrupted by Gabriel: "The fuck?"

"I mean, this is a place of business. You can't have your employees causing such a scene," I continue.

Cap's rare smile is tender as he ushers me into a chair in front of his desk. "Sit." He orders Gabriel to do the same. Surprisingly, he does.

"Reese, it's not about you doing something wrong or you having to quit your job. I need you. You're the best damn assistant I've ever had. You're not quitting. Unless you're not happy—"

"No. God, no. I'm happy here." *So damn happy it scares me.* "I want this job, Cap."

I *need* this job. I need a reason to get out of bed and out of my apartment every day, or at least five days a week. I refuse to let my shut-in tendencies steal any more of my life.

"Good. I'm happy to hear that. We want you here."

Gabriel turns his chair to face me. "Ree, we only want to help. Make what happened easier on you. Do what we can to reduce the likelihood of an episode happening again."

I thought for sure I was going to be fired for showing my crazy. "Um, I don't want to set the expectation that it won't happen again. It probably will. But—" I smile at Gabriel before meeting Cap's gaze. "Maybe I could talk to the guys, let them know my triggers. Tell them what to do… Or what not to do when it happens."

Airing my dirty laundry is not my favorite thing, but I'm willing to give them this so I can keep my job. It's my lifeline to humanity—to normalcy.

Cap checks the clock. "Let me talk to the guys. Go have lunch, and when you come back, we can meet with them."

"Sounds like a plan." A scary as fuck plan.

But what choice do I have? Live in solitude or face my demons head-on?

Head-on, which means I have to start with letting the guys know what my deal is. Something I've avoided talking about except with my therapist, who I quit seeing a few years ago. Maybe not the smartest move. I couldn't afford her, and I felt like I'd hit a plateau.

Taking this job outside of the house was a huge step for me.

Talking about my damage to the guys will be another massive one.

I'm on the verge of popping a blood vessel as I pour my Reese frustration into lifting more weight than is sane when my kitten comes into view, stealing my breath and garnering my focus.

I set the bar on the rack, snatch up my water and towel and meet her halfway. Pride bursts in my chest that she headed straight for me, not even pretending she didn't come looking.

"Kitten."

She blushes on a beaming smile. "I was wondering if you had time to grab a quick bite. I've got to be back in about an hour to talk to the guys." She glances round the room. "But I'd like to talk to you first."

"Yeah, sure. Let me just clean up. Give me five."

Running on pure adrenaline, I speed through a quick shower, not bothering with washing my hair as I have more working out to do when we get back.

I find Reese waiting for me as I exit the locker room. It's good to see her in the gym looking healthy and sexy as hell instead of curled up on herself on the floor, freaking out about what, I still don't know.

She's been avoiding my calls.

She missed work yesterday, and she didn't answer her door last night when I knocked knowing good and well she was home. Instead of pounding like I wanted to, I left her food on her doormat and a note to at least text me to let me know she's okay. I understand avoiding what makes us uncomfortable. But I won't be ghosted when all I want to do is be sure she's safe and alive.

She finally replied to my calls and texts with one of her own.

Kitten: *Thank you for the food. I'm good. I'll see you at work tomorrow.*

It wasn't much. But it wasn't a *fuck off* either and confirmed she was alive.

Me: *Thanks for replying. I was worried. I'm here if you need anything. See you tomorrow.*

I didn't get a response. I didn't expect one.

I'd hoped for one but understood her keeping her walls up. She needs time to lick her wounds, regroup, and come out fighting.

She's in fighting form today in low rider jeans and a t-shirt that hugs her slim waist and not so slim tits. She's a wet dream if I ever saw one.

The blood rushing to my cock reminds me of my unwavering attraction to Gabriel's sister as I watch the sway of her ass and the swish of her high ponytail on the way to my truck. With Reese settled in the passenger seat, I squeeze my cock, reminding it who's in charge before getting in.

Subs, drinks, and chips laid out between us on the tailgate of my truck under the shade of trees, we take in the serene landscape behind Cap's new gym. Someone with a shit load of money put in a lake. In the desert, that's no small feat. It's beautiful.

I built my house out here, not far away, but on the other side of the lake. I've no idea how Cap found the property or afforded it, but it's a gem of a location to come to every day, or most days.

"Um." Reese tears off a piece of ham, slipping it between her tempting lips. "I wanted to apologize and thank you for what you did for me."

"You've nothing to apologize for, and it was nothing."

She half smiles and nods like she figured that's what I'd say. "You saw my crazy and didn't freak out."

"Does that happen often?" I quirk a brow and take a bite of my footlong, triple meat, all the veggies, vinegar and oil sandwich.

"What? My crazy showing, or someone freaking out over it?"

"Both, I suppose."

"Most people can't handle it." She takes a bite, and we sit in silence, eating until she continues. "As for my damage…" She shrugs. "There's no predicting it."

Damage. Crazy. I don't like her referring to herself like that.

She ignores my scowl. Given her brother has a permanent one, she might not even realize it's not a normal facial expression worn all the time. "Cap is getting the guys together. I'm going to talk to them when we get back."

"What?! Why?" That's ludicrous. "It's none of their damn business."

My Kitten's smile is doing things to my body she wouldn't want to know about. "It's okay, Cam. I need to do this. I need to own my crazy. Give them a heads-up so they don't freak out or try to help in ways that'll only make it worse."

"I can help you." *You don't need those other fuckers.*

"You can't always be there. Gabriel can't always be there."

The fuck we can't. We could set up a schedule, follow it to the letter.

"Besides, I need this. It's time."

Well fuck. I can't take the wind out of her sails, but I sure as shit can be there to ensure she doesn't drown.

CHAPTER 6

THE MURMURS COMING FROM THE GYM GIVE me pause as I stop before Rowdy opens the door. Am I really doing this? The blood pulsing in my ears gives me something to focus on other than what's happening on the other side of those doors.

Reading me like a book, Rowdy steps toward me, his fingers tilting my chin until our eyes meet. "You don't have to do this. You don't owe these fucks anything." His intensity sends a tingle down my spine and eases my worry. He motions to the entrance we just came through. "I can take you out for dessert. We can forget all about this."

God, he's so sweet.

"What kind of dessert?" I have no intention of leaving, but I like this side of Rowdy—sweet, doting, protective. Besides, I'm not one to turn down sweets.

"There's a bakery not far from here. I've heard their seven-layer chocolate-chocolate-fudge cake is awesome."

"I thought you didn't like chocolate." I've never seen him eat a cake that sounds so decadent, much less any other regular sweets—he barely tolerates chocolate chips in his chewy granola bars.

"It's the devil."

A laugh bubbles free. "The devil? That bad, huh?"

"No, Kitten." His fingers graze my cheek.

My head spins at his term of endearment, the heat in his eyes, and the feel of his touch. A touch I've craved for so long but didn't know I could withstand.

To be touched in general is a big deal. The fact *his* touch feels safe when no one else's does—and feels so incredible on top of that? Basically, a miracle.

"That *good*. It's my downfall. I'm in training. I don't eat sweets. But I'll gladly sit and watch you, fantasizing about…" He stops like he hit a mental barrier.

"Fantasizing…about?" Does he fantasize about me? Would he be shocked to know I think of him more than I should, given I'm not capable of doing any of those things my dirty mind keeps showing me?

He clears his throat and averts his gaze, jaw tight as he swallows like he's in pain. "We should go in if you're gonna do this."

I stare at his profile, see if he'll turn his sweetness back on me. When I'm only met with his stiff stature and the side of his face, I step back. "Right." I guess we're done flirting.

He's the sexy fighter from Texas. Women, ring chasers, throw themselves at his feet. He's charming with impeccable manners and a giving heart. He's a catch.

What does he need from a broken mess like me? Not a damn thing.

Stepping around him, I swing open the door to the elite fighter's gym and enter like I'm not terrified of each of these larger than life men waiting at the other end, talking and laughing like they're at a social gathering, only they're in a gym, in tight workout gear, hands holding towels or bottles of water instead of beers.

"Reese," Rowdy calls from behind.

I don't stop walking. "It's fine."

The last thing I need is to break down in front of the guys I work with and admire again, showing them I'm just a silly girl who got her feelings hurt by a big, bad fighter who doesn't want her form of crazy. He might feel protective over me, some misplaced, leftover affection for Frankie. But when it comes down to it, he doesn't want me. Not like I want him.

I don't know what I was thinking. Even if he did want me, I'm not sure I could give him what a sexy beast of a man like him would need—my body, completely, in ways I was suddenly picturing might not be impossible… His touch—*he*—feels so good. So right. But my damage may be too much for either of us to overcome.

There's no point even trying. I'll only embarrass myself further.

My father always said I was a *silly girl*.

"Dammit, Kitten, wait." He grabs my arm, but I jerk away.

"Don't." I lock eyes with him and swallow around the lump in my throat. "I get it." My glare must be sufficient as he steps back flashing his palms in surrender.

"You don't." He licks his bottom lip, and I just want to sink into him and find out what that lip tastes like—what *he* tastes like. Are his lips soft? Would he kiss me back? Would his kiss be hard and demanding or soft and giving? Would he be turned off by my inexperience?

Shit. Not the time, Reese. Get a grip.

My tormentor glances behind me, murmuring, "But this is not the place."

Whatever is going on with us will have to wait. I've got bigger demons to filet. I sigh and face our audience, finding all eyes on me, except for Gabriel, glaring plague on poor Rowdy.

Cap gets everyone's attention as I drop my purse at my feet and join the loose circle of fighters. A flash of panic sets in. I should have thought this through, figured out what I want to say before standing in front of them. I take a deep breath and blow it out. "I wanted to meet with you all to apologize—"

"You don't owe anyone an apology," Gabriel interrupts, his sullen scowl deep enough to cause permanent lines.

I ignore him. "—for freaking any of you out. Sometimes my crazy—"

"No one freaked," Gabriel hisses as Rowdy growls, "You're not crazy."

"Oh my God, you two! Can you let me talk? This is fucking hard enough without you negating each and every word out of my mouth. Chill or leave." I stink-eye them both, ignoring the snickers around the room. I'm sure the guys think of me as the meek girl they see slipping through the halls, trying not to be noticed. But here I am, front and center, demanding two guys who could stomp me to dust shut the fuck up.

"As I was saying, I'm sorry you had to witness my very unprofessional meltdown. I'd like to say it won't happen again, but honestly..." I shake my head, study my shoes for a beat. "It probably will." I meet their gazes. "It's like PTSD—"

"It *is* PTSD," Gabriel interrupts.

I merely glare at him, continuing, "I thought it might be good to open up a dialogue, give you a heads up, tell you what my triggers are and how to deal with me when I'm deep in an episode."

"PTSD from what?"

"What happened?"

"Who hurt you?"

"We all got issues."

The rapid-fire questions and comments catch me off guard as I try to figure out who said what.

Cap steps forward. "Why don't you tell us what your triggers are?"

Thank you. I smile my appreciation. "Right. Triggers. Loud noises, like fireworks, gun shots, any kind of loud bang."

"A weight rack falling over?" Jonah asks.

I nod, giving him the best smile I can muster. He tried to help me last time, and if I could have, I would have bitten his hand off when he was simply trying to comfort me. He doesn't hold it against me.

But I do. "Yeah, a weight rack falling over would definitely do it, especially if I don't see it coming."

"That's what triggered you the other day?" Cowboy asks. He's one of the new guys who came onboard the same time as Rowdy, according to Frankie. He's cute and also from Texas.

Maybe I have a Texas thing.

"Yeah." I blush my response and catch Rowdy glaring daggers at Landry, a.k.a. Cowboy.

"Okay. We got loud noises," Cap interjects. "What else?"

"Dark." I focus on Gabriel as my throat seizes, and I try to catch my breath.

He's in front of me in seconds. "Hey. It's okay. Look around, it's bright as fuck in here. Breathe, Ree."

"Shit. You're scared of the dark?" Sloan's surprise matches most of their responses.

"Not crazy about the dark myself," Jess offers up his own phobia.

I'm sure he's not really scared of the dark like I am. He's just being nice, taking the heat off me. I appreciate it, and it gives me the strength to take a breath.

"Yeah." I touch Gabriel's arm, letting him know I'm alright. "I'm not good in dark places. When I can't see what's coming."

He was always there in the dark.

"Anything else?" Rowdy asks, moving the discussion along.

Of course, it would be him who asks me this one.

"Touch." The backs of my eyes sting when he winces. I look away, not wanting to see his or any of their worried, sorrowful expressions.

"No touching Reese, guys," Cap states what's caught in my throat.

"Damn, okay." I think that was Walker, but I'm too far down the rabbit hole to be sure.

Warmth envelops me. "It's okay, Kitten. You did good." Rowdy kisses my head as I sink into the safety of his chest.

"Hey, what the fuck? Don't touch her!" Cowboy steps forward as if to intervene.

Gabriel stops him cold with a hand to his chest, growling, "Only he and I can touch her."

"Well, fuck. Okay then." Cowboy steps back.

"Reese?" Cap garners my attention.

I pull away from Rowdy and swipe at a stray tear. "Yeah, Cap."

"If an attack happens, what do you want us to do?"

"Don't touch her," Gabriel and Rowdy bark in unison.

"Damn, it's Gabriel and his Mini-me." Jess laughs.

It is kinda funny how in sync these two are.

"Fuck off before I sic my *Mini-me* on you," Gabriel taunts.

"Hey. I'm no fucking Mini-anything. I'm Rowdy, also known as Darkboy, and I'll sic my darkness on you so fast you'll wish I was only the devil himself," Rowdy growls.

Gabriel holds him back.

"Whoa, calm down, there, Ponyboy." Jess is asking for trouble.

"Darkboy," Jonah corrects.

"Who the fuck named you *Darkboy*?" Landry laughs.

"Frankie." "My Angel," Gabriel and Rowdy answer in chorus. They're good at that.

"Enough!" Cap, ever the ringmaster, steps into the fray. "Reese, please tell us what to do or what *not* to do if you have an episode."

"There's not much you can do." I shrug and work on meeting each of their gazes. "If it's dark, power outage or whatever, turn the lights on as soon as possible. Get a flashlight. If it's a loud noise, try to stop it from happening again. But don't, whatever you do, touch me. You can sit with me. Talk to me. Tell me it's going to be okay. Tell me whatever set me off is over, is gone. Just talk to me, softly. Help me focus on where I am. Try to keep me in the now instead of getting lost in my head. Music sometimes helps." The worry in Rowdy's eyes has me glancing back to Gabriel. It pains me to say the next words, "Tell me *he's* not here. *He's* not coming. That I'm safe."

"Fuck," Gabriel sighs and runs his hand through his hair.

"Who is *he*?"

"What did *he* do to you, Reese?"

Questions I can't answer. Thankfully I don't have to.

"It doesn't matter. She just needs to know she's safe. So whichever one of you fucks is around when it happens? Sit with her, keep her grounded in the moment, remind her she's safe and that you won't let anything happen to her. Clear?" Gabriel charges forward.

"Clear."

"Got it."

"No worries."

"And someone needs to call me," Rowdy advises.

"And me," Gabriel insists.

"No," I speak over their voices. "You don't need to call anyone. I just need to know I'm safe. I'll come down on my own." I look between the two of them. "There's no reason to call either of you."

"You fucking call me or Rowdy," Gabriel puts his hand up to stop my rebuttal, "or we'll kick your asses. Understood?"

"Yep."

"Got it."

"Was gonna call you anyway." Jonah winks at me.

Gah, protective assholes, all of them.

I leave them to get back to working out, spreading their testosterone around the room to determine who's top dog. For all I know, they pee in the corners and on the workout equipment, marking their territory as they go.

As for me, I'm exhausted. I grab some files and my laptop from my desk, and send Cap a text letting him know I'm finishing my day at home.

I can only take so much.

My brave meter has run dry.

I've no doubt Rowdy and Gabriel will come looking for me again to talk. I can't face them. The sadness in Gabriel's face when forced to hear how fucked up I am over our father and the fact I had to share my crazy with his extended family. I probably should have quit instead of putting him through that. But, like I said, my brave tank is empty, and I need this job.

Then there's Rowdy. He's only grazed the surface of my damage, but now he knows the extent of my triggers, my fear of the dark like a silly five-year-old who needs her nightlight to feel safe. Not to mention the whole touch issue.

Why he can touch me when no other man, besides Gabriel, can, I don't understand. But it's obvious Rowdy has no intention of touching me more, or doing anything else with me unless I'm having an PTSD episode. Then he's all in. Yay for me.

Pity-driven protectiveness I neither need nor want.

My phone buzzes on the drive home. I don't look. No matter who it is, I don't want to talk. I don't want to be reminded of how *not* normal I am.

For a few blissful minutes I just drive, and drive, and drive.

I thought I was going home.

Turns out I was going to Gabriel's.

I hope Frankie and Ox don't mind a visit from Auntie Crazy.

CHAPTER 7

"**Y**OU GONNA LET ME TAPE UP YOUR HANDS before you bust a knuckle?" Jonah circles the punching bag, giving me a decent glare before accessing the sound system on his phone and turning down the music.

I've been here for an hour, no one else around, so I blared some punk rock the guys can't stand. I'm not overly fond of it myself. I'm more of a Chris Stapleton kinda guy. But the hard, fast stuff gets me going, and I've got energy and aggravation to burn.

"I'm good." I punch the bag so hard it nearly swings into him before he grabs it, but it's the sting on my right hand that has me pulling back to find my middle knuckle split. "Fuck."

"You assholes never listen," he mutters under his breath. "Come on, let's get you patched and properly geared up. Cowboy will be here soon to spar with you."

He continues to grumble as he tends to my busted knuckle and tapes me up.

I know better. It was a stupid move. I'm... out of sorts.

Reese is avoiding me—again. I fucked up after our lunch on Friday, letting it slip I might fantasize about her and a piece of chocolate cake.

Being boldly sexy with her felt so natural in the moment. Such an insensitive slip up. I was feeling it, the connection, and for a split second I forgot who she is. I can't treat her like some chick I've got the hots for. She will never be just another fuck—or even *a* fuck.

Besides the fact she's Gabriel's sister, she's been through stuff I don't even know about but can imagine. Things so dark, I try hard *not* to think about.

"What's got you stupid today?" Jonah asks like he doesn't know. He's the most intuitive fuck I've ever met.

"Nothing."

"Well, *nothing* better get sorted before you blow your fight. You've got less than a week."

Yeah, yeah, way to rub it in.

After a beat of silence and his haunting eyes studying me, he finally speaks, "You're good for her. Don't let her push you away or let your stupidity stop you from fighting for what you want."

"Who?"

Jonah chuckles. "Gonna play it like that, huh? Okay." He slaps my arm. "Get a drink, then get in the ring."

As Cowboy enters from the locker room a second later, Jonah tells him, "Warm up. Rowdy will be ready in a minute."

I slip on my Beats, hit play on "Natural" by Imagine Dragons, and bounce on my feet, shadow boxing between hydrating.

Sparring with Cowboy is what I need. The strikes he lands only center me, give me focus to dig in and fight for what I need. What I want.

It could be to love a dark-haired kitten, but at the moment, it's to destroy the asshole across from me trying to take me down. Not happening. Cowboy, Landry, is good. I'm better.

Showered and walking the parking lot to my car, I dig my phone out of my pocket when it vibrates. I hate that I'm disappointed it's not Reese calling, but my mom. I'm such a shit son. She's called me twice in as many days, and I haven't called her back. My funk is not her fault.

I chuck my bag in the back seat as I answer. "Hey, Mom. I'm sorry—"

"Finally, Cameron. I was so worried." Mom tends to overreact. Silence means I've died or been kidnapped, not that I'm a bad son and forgot or *chose* not to call her back.

"I'm sorry for worrying you. I've got a fight coming up next week." I pull out of the parking lot. "I'm distracted."

Not a good excuse for ignoring the woman who gave birth to me and always made me feel like I belonged in our family, when, in fact, I rarely felt like I fit. Square peg. Round hole. That's me. I'm the only un-civilized one. My great-grandfather made our money from the oil fields in West Texas. We've since moved on to greener resources like wind turbine farms, but I'm the only one not *in the business.*

Business savvy is my older brother Drake's strength, something he reminds me of at every opportunity.

I'm the dumb jock.

He's the brilliant businessman.

Only I'm not dumb. I just don't give a fuck. Renewable energy is crucial to humans and something I care about, but I'm not a suit-and-tie-let's-talk-numbers kinda guy. My ability to withstand a corporate environment—even my family's company—is not a renewable resource...

Drake and my dad can handle the business.

"Oh..." Her disappointment is evident.

"I'm sorry. I'll do better."

"No, no, it's not that. I was just hoping you could come home this weekend."

"I can come after my fight. What's going on?"

She hesitates. "That would be nice. I'd like to see you."

"What's wrong? Is Dad around?"

"Oh, you know your father. He's at the office." He's always working. She loves him, but she'd like to see him more.

"Mom." She's avoiding my question, and she sounds off.

"Just come home when you can."

In a t-shirt and sleep shorts, face washed, hair up, I'm about to dig into the fully loaded pizza I picked up on my way home from Gabriel's when there's a knock at my door.

I freeze. My heart races. Is it my father? Has he found me?

I take a deep breath, trying to settle my wayward thoughts. I hate how he's always my first thought when I'm caught off guard.

After a second knock, I consider ignoring it like I usually do when I'm not expecting company. Gabriel and my mom know to call or text before showing up. Frankie never just drops in, and considering I just spent Friday night and most of today at their place, I doubt it's them.

No one else really has the address. I don't *like* company.

Creeping to the door, I grab the bat resting against the wall before daring a peek through the peephole. I really should install a security camera or one of those video doorbells. I've been saying that since I moved in here nearly two years ago.

Procrastination for the win.

One glance has my heart racing. I jump to unlock the door, barely giving my fear from a moment ago a second thought. "Hey." I tip my head, trying to catch Rowdy's eyes before he swings around, facing me full-on.

"Hey. I'm…" His words are lost when his sees the bat in my hand. "You always answer the door with a bat?" Worry riddles his eyes as he steps forward, stealing the oxygen from my lungs.

I step back, needing the space, and set Slugger, my protector, down behind the door. "Yes." No need to elaborate. I'm sure Rowdy can figure out why. "You want to come in?"

He tips his chin and waits for me to move out of the way before he enters, closing the door behind him, locking—all three deadbolts—without my prompting.

Thankfully, I didn't have to ask. No need to advertise my

propensity for excessive locks or highlight my damage—more than the bat just did.

He stops in the living room, noting the pizza and the paused show on the TV before facing me. "Listen, I know things are off between us." He grips his man-bun, frowning. "But do you think we could pretend everything is okay? I—"

"Yes," I jump on the idea. "What's wrong?"

Rowdy shakes his head. "Could we..." Burying his hands in his pockets, he assesses the room as if he might find answers hidden in my walls or sofa. "Maybe we could sit and do whatever you were doing... for a while."

"I was getting ready to eat pizza, veg on the coach, and watch a movie. You want to—"

"Yes." His response is too quick. I'm not even sure he cares or comprehends what I'm doing. It's obvious something's wrong, but he's not ready to talk.

"Sit. I'll grab another plate." I disappear to the kitchen, taking a second to catch my bearings.

He's clearly only here because he doesn't want to be alone.

He chose you to spend time with because he thinks you are weak and vulnerable because of your issues—not because he wants to "hang" with you. Don't read anything into it.

"All I've got are soda, juice, or water," I call out to the other room, staring at the ceiling until he answers.

"Water, please."

Please. So well mannered. His mom should be proud.

Plate, napkins, and water in hand, I still when I turn the corner and see he's sitting in the middle of the couch, facing the TV. I'll have to sit next to him, or in the loveseat that'll give me a crick in my neck after being craned left to watch the movie. I guess I'm sitting next to him. I could ask him to scoot over, but, really, why would I do that?

"What are we watching?" He plates a few slices of the fully loaded pizza, hands me my plate that I left sitting next to the pizza box.

I bite my lip, feeling silly. "Um, well... It's... We can watch something else." I hand him the remote, but instead of searching for a new movie, he hits play. I side-eye him, nervously waiting for the judgment.

He smirks. "G.I. Jane?" His head slowly turns toward me, his eyes taking in my drawn lips and settling on my eyes. "It's a good choice. Demi is kick ass in this movie."

Shocked, all I can mutter is, "Yeah."

She's my hero. I want to be as tough as Jordan someday. She takes no shit, but she wasn't always that tough. She worked for it. I'm working for it too.

Before long I've finished three slices of pizza. Two is usually my limit, but Rowdy kept refilling my plate when he did his. I motion to the fourth slice on my plate. "I can't."

He eyes it, then me. "I'm sure you can manage."

"I'm sure I don't want to." Plus, it's the last slice.

He's barely full, I'm sure. "Okay," he takes my plate, "but next time, it's my treat."

Next time? I'd like that.

I settle in, full tummy, great movie, and a guy who makes me forget I'm a little broken and nobody special.

Pizza devoured, the two of us slumped down on the couch, the sides of our bodies fully touching, the credits rolling, Rowdy looks down at me. His eyes settle on mine, his lips so close.

Is he going to kiss me? God, I want that.

For a split second, I think he might.

Then the pain and uneasiness from earlier seep across his face before he says, "My mom has cancer."

CHAPTER 8

ANCER. *MY MOM HAS CANCER.*

Those four words knock the wind out of my sails and send me into his lap, curling around him like a python getting ready to squeeze the life out of its next meal. Except it's Rowdy— and it's me, the girl no one can touch without sending me into a PTSD episode.

No one except Rowdy.

The guy I've had a crush on since day one…

"God, Kitten." He holds me like a lifeline, like I'm his connection to the world, only it's him who's *my* anchor. He grounds me, not to the here and now, but to *him.*

He is my here and now.

"I'm so sorry, Cameron. Is it bad? Is that why you didn't want to talk about it?" His hold tightens.

With his head buried in my shoulder, I barely make out his reply, "I didn't want to be alone. All I could think about was getting to you. I needed you."

Air rushes from my lungs, but in a good way I've never felt. I've never been needed before. I'm the one usually doing the needing.

Growing up, my mom needed Gabriel, not me. In fact, things might have been better for her if I hadn't been around.

Gabriel definitely didn't—doesn't—need me. He's always been the protector.

My father... Nope not going there.

"Thank you," I whisper in his ear so softly I'm not sure he hears me.

Rowdy edges back, studying my face. "Why are you thanking me?" His warm hand cups my cheek, and his fingers sink into my hair. His eyes, such a light blue, seek out my darker ones. His thumb brushes my cheek when I don't answer. "Why?"

My head shakes, and I bite my lip, not wanting to admit, "No one's ever needed me."

"Fuck, Reese." He presses his forehead to mine. "That's not true. I need you more than I should." He puffs out a breath, each word producing a new ache in places I didn't even know were possible. "Cap needs you."

"He needs my organizational skills," I scoff.

"Gabriel needs you."

"No. I'm a burden to him just like my mom. I've always needed Gabriel. He never let himself need anyone before Frankie."

"Yeah, I can see that. Your mom?" He's running out of people, and I'm running out of pride.

"No. She needs Gabriel. I've only ever been a hardship for her."

"Kitten, you're killing me." His grips on me tightens. "Can it be enough that *I* need you?"

Heat pools between my thighs when he hardens beneath me as if my body needs any encouragement to be turned on by him. Instinctually, I squirm, rubbing against his length. I have no idea what I'm doing, mindless pleasure-seeking genes must be taking over. But moving against him is the only thing I can think of as I try to get more air into my lungs.

He groans and seizes my hips. "Ignore that."

Is *that* the *need* he's referring to?

Sure, I'm shamelessly grinding against him, but I thought he meant he needed me as a person, not as a...

Frowning, he tips my chin. "Me sporting wood doesn't mean that's the *need* I'm talking about, Kitten."

I can't stop the next words from coming, but I have to know, if he's here for *me*, is he here for *more* with me? "Is this..." I look down at his lap. "Is this just an automatic response?"

"There's a gorgeous woman on my lap."

"You think I'm gorgeous?" If blush was clothing, I'd be wearing it from head to toe.

His dimpled smile lessens the sorrow in his eyes and voice. "Yeah, I do." His gaze, feeding on my reddening skin, lands on my lips before meeting mine. "I want to kiss you."

The damn air in the room is getting harder and harder to come by. How does he do that? "You don't sound like you do."

"I'm telling myself it's a bad idea." His blue eyes darken as his pupils enlarge.

"Is it?" Shit. *Is it?* I hunger to taste him—to be tasted.

Fear, my normal companion, has fallen asleep, for what I feel for Rowdy is definitely not fear. I'm nervous and anxious but in a good way. I think. I'm not sure. I've only ever felt this way around him. Other men make me anxious and nervous for completely different reasons. I fear their touch. I don't fear his.

He rubs my side, his nose trailing up my neck. "I don't *only* want to kiss you." He kisses the corner of my mouth, soft and tender, with reverence, taking in a deep breath, breathing me in.

I'm lightheaded. The contact has me buzzing and rattled in the best, unfamiliar way.

I'm not afraid.

"Do it again," I whisper to his so-close lips.

His brow furrows. "I don't just want to kiss you," he reiterates before pressing his mouth to the opposite corner of mine.

When he breaks contact, I want to touch my lips to see if they're as scorched as they feel.

"I want to devour you. I want to mark you. I want to claim you, make you mine," he growls low and sultry with a tinge of sadness as his savage eyes rake me in.

All that's holy, I must have died to be hearing those words come from the man I've fantasized about since the day I met him.

"Yes. Do that," I practically whimper.

"Fuck." The gravel in his tone only amps up my need—the ache becoming unbearable. "You can't look at me like that, Kitten."

"Like what?" Does it show? Do I have a sign over my head asking him to take me, teach me, devour me?

"Like you're anything but afraid of me and my dirty mind."

Emboldened with desire, I run my mouth across his jaw, his scruff tickling my lips. "I'm not afraid, Rowdy. Not of you." It's hard to remember I've ever feared intimate contact when he's near.

"Fuck, baby." His fingers flex on my thighs, and my hips jump forward, pulling a moan from us both. "I am."

His admission deflates my hopes of finding out what normal feels like. "You're afraid of me?"

"Of this. Of you. Of wanting more than you can give. Of hurting you."

Gah, this man.

"I don't know what I have to give, but at the moment it feels like everything." I hold his face between my hands, capturing his gaze. "Kiss me."

Let's see what I'm capable of.

The confidence and desire in her eyes takes me aback. There's my lion. "Kitten."

"I'm afraid so much of the time, Rowdy. But at the moment, I'm not afraid of you or what you want. Kiss me. Please, don't make me beg."

Fuck. If she only knew how much begging turns me on. From *her*, it would be an inferno burning through my body to pleasure her in whatever way she desires.

"Only a kiss," I growl. I shouldn't be doing this. She's not ready for me. My need for her is already too big to contain in my head. In my pants, my cock is planning ways to drill through my jeans to get to her.

"To start." She leans in, so fucking eager and sweet. So, so sweet.

Fuck it.

I aim for a center-of-her-lips, closed mouth, gentle and slow kiss.

What I get is her tongue sweeping out to lick my lower lip the second our mouths connect.

All sanity leaves the building.

She wraps around me, grinding her hips as if she knows my cock is seeking its way to her.

A gasp from her, a parting of our lips, and our tongues are tangoing like they didn't just meet.

Her mouth is heaven, if heaven is a fiery pit of temptation and lust.

"Damn, Kitten." Am I dreaming? I lean back to be sure it's her I'm kissing.

I'm met with a whimper and her hands sinking into my hair, drawing me back to her mouth.

"Take what you need," I breathe against her lips what might be my final words as she sucks my tongue and reduces the air in my lungs by half.

Blood rushes to feed the cocky sucker in my pants, nodding like he has any idea what he's getting himself into.

Cocky, have you met Blue Balls?

I think you're about to become good friends.

A frenemy situation.

Her hunger unleashed, she attacks my body like a starving carnivore that's been stuck on a deserted island and just found fresh water and red meat. All I can do is hold on, take what she's giving, devour her taste as she eats at my lips and feeds me her tongue over and over, deliciously hard, deep, and wanton.

She's killing me.

Straight out murder by kissing.

Who knew kissing was lethal?

What a way to go.

As lost as I am in her, I'm careful to let her lead as much as I can. Her animalistic sounds and hunger make it hard to remember I can't flip her over on the couch, wrap her hair around my fist, and rut into her as her sweet, innocent pussy squeezes the life out of me, drilling her until she screams my name, coming all over my greedy cock as my cum marks her beautiful body inside and out.

Yeah, I can't do that.

But I can let her use me, experiment on me, find her pleasure using my body in any way that makes her feel good, safe, needed, and most desperately wanted.

"Rowdy," she mewls in the seconds between one kiss ending and another beginning, rocking her hips, moaning and gasping for air.

She lights fires everywhere her hands touch and claw at my shoulders and the back of my neck. The way she pulls my hair free and her fingers skate across my scalp, massaging and tugging to get me closer, drives me insane with want.

My cock begs to be freed. *Just an inch is all I need.*

Crazy fuck thinks an inch inside her pussy would ever be enough.

It's a start.

Shut the fuck up. This isn't about you.

Not possible. I'm a dickhead, remember? It's always about me.

"Tell me what you need, Kitten." *Please, say it's my cock. My tongue on your clit. Your nipples in my mouth.* "Tell me."

"I… don't know." She sounds lost.

Of course she doesn't know. She's as innocent as the Virgin Mary.

God, why'd I have to bring *her* into this?

"Trust me?"

"Mmm, yes," she pants across my lips before diving in for more. Christ, this woman.

She's so much more than I dared to imagine.

Hyper-focused on her cues, I slide my hand down her belly, slipping my hand inside the waist of her tiny shorts, my thumb finding her wet heat coating her panties. "So wet, baby."

I rub circles around her clit, her slickness seeping onto my thumb. "I want to taste you. Would you let me do that, someday?"

I'm not pushing her boundaries or my willpower by trying to do that now. I have my hand in her pants. I never thought I'd get to kiss her, much less rub her to orgasm. I don't need to push for more right now.

Her hips buck as she nips my jaw, seeking my mouth, humming, "Hmm."

"Yeah, you will. My little kitten wants me to lick her clean after getting her dirty and wet."

Fuck.

I'm trying to get *her* off, and *I'm* about to blow in my jeans, my words doing a number on myself.

Arousal coats the air, thick and hot. Sweat beads on her brow. Perky nipples push against her t-shirt, braless and begging for my mouth, but I don't dare.

One step at a time.

As she shakes and crushes her mouth to mine, her grip on me tightens, her movements jerky, uncontrolled. She's primed to blow.

I could bite her nipple. Tell her to come and send her sailing, sucking and soothing her through the roof and back.

My balls tingle at the thought of doing her rough and her loving it, begging me for more. To see her free and fearless with me.

"Cam, I—"

"I know, Kitten. I got you." I kiss up her neck, nip at her pulse point and suck the sting away before whispering in her ear, "You're so hot, you gonna make *me* come."

Her nails scratch my scalp as her head is tossed back. A moan builds as her body trembles. I bypass her panties and nearly have a coronary when I feel her flesh against my thumb, skin to skin, slick and warm, and so needy. Her bundle of nerves is hard and ready for my mouth to lick and suck. "Come for me, Kitten."

And damn if she doesn't.

Flailing in my arms, electrocuted with zings of pleasure, my girl comes undone, calling my name, begging me not to stop, like I would—like I *could*.

If given the choice, I'd never stop making her come.

I'd spend the rest of my life feeling her limp and satisfied in my arms, taking her over and over again until she begs me to stop.

Then working her into a frenzy until she's begging me to *never* stop.

CHAPTER 9

PANTING AND TREMBLING IN HIS ARMS, THE horror of what just happened—of what I did—of what I let him do, blankets me like a shroud of shame.

He came to me for comfort over the news of his mother, and here I am, selfishly finding pleasure in his arms, mouth, hands, and body.

Oh, God. What have I done?

He's hard between my thighs, his hand that was in my panties—touching me *there*—is now caressing my back under my shirt, and his lips skim my brow, whispering sweet, soothing things into my skin.

What have I done?

I've *used* him.

And I'm a horrible tease, because what happens next when he wants more and I freak out?

Would I freak out? My body is humming. My muscles have never been this relaxed… But that doesn't mean an attack isn't on its way to remind him I'm broken.

"I should go," I mumble and fight to disentangle myself from his lap, his hands trying to hold me.

"What?" He laughs as he grips my arm, keeping me from stumbling over the coffee table.

I pull back, straightening my shorts and t-shirt. "I should go."

I'm a horrible person. *I'm so sorry, Rowdy.*

"Go?" He frowns and steps toward me as I edge back. "This is *your* place. Don't freak out on me, Kitten."

"Oh, right." He came to *my* apartment. Gee, I'm genius-level smart and well-adjusted to life, obviously.

God, this is awkward.

"Reese."

The first time I saw Rowdy, Frankie introduced us at Gabriel's championship fight—the night before she became my sister-in-law.

Rowdy was hot. Tall, strong with muscles for days. Long light-brownish-blond hair that danced on his shoulders when he spoke, scanning the room for potential danger with ice-blue eyes that stole my breath and dimples that zapped my clit, making me uncomfortably wet in public for the first time ever.

The way he fawned over Frankie, sweet and gentle, ensuring she was comfortable and safe, made me envious.

Gabriel had been in love with Frankie since the beginning of time.

He didn't know it.

I did.

But Frankie, she had to find her way to Gabriel via a horrendous path through Austin, her first boyfriend and Gabriel's former best friend.

But as I watched Rowdy being protective over her, all I could think was *I want that.*

I want a man to look at me the way Rowdy looked at her. The way Gabriel looked at her when he thought no one was watching.

They were both so protective of her, like guardian angels but better.

I wonder if Gabriel knows Rowdy was in love with Frankie.

Was?

That's a sobering thought.

Is he still?

"Do you love her?" I gulp down my embarrassment for coming on his hand. I ignore the darkness lapping at my heels, the buzzing in my ears.

Rowdy touched me.

He. Touched. Me.

What if Dad finds out?

Go away, crazy. I've got no room for you between Rowdy and me.

I can't ruin this more than I already have with my damage.

"Who?" Rowdy moves like lightning and captures my face in his hands. "Don't." His lips brush mine. "Don't freak out on me, Kitten."

He means crazy. Don't go *crazy* on him.

Too late.

I came this way.

There are no returns.

No exchanges.

Final sale.

All items must go.

Placing my hands over his, I bore holes into his gaze. "Are you. In. Love. With Frankie?"

He flinches. His concern for me morphs into understanding and then sorrow.

He does.

I release his hands and step out of his grasp.

He loves her, and he made out with me like it mattered—like I mattered.

"I don't blame you. Frankie is amazing. She's beautiful... And tough." *Not crazy like me.*

I pick up our plates, glasses, and pizza box. "Smart too. She sees things." I dump everything on the kitchen counter. "I feel like she knows me when barely anyone does. She just gets me." My jealousy doesn't negate the fact she *is* an incredible woman who has been there for me.

"Reese."

I start washing the plates. "She has such a big heart too, though she keeps it locked up tight most of the time. Except for Gabriel. She's dumb, stupid in love with him... And Ox, of course." I set the plates on the drying rack.

"Kitten."

No point in using the dishwasher for so few items. It's usually just me, so I rarely use it.

I start on the glasses. "They're a forever thing. You know that, right?"

His gaze drills into the side of my skull, practically begging me give him my eyes. But I can't. I can't face the man who's already stolen my heart but has kept his for a woman who can never be his.

We're both screwed.

Well, not literally since I've never done that.

Probably never will.

I came for him tonight.

He touched me, and I didn't have an episode.

But he loves another woman.

He's not mine.

Kitchen clean, I throw away the pizza box, avoiding eye contact or any contact whatsoever. I fluff the pillows on the couch, turn off the TV. Then stand at the door. Waiting.

Waiting for him to come to the same conclusion.

He doesn't.

I unlock the door, still waiting for him move from his spot in the middle of my living room.

"It's not what you think," his pained rasp has my downcast eyes pricking.

"It's fine. Really." You can't help who you love.

I still love a man who hurt me in ways no father should.

How sick is that?

Who am I to judge?

"I hope your mom will be okay." That's what's more important here, potentially life and death. Cancer is a mean fucker. I really do pray she'll be alright, kick cancer's ass.

Silence radiates like beams of light, bouncing off the walls, casting shadows, shining too brightly in some places, making me want to hide.

I can't ask him to leave. I can't be rude, but I can't stand here and take his broken-down demeanor either. He takes up too much space, sucks the oxygen out of the room, making it hard to breathe. I'm forever short of breath when he's around.

"Please lock the door when you leave." I all but run, darting for my bedroom, locking the door behind me and slumping to the floor.

I'm such a chicken shit.

A knock and jiggle of the doorknob has me crawling away from the door. "Reese." He knocks again. "I don't want to leave things like this."

"It's fine. Let's just pretend tonight never happened." *That you weren't using me to find comfort from your bad news instead of going to Frankie, who I'm sure was your first choice.*

"Dammit, Kitten. I'm not talking about this through a fucking door. When you're ready to talk about this like adults, you find me." He stomps away, but halts after a few steps.

Then his footfalls return.

"I'm not mad at you. I need you to know that." His exhale nearly blows my hair from the other side of the door. "This will be a hard week. My fight is next Saturday. If I'm distracted, distant, it's because I'm in my head. Not because I'm mad at you or ignoring you. Because I'm not. And I don't want to pretend tonight never happened."

His insistence makes me smile. I rise to my feet and slink to the door, placing my hand over the cool surface as if I can feel him through it.

"Kick ass, Rowdy. Win your fight," I whisper to the dead tree that separates us.

"I heard that. Please, open the door." A thud hits the wood, and I imagine it's his forehead. "Let me kiss you goodnight, Kitten."

My hand moves on its own accord, unlocking the door.

Oh, shit.

I step back.

Slowly the door creaks open. His darkness fills the doorway, seeping forward like smoke. He snakes an arm around my waist, his hand on my back holding me in place as he advances. Capturing my cheek, his fingers sink into my hair.

I whimper my acquiescence, making him chuff seconds before his mouth crashes over mine.

If I thought he was kissing me before, I was wrong. So very wrong.

He was going easy on me.

This is a kiss of anger—though he said he wasn't mad—and passion. So much passion.

He nibbles and sucks my lips until I open fully, then his tongue plunders, diving in, taking mine hostage.

He fucks my mouth with his, wrenching me closer, devouring me with abandon, without care for my crazy.

And, oh my God, I'm done for.

Wring me out and hang me up to dry.

This man can kiss.

My toes curl.

My fingers lose feeling digging into his shoulders and hair.

I want to climb him, build a treehouse, and never leave.

He squeezes my ass and breaks our kiss. His eyes, blazing with hunger and anger singe my skin. "If I were *in love* with another woman, I wouldn't be here kissing you like a starved man. Got it?"

Kissed stupid, I nod and suppress the need to beg, *please, sir, may I have another?*

Satisfied with my agreement, he quickly scans the room, then quirks a brow at me. "It's dark in here."

"What?" It's nighttime. Of course it's dark.

He runs a callused thumb along my cheek. "You didn't turn on the light, Reese." His lilted smile is full of pride. I'm not sure if it's for me or him.

It's dark in my room. I forgot to turn on the light. What is he doing to me?

His soft, scorching mouth finds mine, kissing me tenderly before releasing me to step back. "Night, Kitten."

"G'night, Rowdy," I manage as I sway to the door, watching his smartass swagger, so satisfied with himself.

I fall into bed after locking up, replaying the night on repeat. I may or may not touch myself before drifting into a dreamless coma.

CHAPTER 10

IF YOU ASKED ME EIGHT DAYS AGO IF I WOULD WIN my fight tonight, I would have said *yes*, hands down. Now, a week after finding out my mom has cancer, kissing Reese, and seeing her come face—it's spectacular, by the way—I'm distracted and finding it hard to concentrate.

This week's a shitshow of relentless anger at my mom's situation, fear of losing her, fear of fucking up with Reese and losing *her*. Cowboy, Jess, and Jonah were the main recipients of said rage, taking it like the men and friends they are, redirecting it toward my fight prep.

My flight home is booked for Monday, giving me a day to recover from my fight. Cap is good with letting me take a week or so off to be with my mom. She's not giving details of her cancer or her plan of attack. Every time we talk, she distracts me with a memory from my childhood or asking about my friends and family-by-choice here in Vegas.

We even talk about Reese, a topic she is all too fond of.

Moms always know.

Even if I didn't allow myself to hope for more with Reese, I guess Mom always saw the way I talk about her.

"Tell me how she makes you feel, Cam," Mom asked two days ago.

She never calls me Rowdy. That nickname came from my dad and my ability to get in trouble.

He said I'd find trouble in an empty room with no windows or doors.

The thought is disturbing, locked in a room with no exit, but I get what he meant now. As a kid, I thought he was weird as fuck and totally unrelatable.

"Like a man." It may sound corny, but it's true. I feel like an adult, like a guy who finally grew into himself and could be the man Reese needs if she'd let me.

I don't mention she also makes me rock hard with the desire to drill her to the floor.

Some things a mother doesn't need to know.

"That's good. Means she respects you, looks up to you. It's a great start, honey."

Yeah, my mom also calls me *honey*. It's a southern thing.

"But there are things in her past... Her dad... He..."

Hell, I don't even know for sure what he did, but I suspect it's not just physical and emotional abuse but sexual abuse as well.

I have no business sharing her secrets. "It's complicated."

"I'm sure it is." She sounds so tired.

I'm second-guessing my decision to wait to fly home.

I could fly out tonight.

Should I leave now? Skip my fight?

"Most things worthwhile are quite complicated, baby."

Mom calls me *baby* too. Essentially, any term of endearment you can think of, my mom has probably called me it at one time or another, including *sugarplum* and *pumpkin pie*. Not very manly, but it's the way she shows her love, one sugar-laden nickname at a time, packed with love and adoration.

That's my mom in a nutshell.

She loves hard and deep with no qualms of showing you just how much.

"What most women need is a safe place, Cameron. Make her feel secure and believe there's nothing she can't tell you, lay at your feet, that you won't still love her through. That's all we need. Men think we're all complicated. We're not that hard to understand. We want to be loved as we are, where we are, and with what gifts God gave us or chose not to give us. Make her feel respected, cherished, and seen every day, and that right there will be a woman who will fight the devil himself for your soul."

My mom, the philosopher, soothsayer, great advice-giver, breaks it down into manageable chunks.

There's no one else like her.

"I love you, Mom."

"Ah, honey. I love you too. You've always been the light of my life. You remember that when things seem dark. I know you got that Shadow chasing you, but when you need to, you turn round and shine the love I put in your heart and chase that demon out. Plain banish it with the tender heart God gave you. He gives us light and dark, baby. All of us have it in us. You just have to find your balance. Maybe Reese can be your Wendy, staple that Shadow to your feet, where it belongs, under your control."

Damn, my chest aches and warms with the idea that Reese could be my *Wendy*, my dark-Shadow whisperer.

"You can't have rainbows without a little rain."

Mom's voice trails in my head as I stare at my phone minutes before my fight, calls to my mom unanswered and my text unread.

I talked to her last night. She was fine.

A tug on my gut drew me to reach out again.

It's stupid, really. She's never been one to keep her phone in hand or even at her side. It's usually on her desk or in the kitchen until she needs it.

"You ready?" Cap clasps my shoulder.

I tuck my phone in my bag and don my Beats. "Ready."

Coach and Jonah mill around in the corner, talking. Walker and Jess are at the door, taking inventory, which is code for looking for girls.

"Concentrate on your fight. Put your worry and frustration into the ring. Make that motherfucker yours." Cap gives me another squeeze before sauntering out the door, heading for the arena and his front row seat.

I invited Reese. I doubt she'll show. Crowds are not her favorite, and it's not her MO to come to the fights. Gabriel's championship fight was the last one she attended, as far as I know.

Instead of letting the sinking feeling in my gut take hold, I choose to believe Reese is here fighting her fear to support me. But I won't hold it against her if she's not.

Grumbling under my breath, I hit play and get lost in "Wolf Totem" by The Hu, bouncing on my feet, closing my eyes and staring into the deep blue ones I hope to see shortly.

Agitation is a close friend, keeping me company more times than not.

Not a good friend, but always close by like a nosey neighbor.

My leg bounces, keeping time with a beat I can't hear. I stop it, only for the other leg to take up the cause.

I scan the arena, watching the throng of people mulling about acting like fools, hyped up for the main event.

My thumbs run endlessly around my fingertips, feeling for rough nails or hard cuticles and, if they find any, continuing to rub until either that finger or thumb is sore. It's a nervous habit. I try to keep my nails short, well-manicured to avoid such things from happening. Thankfully, I'm all good, but it doesn't stop my thumbs from searching.

"You need a beer." Landry leans in, his gaze darting to my legs and hands.

My skin tingles.

He's going to touch me.

Please don't.

"I need a Xanax," I mutter.

He laughs, and his brows hit his hair line. "You have one?"

"No." I don't take meds, but I know from my mom, they make social situations more bearable.

"A beer would ease your nerves," he offers. He's sweet to sit here with me.

"Weed would work too," Jess offers from my other side.

I'm in a Jess and Landry sandwich.

My gaze swings to Jess. "You smoke weed?" I can't imagine Cap would be okay with that.

"Nah." He bumps my shoulder with his. "I wish."

I suck in air, my vision closing in. I grip my legs.

It's okay. It's okay. It's okay.

"Oh, shit." Jess shoots to his feet to give me space, his hands raking his hair. "Fuck, Reese, I'm so sorry."

"Fuck, man," Landry chastises. "We had one fucking job tonight, and you go and fuck it up."

Eyes screwed shut again, I nod incessantly. "It's okay. It's okay. It's okay." The buzzing in my head starts to fade.

"I'll grab us some beers." The wind from Jess' departure wafts my hair off my neck for a second before settling along my back.

"You alright?" Landry's timbre is edged with worry.

"Yeah, I just need a sec." When the panic wanes to a manageable level, I open my eyes on a long exhale.

If Landry scoots any closer, he'll be touching me in multiple places. My pulse ratchets up further. This was a bad idea. How did I expect to be in the middle of so many people and not be touched or knocked into by an unknowing bystander?

"If I were to sit close enough so our sides were touching, would that make you feel safer or make it worse?" Landry asks.

Biting my lip, I eye his body, considering if I'll panic if I *know* the touch is coming.

He shrugs. "I was just thinking, if I was already protecting that side of you with my body, maybe you wouldn't get bumped because we're in contact already."

What he says makes sense.

"I don't know." I've never considered it.

"If I sit still and keep my hands to myself... can *you* touch *me?*"

I frown. I normally don't touch people, but when I have, it doesn't trigger my crazy. If it did, I'd never be able to work with anyone in the career I have. I tentatively lay my hand on his forearm, holding my breath, waiting.

Nothing happens.

Landry grins. "Don't move your arm. I'm going to sit right next to you and wait for you to move until the side of your body touches mine." His gaze keeps mine. "I won't hurt you, Reese, and I'll kill any of these fuckers if they try to touch you."

I nod, believing him.

I concentrate on my breathing as he scoots back in his chair. "Trust me."

I do.

He's Rowdy's friend.

He's part of Cap's family.

He holds his hands up. My hand still resting on his goes up too. "I won't move."

He wouldn't hurt me.

I know that logically, but my damage is rarely logical.

I slowly sit back in my seat and edge closer to him. A cell at a time, I make contact with the side of his body: shoulder, arm, thigh. My hand remains on his arm, moving down to rest on his hand, not holding it, just making contact.

There's no panic.

It's just... touch.

A cleansing breath fills me with relief.

I can do this.

Holy shit, I can do this.

CHAPTER 11

THE FIRST TIME SOMEONE'S TOUCH SENT ME into a panic was in middle school.

A new guy to our school—who I thought was cute—walked up to me, humor blazing in his eyes, and slung his arm over my shoulder. In an effort to escape him, I went down like he'd saddled me with a fifty-pound bag of potatoes.

He didn't know.

He thought he was being cute and charming.

I reactively thought he was trying to hurt me.

He wasn't, of course.

But my crazy—that I didn't even know existed—took root that day and preened like a big ole peacock. Its tail splayed, swaying back and forth as it stalked the hall, shaking its feathers, putting on quite the display.

Meanwhile, I cowered on the floor, my face buried in my knees, begging him to stop, not to hurt me.

Not my proudest moment. Sadly, not my worst moment either.

Not then, nor any episode since, have I thought I could sit here in a crowded arena of thousands, sandwiched between two big men—Landry and Jess—touching me from side to side, and beam at Rowdy as his fight song, "Wolf Totem," plays on the sound system, watching him walk to the stage—octagon—like he owns the world.

The noise of the crowd is deafening.

It doesn't set me off.

The three of us don't move. We don't stand up. Even as everybody around us is on their feet cheering for our guy, we stay put. They've sacrificed for me.

And I don't let them down. My crazy peacock is asleep—or dead if I'm lucky.

Sorry, peacocks. Nothing against you. I like peacocks. They're beautiful, majestic birds. But Crazy Town doesn't need a mascot—it needs shutting down.

When Rowdy passes our seats, he pauses, tensely doing a double-take, his eyes flaring between Jess and Landry plastered to my sides. His scowl is incriminating until his eyes land on me. He bathes my face in his light blue gaze. One brow twerks, and his mouth twitches, fighting a smile when he sees I'm okay.

I don't move. I barely breathe, but I try to convey my state of mind: *I'm okay.*

He doesn't need to worry about me or pause to celebrate my tiny victory when he has a bigger one of his own to win.

Focus on your fight, my Shadow.

He hesitates a beat more before giving a slight nod and moving on.

Jonah and Coach Long have his ear as he removes his hoodie, but his eyes zoom in on me at every opportunity.

Heat. I can feel his from here. It's all consuming. My skin tingles, and my body clenches, preparing for an onslaught of what his gaze promises: *I'm coming for you, Kitten.*

I tremble with anticipation. Endorphins rage through me.

"You okay?" Landry whispers in my ear, mistaking my reaction.

"Yeah." I haphazardly nod. My only focus is the man getting ready to kick some ass in the ring.

63

Rowdy's eyes narrow to slits, taking in our interaction as his competitor enters the ring.

The world narrows. It's just the two of us. Everything is swirling around us, but in the vortex of Rowdy's locked gaze, time stands still.

He bounces, fists jabbing at air, his pecs bouncing in rhythm with his feet. Nostrils flare, chin juts outs only to be tucked back in. Hooded eyes glare daggers at the world—at his opponent—only for me, they are all heat and want, teaming with protectiveness.

If I believed in God, I'd be praying for my soul.

As it is, I pray for Rowdy. He needs the protection, not me. And though I might believe God has dismissed the Stone family as a lost cause of sin, pain, and anguish, I don't totally reject the idea that He might have brought this dark Shadow into my life for a reason.

Yeah, I know I said I don't believe in Him. Perhaps what I really mean is *He* doesn't believe in me.

The ref's voice comes over the speakers, talking about a fair fight. Rowdy rolls his shoulders, dips and dodges, knocks fists with the other fighter—whose introduction I totally missed.

I don't really care. The only man who matters is the one I'm rooting for. The one who ties my insides in knots and loosens them all at the same time.

Right before the bell rings, Rowdy breaks our gaze. His eyes swing to the dipshit in front of him. As his opponent bounces around, a smirk on his face, and says something no one but Rowdy can hear, Rowdy's face morphs from confidence and dominance into pure, murderous rage.

It's a split-second action. If I'd blinked, I would have missed it.

Rowdy hits the guy with a left cross.

His opponent staggers, blinking in confusion, shaking his head.

But Rowdy isn't done.

The right-handed uppercut hits the guy square on the jaw, sending him flying backwards.

The roof on the arena vibrates from the sheer volume of cheers.

"Holy fuck." "Goddamn." Jess and Landry scream, exploding out of their seats.

I hug myself, trying to replicate the security of their protective bubble. But I'm so happy and struck by what I've just witnessed, I don't register panic or fear, only awe for the man in the ring, standing over his opponent—who's out cold—bending down, saying something into his ear.

Coming to his full height of about ten feet tall, he swings our direction, his arm raised by the ref, who announces he's the winner by KO.

It wasn't even a thirty-second match.

That has to be a record for him.

In my books, it's a history maker.

Rowdy locks on me, points squarely in my direction. Breathing hard, nostrils flaring, he growls, "You. Are. Mine!"

Blood pounding in my ears, brushing off the announcer, ref, coach, and Jonah, I push through the crowd to get to Reese. She stands stark still, hand over her mouth. Her eyes, as big as saucers, caress me the entire way.

I can't get to her fast enough.

Cowboy and Mustang, protecting her like bookends, step back to give me space when I sweep in and wrap her in my arms, crashing my mouth to hers.

Mine.

Her whimper is fuel to my I'm-claiming-you kiss. Her heat blisters my lips, singes my soul, and extinguishes the rage that asshole ignited.

She's shaking by the time I put her down. Forehead to forehead, I rasp, "Go with Cowboy. He'll get you home. I'll meet you there."

Wordlessly, she pulls me in for another kiss. Strong and demanding, her fingers dig into my hair.

I grunt my approval as she presses her mouth to mine, lashing me with her tongue with a quick suck, then pulling back, tugging on my bottom lip before finally releasing me with a *pop*.

Fuck. Me. There's my lion leaving me in a sex-laden stupor. "Kitten."

"You won." Her sweet breath puffs over my face.

"You doubted me?" I tease.

"Not for a second." Her smile and confidence wreck me.

Damn.

I'm done for.

I'm a goner.

Watching long enough to confirm Cowboy has her, I let Jonah usher me out to finish my fighterly duties for the night.

After all the hoopla, before I can step into the shower, Cap stops me. "What did that fucker say to you in the cage?"

Anger steeps thinking about it. "He said he and his team would show Reese how real men fuck if I wasn't up to it."

Jonah's bark of laughter over Cap's shoulder eases the tightness in mine. The rest will release once I have my Kitten in sight.

"Well, that sure backfired on him, didn't it?"

"Yeah, Cap, it sure as shit did."

"I'm proud of you, Cam. You did good, son." Cap clasps my shoulder. You go see your momma. Take all the time you need. We'll be here when you get back."

I swallow the lump in my throat for his kind words and the reminder of my mom's state of health, and reply in the way she taught me, "Yes, sir."

A crick in my neck has me groaning as I blink awake, looking around my living room, confused. Lights are on, and the TV's playing a show I wasn't watching the last time I looked.

I sit up and take a drink of water as the brain fog dissipates.

It's 2 a.m.

Oh no. No. I missed him.

I had a snack when I got home, plopped down on the couch with every intention of watching TV until Rowdy showed.

My body had other plans.

Did he not show up?

Checking my phone, I have a missed call from Rowdy and a couple of text messages. My stomach sinks. Did he show, and I was too dead to the world to hear him knocking? Surely not. I've never been that deep of a sleeper. A part of me is always alert, prepared for *him* to show up. In the dark…

I shake the thought away.

Rowdy. I hit "call" before I even listen to his voicemail or read his texts.

The call goes straight to voicemail. I hang up and pull up his texts.

Rowdy: *My mom died.*

"Oh, Rowdy." My heart aches.

I continue reading his next text.

Rowdy: *Catching the redeye.*

Then, a few minutes later:

Rowdy: *Need you. Come.*

Need you. Come. I reread. Then reread it all again.

I missed him by a few hours, and he's been in so much pain.

As tears fall, I listen to his voicemail while frantically trying to fig-ure out what to reply: "Kitten…" his voice breaks, and my heart cracks. He clears his throat. "Read your texts. I need you." The line goes silent, and I think that's it, then... "There's a ticket waiting for you. I emailed you the details. Please come."

I switch to my email and find an e-ticket with an early morning flight and his address in Texas. He tells me again: *he needs me* and to *please come.*

Swiping at my eyes, I quickly text Cap and Gabriel, then finally text Rowdy:

Me: *I'm coming.*

CHAPTER 12

I NEARLY KEEL OVER WHEN DAD SAYS, "YOUR MOM *passed, Son."*

After showering, I checked my phone and found missed calls from my dad and sister. I knew something had happened to Mom.

It's telling my brother didn't call. Asswipe.

"Why didn't you call me sooner?" *There's no missing the anger in my tone.*

"She didn't want me to. You had your fight. She always supported your dreams." *Dad attempts to justify keeping how sick my mom truly was from me.*

As for supporting my fighting career, she was the only one. She made sure my finances were locked in despite not being a part of the family business. She's the one who pushed me to move to California, to seek out Cap. My mom was a researcher by nature and career. She dug in deep when I shared my dream of becoming a professional mixed martial arts fighter. Her knowledge of the sport and the big players rivaled my own.

Now she's gone. My biggest supporter.

"She didn't want to be the reason you didn't win tonight. You did win, didn't you?"

Fuck, like that matters now. "I'm catching the next flight out. I'll be there as soon as I can."

"Send me your flight details. I'll send Chuck to get you."

I splash water on my face, needing to knock the groggy loose and stop my mind from replaying the call with Dad.

Spending the night at the airport is not how I pictured my night would go. I won, for fuck's sake. I should've been celebrating with the guys or tucked in next to Reese watching a cheesy movie or five, not making the trek home to bury Mom.

Mom. Jesus.

I landed hours ago, but instead of getting a hotel room for a handful of hours, I chose to stay put after reading Reese's text that she was catching the first flight out.

Before leaving Vegas, I'd given Chuck the heads-up that I was waiting for my girl so he didn't need to come till morning. I didn't even know if she'd be on the plane, but I wasn't taking a chance on missing her.

As I dry my face, I'm rethinking the no-hotel logic. A hot shower and clean clothes wouldn't have been a bad idea.

Too late now.

My kitten will be here in less than an hour. I can't wait to see her. That kiss, after my fight, I thought I was claiming her. She was claiming me. Thank fuck. I need to tell her I'm hers just as much as she's mine. I was deep in the emotions and adrenaline from his fighting, slanderous words. No one is touching her besides me.

It's more than that, though. I need my girl by my side, now more than ever.

I brush my teeth and change my shirt. It's the least I can do. Then I saunter to the cafe that's finally opening its doors. I need a Texas-size cup of coffee and a bear claw, if I can find it, now that I'm out of training for the fight.

I could eat a horse I'm so hungry, but I'll wait for Reese. She'll need sustenance.

"We all work, Drake. Don't pretend what you do every day puts food on this table." Rowdy's bite hits home, and Drake's anger morphs into a cold stare as his eyes ping between Rowdy and me.

"It was nice to meet you, Reese." His smile seems genuine, and for a split-second pain flashes through his eyes before he hides it away.

They're all hurting.

"Have a good day, Son." Barrett's eyes remain on his paper as if his sons didn't have a sharp exchange.

Must be old news.

But the tension is palpable.

I decide trying to eat is a smart move.

I'm going to need my energy to keep up with this family.

My phone pings with a text.

Chuck The Man: *20 minutes out.*

I quickly text him back, letting him know Reese's ETA and that we'll meet him outside of baggage claim.

Chuck has been my family's driver as long as I can remember. We have a fleet of drivers, but Chuck is dedicated to the family. And though I love the guy *like family*, it hurts Dad isn't coming himself.

He just lost the love of his life. Give the guy a break.

Yeah, okay. I'd be devastated if I lost Reese or Frankie, and I haven't been with them for over thirty years. Haven't really been with either of them, if you get right down to it. Not ever with Frankie, and not *yet* with Reese.

My love for Frankie is tied to our connection and understanding of each other's flaws. She gets me—I get her. But she's right, I'm *not* in love with her. I was in love with the idea of her, the dream I conjured in my head before proposing to her. I knew she was still in love with the devil himself—Gabriel.

I love Frankie fiercely, but she's not my one. She was my bittersweet could-have-been.

As for Reese.

Fuck.

What I feel for that woman is hard to put into words. It's a completely different stratosphere of emotions wrapped around a protective streak that wants to impale anyone who looks at her wrong, causes her a moment's pain, or makes her second guess herself, and an inappropriate drive to drill her to the floor, sink into her sweet heat so deep she can taste me in the back of her throat.

Calm down, cock. That's not going to happen, and it's not why we're here.

Mom.

Fuck.

I rub my chest at the idea of losing my other half after decades together, the way my dad has lost his.

If I lost Reese…

I can't go there.

Grabbing a coffee, I forgo food and pace the gate area, waiting on the world to wake up and my Kitten's plane to land.

Walking the jet bridge like cattle has me edging to break free from the herd and elbow my way to Rowdy. I slept most of the flight, waking in time to freshen up in the bathroom before the pilot came on asking us to prepare for landing.

I've only flown one other time, and after that trip, I swore I'd never do it again.

But Rowdy…

He said he needs me.

I'm like an addict, needing my next Rowdy fix.

He makes me buzz in a good way.

And… He needs me.

What else could I do but put my crazy aside to be here for him?

He needs support. I'm there, no hesitation.

Luckily, I had a window seat with no one next to me.

I didn't make it unscathed, though.

I fought back panic more than a few times while boarding and braving a trip to the bathroom.

The rows of bodies like landmines—any second one could touch me, rub against me, jump up and bump me. I walked the aisle like a germaphobe, veering and dodging all contact, my heart racing, convinced I'd die of a heart attack before making it to my seat or the bathroom and back.

Now, I'm almost free.

Daylight beams through the open doors leading to my Shadow.

On tiptoe I stretch to see over people's heads. I'm not short at 5'8", but so far, I can't see him as people disperse on the other side of the doors.

Ten feet.

I'm nearly there.

Seven feet.

No sight of him.

Five feet.

Nothing.

Two feet.

Breaching the doors, I scan left, then right.

I don't see him.

A few more steps.

Then—

"Reese." Rowdy prowls from the side, sweeping me up in his strong arms. Finally, I'm safe. My name is spoken, muffled, again and again as he breathes into my neck, calming my panic and stifling my gasp.

"Hold on." He bands one arm around my waist, and I cling to his neck as he grabs my bag and carries me out of the throng of people. Stomping to a sequestered corner, my butt lands against a chrome railing, my back to the windows. He slips in between my legs and wraps around me like a privacy curtain.

He kisses along my jaw before we're tucked into each other's necks. His warmth is all encompassing. Our breaths erratic, our hearts beat heavy in our chests as if they're trying to reach their other half.

"You're here." His voice cracks with emotion.

"Couldn't not be." I squeeze him tighter. "I got you."

"God, Kitten. My mom..." he trails off. No need to finish that statement.

She's gone.

God, his mom is *gone*.

And he wasn't here. He didn't get to say goodbye.

His shudder releases my tears. His hold has me wanting to crawl under his skin to protect the little boy who just lost his mother.

Give me your pain, I breathe into his neck.

Years later he sniffs and swipes at his eyes, glancing sheepishly at me. "We should go."

I nod and wipe at my own tears. "Yeah, sure."

His bag slung over his shoulder, my bag rolling behind him, he laces our hands and guides me out of the airport. Safe in his bubble, I don't even think about avoiding people's touch. It's like his assuredness passes through our contact. People move out of *our* way, not the other way around.

As much as I hate the reason I'm here, I'm so glad I am.

He needs me, and I'm not about to let him down.

CHAPTER 13

I F I THOUGHT I UNDERSTOOD THE EXTENT OF Rowdy's family's wealth, I was mistaken. Frankie told me they had more money than God.

I greatly underestimated God's budget.

The sprawling mansion comes into view as Chuck—his driver—maneuvers us through the winding mile long driveway.

Could I take a picture?

The fact I want to take a picture of someone's *home*…

I mean, people really live like this?

And he left?

Voluntarily?

My circumspective frown falls on my Shadow, whose smile pops out his dimples.

Be still my heart.

"We're just as fucked up as any other family, Reese." He motions to the house growing larger by the second. "It's just money."

"Only people *with* money say *it's just money.*"

He chuckles and kisses my forehead. "Touché."

I've been tucked into his side for the last hour or so as Chuck drove us from the Houston airport.

We didn't talk.

We grabbed some food, consuming it like starved urchins, then he pulled me into his arms, kissed me once—no tongue—and fell asleep.

Amped up on caffeine, I couldn't sleep. I just laid there in his arms, reveling in the feel of him and the simple fact that I could do it without freaking out. It's him. I couldn't do that with anyone else—I wouldn't want to.

It gives me hope. *He* gives me hope.

Maybe I can get past my issues and be intimate with Rowdy in the truest sense. Maybe Dad didn't ruin me for life. A shudder runs up my spine as it usually does when I think of *him*.

Sitting up, Rowdy pulls me into his lap. "You okay?"

His eyes seek mine, and I give them freely. "Yeah, I'm good."

"Don't be nervous. But…" He squeezes my thigh. "Stay away from my brother. He's an asshole to the nth degree."

"Stay away? Seriously?"

He sighs and wraps his hand around the back of my neck, fingers flexing before holding firm. "He hates me. Always has. I have no idea why. I could see him trying to use you to get to me."

"That sounds ominous." I squirm on his lap.

His fingers tighten, holding me still. "I won't let him hurt you. He's an ass, not a predator. His forte is of the verbal nature. I'm the only one he beats up—or used to." He smirks.

Rowdy is a big guy at 6'5" and 230 at least. I can't image him ever being small enough for someone to hurt.

"I won't let him get near you. I just wanted you to know what the deal is."

"Okay, I'll avoid him." I'm good at being invisible. Operation *Avoid Rowdy's Asshole Brother* underway. Check.

"Right by my side is where I want you. Where I'm keeping you." His lips graze my forehead, and I shiver for a whole other reason.

Stepping into my family home, my mother's absence hits me square in the chest.

She should be here to greet me, running down the front steps if she saw me coming or dashing from another room if she heard the front door open.

She was always the first one to wrap me in a hug.

Comfort. Warmth. Home.

That was Mom.

Now, we're greeted by an empty foyer. The silence, the stillness, the emptiness seems cavernous without Mom to warm it up, filling it with her voice, with her hugs, with her love.

Breaking the silence, Chuck advises he'll put our bags in my room.

My room. Shit.

I turn to tell him to put Reese in the guest room closest to me, but her hand rests on my chest, and her next words steal my voice and my next breath, "I'd like to stay with you. If that's okay."

Her big blue eyes shine as she gazes up at me. All I can do is kiss her blessed mouth and say a silent prayer of thanks. I won't have to sleep alone in this menagerie of memories and haunting rooms my mother will never occupy again.

"God, yes," I find my voice. Forehead to forehead, my pulse evens out. "Let's go find my family. Get the introductions over with. Then I'm stealing you away." Though there are a million things to be done, napping with my Kitten sounds like a brilliant plan.

As I hold on to Reese, we trek to the back of the house toward the kitchen, keeping my eyes off the other rooms where my mother could usually be found.

"This is gonna suck," I mumble to myself seconds before entering the kitchen, where I can clearly hear my family moving around.

Reese squeezes my hand, and with one quick glance of reassurance, we come face to face with my family—what's left of them.

If trepidation was a cologne, Rowdy would be bathed in it. He's usually so confident and commanding. It should throw me off, make me uneasy, but it emboldens me to straighten my spine and give him the strength he needs to get through this.

I don't know what I thought I'd find beyond the walls of this glittering fortress, but it wasn't the slight man standing before me, hugging his son like he's the second coming of Christ.

"Dad." Rowdy's shoulders shake as he dwarfs his father in a soul-encompassing embrace.

God, my eyes burn, and my chest aches at the emotions thickening the air in the room.

His dad pats him on the back repeatedly, his face buried in his son's neck, shaking just the same. "I'm sorry I didn't call you sooner."

Someone moans in agony. I look away, unsure if it was me or one of them.

"Hey." A teary-eyed blonde about my size and age tentatively approaches. Her eyes dart to the heartbreaking spectacle of a son finding comfort in his father, or maybe it's the other way around. "I'm Taylor. Cam's sister." She sticks her hand out. "You must be his Reese?"

His Reese?

Ignoring the shock of her even knowing who I am, much less claiming I'm *his*, I shake her hand without hesitation. It's not women I fear.

"Yes." Strangely, I find myself wanting to hug her, give her more physical comfort than just a heartless handshake as though I routinely hug people I've just met. "I'm so sorry for your loss."

Her head dips as her smile fades. "Thanks." Her gaze lingers on her brother then rests on the buffet of food on the counter. "Helga made more food than we can ever eat. Please make a plate and join me."

"Helga?"

"Our cook," she says matter-of-factly, like everyone has their own chef.

"Ah, it looks amazing." I don't have the heart to tell her I couldn't eat even if I were hungry. I spoon up eggs, bacon, and biscuits from the chafing dishes.

Chafing. Dishes.

Lord, I've hit my head and found myself in an episode of *Dallas*.

I only know that show because the grandmotherly lady who used to watch me when I was young watched it on an endless loop from her massive DVD collection.

"Coffee?"

"Yes, please."

She shrugs at the men in her life talking low and staring into each other's eyes. "They're going to be a while. It's the prodigal son returning, you know."

I follow her to the dining room.

The. Dining. Room. Who eats breakfast in the dining room?

Oh, right. *Dallas* or maybe this is *Dynasty*. My surrogate granny used to watch that one too and *Knots Landing*. Her TV viewing tastes ran in the incestual shows genre. She said you can't find good shows like they had back then.

I beg to differ, but I was five. What did I know?

A cool brown gaze halts my progress. He tips his chin. "Taylor, aren't you going to introduce me to your friend?"

She sighs and pats the seat next to her. "Reese, this is our oldest brother Drake."

I sit, keeping my stare guarded. Ah, so this is the asshole I'm supposed to avoid.

He doesn't look a thing like Rowdy or Taylor. He's short like his dad, small stature.

"Drake, this is Reese, Rowdy's girlfriend," Taylor continues the introductions.

His brow hitches. "You're his?" The distain in his tone can't be missed.

"Yes. She's mine." Rowdy's hand finds the back of my neck as he practically growls at his brother.

Possessive much? Not that I mind. I've known brotherly protectiveness, but when it comes from Rowdy, it's different—so, so different—a make-my-panties-wet kind of different.

"It's nice to meet you." Not really, but we are in a TV show, so we must keep up appearances.

Drake's lip twitches as he sneers. "That it is."

Rowdy sits with two plates piled high like a bunkbed. "You missed the pancakes, Kitten. Helga's pancakes are not to be missed. Share mine." His smile is sweet and sorrow-free. He may have dreaded coming home, but it's obvious he needed the time he had with his dad.

Speaking of…

"I'm sorry, Reese. It's been a while since I've seen my boy. I needed a minute." Rowdy's dad offers his hand over my shoulder and a kiss on my cheek.

Panic tightens my spine and steals my breath. Rowdy's hand finds my thigh, easing me just as fast. "Dad, Reese doesn't like to be touched."

"Oh, I'm sorry." His dad pulls back, eyes widening in surprise.

"No problem, sir." I hide my embarrassment by studying my plate.

Rowdy kisses my cheek, whispering, "It's okay. You're good." He hesitates for a second before speaking louder so everyone else can hear, "Reese, this is my dad, Barrett O'Dair."

"Bear. Call me Bear or Barrett. I'll answer to either. Mr. O'Dair was my father and is for the boardroom, not family."

Family. He considers me family?

He continues, "I'm glad you could come with Cameron. It's good he has you."

Rowdy's hand finds mine on my lap, and he squeezes with a wink.

"Thank you, sir… err, Barrett." It feels wrong calling him by his first name. Maybe Bear would be better. No, probably not. Sounds like a bedroom name. Yuck.

"Well, if you'll excuse me." Drake stands, tossing his napkin over his plate of barely touched food. "Some of us have to work for a living."

I scowl. Was that directed at Rowdy?

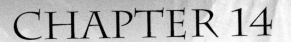

CHAPTER 14

"**Y**OUR SISTER IS SWEET."
Your brother is an ass.
Your dad is smaller than I thought he'd be.
I linger near the door, awestruck by his massive bedroom.

It's bigger than my one-bedroom apartment.

"Yeah, she's good people." His gaze burns a trail up and down my body before he sets our bags in his walk-in closet, which is the size of my kitchen.

Christ on a cracker.

I've never felt so poor in my life, and I've been on welfare. I've stood in line to get food stamps with my mom. Frequented the dollar store to buy groceries, clothes, and shoes. I thought I was doing pretty good for myself with a job, paying rent, buying food. Sometimes I even give money to the homeless when I have a few extra bucks in my pocket. It's not much, but it's a life I've built for myself. Unassisted. Gabriel helps Mom, but I haven't taken a dime from him since I was eighteen.

My tainted history has me looking at Rowdy in a different light. One I'm not so proud of. Has he ever gone hungry? Faced eviction? Feared for his life because he could only afford to live in the worst neighborhoods? He faces guys as big as him for a living. Fear is not something he knows.

I, on the other hand, know it intimately on many levels.

"You can shower first, if you want."

Nodding, I grab my toiletries, a change of clothes and get lost in the bathroom big enough to park two cars in. This is not my life. This is a TV show.

Scrubbed clean, fresh breath and clothes, and a less judgmental attitude, I wait on the bed while he showers.

Scanning the shelves across the room, I spot Lego masterpieces of the thousand-plus-pieces variety; books; model airplanes and cars; pictures; DVDs; football, wrestling, and soccer trophies; and all kinds of trinkets from childhood. The mahogany built-in matches the room's décor, and it's beautiful while being masculine, like my Shadow.

His bed is massive, like the man. It can't be a standard king. It seems way bigger in width and length. A custom job to be sure.

The bathroom door opens, and through a puff of steam, Rowdy materializes like a god emerging from a heavenly portal, wearing only a towel.

Sweet Mary.

I bite my lip and sink down. Maybe he won't be able to find me in this Texas-sized bed of his. One minute ago, I was feeling confident about my experiment, ready to take a chance, try something I never thought I would *want* to do.

But now I'm second-guessing my sanity.

How do you tell a guy richer than God and bigger than the state he's from that you want to suck his cock?

Do you just throw it out there in passing? Or do I need to have his butler deliver an invitation for him to RSVP: *Yes, please, suck my cock,* or *No, thanks, I'm good…?*

Do I need to sign a non-disclosure agreement? *Sign here to agree to never share the details of Mr. Cameron Jenkins' massive cock, what his O face looks like, or expect that his enjoyment entitles you to any portion of his life or fortune.*

I'm going to puke.

"Kitten?" Rowdy stands over me, wearing gray sweat shorts and nothing else. He grazes my cheek with the tips of his fingers.

"You found me."

He barks out a laugh. "You doubted me?"

"Your bed is huge."

Still chuckling, he climbs over me and plops down on the other side, pulling me in till we're touching. "I'm a big guy."

That he is.

My hand flattens on a pec. His nipple hardens, and my breath quickens. "I've noticed."

Running a finger across my brow and into my hair, he leans in. "What's got you pensive? Regret coming?"

Coming. Lord have mercy.

"No." I prop up on my side, leaning over him as much as my narrow frame allows without lying on him. "I'm glad I'm here." I trace said pec, circle his nipple, before trailing the lines of his cut abs. I suck my bottom lip to stop from whimpering my approval.

"Kitten, what are you doing?" His husk has my panties soaked. If I were wearing any. Oops.

"I want to touch you." Not entirely true, but the butler was unavailable, so I'm going with the *ask for forgiveness, not permission* approach.

"You are touching me." He swallows, and the movement of his Adam's apple has me clenching around nothing and wanting to suck his neck to feel his pulse dance.

Who knew I was so wanton? I didn't, that's for sure.

I thought I was a frigid lost cause who would never know what desire feels like, much less tastes like.

I'm about to find out.

"Not as much as I want to." I straddle his thighs, my heart hammering against my chest.

His eyes scan my breasts as if he can hear it.

My nipples tighten.

He secures a hand on each hip. "Kitten."

"Do you trust me, Rowdy?"

"With my life," he exhales without hesitation.

"Good." I bend over and brush his mouth with mine. Only a taste. I can't resist sucking his bottom lip till he growls.

"Take your cock out, my Shadow. I want to play."

"Jesus Christ." I couldn't have heard her correctly.

Ever since we walked into my room, she's had something on her mind. I figured it was regret for coming. My home, my family can be a lot to take in.

Though I hoped not.

I never in a million years thought I'd hear my Kitten asking to see my cock so she can *play*.

Bashfully, she blinks at me, waiting. "Please don't make me say it again."

"You don't have—"

"I want to. I've just never—"

"Don't say that." If she talks about me being her first for anything, I'm going to come right here in my shorts with her as my witness.

Her mind is racing with a million replies. They all flash in her eyes.

I want—no, need—to know her history. I don't want to fuck this up. "I don't want to hurt you." That's the God's honest truth.

"Then take out the monster growling in your shorts." She edges back, licking her lips.

The cocky bastard bobs against its confinement, dying to be set free.

"You sure?"

This is not a good idea.

It's an amazing idea, Cocky argues.

She nods. "Don't stroke it or tell me to…" she trails off.

There's damage there. Anguish flickers across her face.

"Kitten. We don't have to do anything."

"Please, Cam. I need this. I need to know I can. I want you. You don't scare me. Not in the way…" she trails off again.

I'm a bastard. I'm going to hell.

I cup the back of her neck, pulling her down, garnering her eyes. "I don't want to hurt you." I need to be sure she hears that. "Tell me what you need."

"Take off your shorts. Let me touch you." She bites her lip. She's unsure.

"And?"

"Don't tell me what to do unless I ask."

"No commands. Got it." I hate her father more than ever. The fact that I'm even thinking of him should be a total boner killer, but the lioness on my lap is begging for my cock.

So, there's that. Yep, going to hell.

I edge my shorts down.

She lifts off me enough to remove them completely.

My cock lands on my abdomen and bounces when she stares at it. Fucker's preening.

"You okay?" I touch her leg, needing to know I haven't scarred her for life.

Her smile is a testament to her strength. "It's beautiful." She runs her hands up my thighs, holds on to my waist as she resumes straddling them.

My hands move back to her legs, needing the contact.

She trails soft pecks up my chest. I fight to remain still, my fingers itching to touch every inch of her.

I hold back a groan as she licks at my neck and nuzzles my jaw like a lioness loving on its mate. "You're beautiful." She kisses across my lips.

I'm not the beautiful one in this relationship.

Shit. Are we in a relationship?

We need to talk. I need to nail that down.

"Tell me what else I can't do." Before I lose my mind and embarrass myself.

A soft smile crosses her lips. "No commands. But you can tell me if you like something. How it feels."

"Can I touch you?" Please say *yes*.

Her sigh wafts over my face. "Rowdy, I don't fear your touch. I *crave* it."

Fucking hell. I was wrong.

I've died and gone to heaven.

CHAPTER 15

I'VE SEEN PENISES BEFORE. ONLY MOST WERE NOT in person. In fact, only one was in person.

It was always dark. There wasn't much *seeing*. It was more the motion of his hand as he tugged, angry and rough, that gave way to the shape of it and what it could do to a man—the way it made him feel. Pleasure.

Only that vision is tainted and evil.

I want to replace it with this… The vision of Rowdy, naked before me, hard all over, particularly in one place—his cock.

It's beautiful. Long. Thick. Straight. It really does resemble a snake. I understand that reference now. Avoiding his gaze, I touch it, tentatively at first until he sucks in air, then I wrap my hand around it.

"Soft, so very soft," I murmur in awe. I had no idea.

"Kitten, there's nothing soft about it," my Shadow grates through gritted teeth.

"Am I hurting you?" I start to release him, but he sits up, wrapping his hand around mine.

"No." Our lips are nearly touching. "Just driving me crazy."

Eyebrows pinched. I study his face, contemplating if *crazy* in this context is good or bad. "Do you want me to stop?"

"God, no." He kisses me sweetly, his breath warm on my face. "You're just getting started."

My heart jumps into overdrive.

He lies back, hands laced behind his head, a smirk on his all-too-handsomely-rugged face. "Do your worst."

My worst? That shouldn't be hard considering I've no idea what I'm doing.

I stare at it, dwarfing my hand. My fingers don't even touch. He's huge.

"You're staring at it like it's a puzzle you're trying to solve." Rowdy draws a rough hand up my arm, cupping the back of my neck. "Just touch me, Kitten. You won't hurt me." He tips my chin so our eyes meet. "You won't do anything wrong. There is no *wrong* when your hands are on me."

Crack. That's the sound of my heart breaking open for this man.

I'm scared and intimidated. What if I suck at this? And… I'm thinking entirely too much. I latch onto his wrist still holding my neck. "Kiss me."

He chuffs deep in his throat, meets me halfway, and claims my mouth as if it's always been his, and he doesn't want me to forget it.

What would he say if he knew my mouth has only ever been his?

He was my first kiss.

The only kiss I ever craved.

The only mouth I ever dreamt of.

As he licks at my tongue and nips my lips, a shudder has my nipples hardening and my inexperienced hand slowly stroking his cock in rhythm with his kiss.

The harder his kiss, the tighter my grip.

The deeper he sucks, the faster my hand moves.

His grip on my ass and the back of my neck urge me on.

Our groans and gasps—the soundtrack of our desire—have me grinding against his thighs, aching to be filled with the monster in my hand.

"Jesus, Kitten." He stills my hand. "You're gonna make me come."

Oh, no. I'm not done playing.

Releasing him, I push him down, trailing kisses down his neck, to his chest, scraping his nipples with my teeth and nails.

"Fuck," he hisses, running his hands over my body, kneading and cajoling.

Before I can chicken out, I lick down his velvety shaft, loving the feel of it on my tongue.

"Jesus Christ," he moans, sinking his fingers in my hair. Then he quickly frees me, his brow furrowing with uncertainty. Caution.

"Touch me, Rowdy. I need it. Show me what I do to you." I circle the head of his glorious cock, getting my first taste of his cum beading like a sweet treat on the tip.

"You're driving me insane, baby."

Yes, lose your mind.

Working my mouth around the cap, sucking lightly, has his fingers flexing in my hair, massaging my scalp.

My moan of appreciation has a stream of cuss words flying out of his mouth.

I beam with pride as my confidence grows, daring to take in more of him. "You're so big."

"Fuck. Don't say that." He curls down, capturing the side of my face and kissing my forehead, then my lips. "You're gonna make me blow, and I'm enjoying this too damn much for it to end so soon."

I didn't think my struggle to take him deeper would be a turn on. I'd think he'd be disappointed.

Struggle as I might, I can't take him all. He moans each time I try.

When I gag, he growls, tightening his grip on my hair and easing me off him.

But I'm determined. I won't give up.

Deeper and deeper. I suck so hard my cheeks hollow out.

He curses and caresses my cheeks.

I'm drooling, tears running down my face. I'm a hot mess.

And he looks at me like I'm the most beautiful thing he's ever seen.

Words of praise mixed with his dirty mouth have me soaking my sleep shorts, my hips dipping, flexing to find pleasure.

"Fuck, Kitten. You need my touch, don't you?" He half sits, his abdominals clenched, and slips his hands down the back of my shorts, squeezing my bare ass, pulling me forward till the top of my head hits his stomach.

I swallow him deep and stay there, sucking, running my tongue along the underside of his shaft just as he slips a finger inside me.

Ohmygod! I buck and moan, pulling back and taking him deeper.

"You're dripping for me." He's so proud.

I'm a total wreck as his finger slips barely in and out of me.

I clench around him. Tingles bubble up.

I can't. I'm gonna come.

He needs to come first.

"No," he growls when I wiggle out of his hold. "Fuck, I want your sweet pussy."

Glaring, I push on his chest until he's lying flat on his back. I can't concentrate with him touching me like that. Now that I can think, I lick his seam and relish his animalistic sounds when I suck him down. I work him hard and fast. I worry I might be too rough until his hand is on my neck squeezing lightly.

"Coming, Kitten. Let go if you don't want it down your throat."

Down my throat.

I hadn't thought that far, but the idea of him feeding me his cum is an experience I don't want to miss. I wanted to know what desire tastes like. Here's my chance.

Humming and nodding my consent, I stroke his base and suck him down as far as I can, bobbing my head like I'm searching for apples.

"Now, Reese!" he cries, his fingers lost in my hair, his body flexing and tensing as his cock pulses. Then, like a firehose, warm salty liquid coats my throat in pumping blasts.

I fight to swallow.

I fight to breathe.

I fight not to come too.

He cusses a blue streak.

Pumps his hips a few times.

He caresses my back while I suck him clean, rimming the head a few times, elated when more of his desire pumps free.

I lick every drop.

"You've killed me." He falls limp, arms at his sides, fingers grazing my knees. "Give me a year to recover, then I'm eating my dessert."

CHAPTER 16

WHEN GOD MADE REESE, I DOUBT HE KNEW He was making *my* perfect woman. Innocent and dirty. Confident and shy. Lion and mouse. I can't image He had a dark ass like me in mind.

If he did, I'm sorry for Reese. 'Cause I think she's stuck with me.

I've had plenty of blowjobs. Some quite spectacular. Some mind-blowing. Some forgettable at best.

But the feel of Reese taking my cock down her throat and gagging to do so? I'm done for.

Where do I sign?

Is there a membership fee?

Please tell me there are no recalls, as I have no intention of giving her back.

Come hell or high water, Reese is mine. Now I have to convince her of that.

Slowly, blood makes its way to my brain and outer limbs. My cock—the blood hog—finally sated, I can think again.

My Kitten lies beside me, biting her lip, insecure in her skills. Ignorant of her effect on me.

I can't wait to show her.

A bit sluggish, I face her, securing my hand on her ass and hauling her against me, smiling when she squeaks. Pulling her leg over my hip, pressing her against my half-hard cock, I grind against her. "You've no idea what you've started."

Her eyes widen, then soften into slits as she smiles. She knows.

"What have I started, Shadow?"

Shadow. I like it. She's scared of the dark. But she's not afraid of me.

"You've unleashed the beast, Kitten. The one that's going to taste you and make you come until you beg me to stop." I suck her bottom lip. "And you will beg."

She shivers.

I lick at her lips until she lets me in.

Her fire, burning so damn hot, its flames lash at my balls. Grinding her hips, she opens her mouth, lapping at my tongue, inviting me in, and in, and in.

Before we get carried away, I cinch her neck and tip her head back so our eyes meet, barely any air between us. "I want to taste you. Touch you. Lap at you. Drink you in. But if at any time you want me to stop, just say it. I tease about begging, but I'm not teasing about this. I want you hungry and wanton, not fearful. There's no fear here. No danger. You tell me. It stops. You control what happens. Understand?"

"What if I'm afraid because of inexperience, not because I don't want you?" Blue soulful eyes read into mine.

"If there's something you want to try, want to work through the fear with me, then you tell me. We'll take it slow, talk about it. But if, in the end, you change your mind, all you have to stay is *stop.*"

"But what if I really don't want you to stop?"

This girl. She's going to challenge me.

"There will be times when it feels too good or too much, and your first reaction will be to ask me to *stop.* You either have to be able to acknowledge those times and not say it, or we need a safe word. A word that shuts everything down. No exceptions."

We're not really in safe-word territory, but with my girl, I'm not taking any chances. I'm overly cautious and optimistic.

"A safe word," she contemplates, her finger tapping my shoulder.

"Yeah, not a word you'd ever use during sex. It could be a food, but probably not one you'd say often. But one you won't forget."

"Cucumber?" She shrugs.

"Cucumber?"

"Yeah, I'm not particularly fond of them, and they're big like your cock so I won't forget."

I'm not crazy about her safe word associating my cock with a food she doesn't like. I want her to like my cock. Like she *can't get enough of it.* But it's a good word. "Sure. Why not?"

Now that that's settled...

"Rowdy?"

"Yeah, Kitten?"

She teases her bottom lip. "Do you think you could make me come now?"

Christ.

She will be the end of me. Or the beginning. I'm not rightly sure which.

But one thing's for certain, life will never be the same again.

"Ohmygod." I fist his hair, holding him to my breast as he sucks the hell out of my nipples. One, then the other.

His entire hand cups my privates with only one finger drilling into me, driving me insane. Every touch is fuel to the growing fire inside me. My skin pricks, my walls clench, my asshole puckers, my hips move of their own accord, begging for more. And my gasps are so desperate, I fear I'll never get a full breath again.

I'm dying. This is it.

How does anyone survive this man? Does he have a string of dead lovers trailing behind him? Surely they don't live to tell the tale of Rowdy The Pussy Whisperer.

"Rowdy," I beg as much as plead for him to put me out of my misery.

"I've got you, Kitten." He kisses down my stomach.

My breasts are pissed he abandoned them so easily. I wrench my back when he licks over my hipbone, nuzzles my mound with his nose, then kisses my lady lips straight on.

I've never been so mortified and exhilarated at the same time.

He groans into his intimate kiss, setting off a shockwave I feel to the tips of my toes. Nudging my thighs, he settles in, slings my legs over his broad shoulders, his thumbs holding me open as he pecks kisses around the most embarrassing place anyone has ever gazed upon.

"You're so fucking beautiful. Pink and wet." He's looking at me like he's struck gold.

I squirm and contract.

He teases my opening before dipping inside. "You're squeezing me so good, baby."

"Is that good?"

"Oh yeah." He praises me like I have some kind of control over my body's reaction to what he's doing to me.

When a second finger joins the first, the discomfort is immediate. I suck in a breath, gasping my surprise.

"Sorry." He slows his thrusts and licks my clit, coaxing my body into submission. "That's it."

By the time my brain realizes it's feeling pleasure instead of pain, he's kneading my insides, rounding my nub with his tongue, and his free hand has found my needy breasts. Thank God.

He's a maestro, working my triangle of happiness: nipples, clit, G-spot, playing a chord I've never heard before and didn't even know existed.

The tempo increases.

A chorus of my cries. His grunts join the symphony.

A wave of supersonic proportions builds inside me, shaking me to my core.

This is it. My death.

My vision blurs, ears ring, my body lifts off the bed. Head thrown back, I cling to the only hope of saving me—the man between my thighs, licking me like I'm his favorite lollipop.

The blast inside me explodes. I shatter into a million pieces, skyrocketing into the stratosphere.

Never.

Never.

Never to be seen again.

CHAPTER 17

WAKING UP BESIDE REESE FOR THE SECOND day in a row is my new happy place. Besides her pussy. Oh, and her mouth.

Yesterday was a hellacious drudgery of funeral arrangements, talking business with Dad, comforting Taylor and avoiding Drake like he has the plague. Because he does.

The Asshole Plague.

You've heard of Typhoid Mary? Well, he's Douchebag Drake.

Everything felt like it took extra effort; even breathing and walking felt sluggish and discombobulated. Numb was the feeling of the day, except where it came to Reese.

She was the highpoint. Every thought ended up at her. The feel of her on my tongue. The mind-blowing feel of her mouth on my cock.

It's not just the physical stuff. She centers me. One look, one touch, and my darkness fades, my pulse races for a whole other reason, and her smile notches her place in my chest.

I'm so fucking thankful she's here. She makes today bearable.

I slip on a pair of workout shorts and a t-shirt, then turn to find her ogling my ass. I love her eyes on me. Always on me.

"Morning, Kitten."

"Good morning." She sits up, holding the sheet over her bare chest, naked as the day is long, in my fucking bed. Cue the chest thumping.

"You're up early." She frowns at the clock.

"I'd like to take you somewhere this morning before the funeral. If you're up to it."

We didn't get much sleep. We haven't had sex, but we certainly haven't been keeping our hands—mouths—to ourselves.

One heated look, and I swear my kitten purrs like she was made for me.

She was. I've no doubt.

"Yeah, give me a minute to throw on some clothes." She rubs her tummy as it growls.

"I'm taking you to breakfast."

She beams her electric smile.

Damn this woman gets me going. Cocky jumps in my pants, elongating down my thigh.

Nope. I have vertical plans.

We could do her against the wall, Cocky suggests.

Shut the fuck up.

I kiss her forehead and step back before she can touch me, blowing my *non-sexual* plans for the morning. "I'll see you downstairs."

I make my escape, socks and shoes in hand, ignoring her eyes on my crotch.

She wants a taste, Cocky sulks.

I ignore him too.

I have things to do, things to share before we say goodbye to Mom this afternoon.

Biting back the rage at the injustice of it all, I stalk to the kitchen.

Mom should be here to meet Reese.

To know her grandkids.

The ones you'll have someday with Reese.

Wait. What?

Damn, that just snuck in there.

Mom, was that you?

No answer. Not that I expected one.

I want Reese. There's no doubt. Kids don't seem like a stretch.

That would require sex, though, and we're not having the kind that makes babies.

Yet.

I don't even bother with a shower. I just had one a few hours ago with Rowdy. Man, how far my sex life has progressed to never having been kissed to near shower sex with The Pussy Whisperer.

We got dirty under that shower spray before he was nice enough to clean me up.

He's thoughtful like that.

Slipping into my sneakers, I locate my purse across the room in the sitting area. I wasn't sure it had made it to the room last night.

Rowdy basically threw me over his shoulder and carried me to his wing after a day of dealing with his family. We didn't even eat with them. He had dinner waiting for us in his room. Thank you, Helga.

We snuggled and watched TV as we munched on the most delicious hamburger and steak fries I've ever eaten.

And for dessert? Him, of course.

I grab my purse on my way out to find my Shadow.

Today's gonna be hard. Whatever he needs, I'm here.

After a short drive with the sunrise breaking over the horizon, Rowdy pulls into a marina. I knew we were close to the water, but I didn't realize how close.

"Come on." With a bag slung over his shoulder, he takes my hand. "You don't get seasick, do you?"

I trip over my feet. "Wha… We're going out on a boat?"

He nods like it's no big deal and keeps walking, but now I'm tucked under his arm to avoid a future trip, I suppose.

"We can't. What about…" What am I balking about? If he wants to miss his mom's funeral, I'm not going to stop him. Whatever he needs today, I'm his girl.

"Only a few hours, Kitten. We'll be back in plenty of time to shower and dress." He stops in front of what I can only describe as a yacht. It definitely is not the kind of boat I was envisioning. His light eyes rival the water glistening below our feet. "I need this."

Yep, totally in. "Then what are we waiting for, Shadow?"

His dimples stir hormones and warm my heart. "Not a damn thing." A quick kiss and he's pulling me up the gangplank to be greeted by the crew.

Crew. He has a yacht and a crew.

I'd nearly forgotten we're on a TV show. Otherwise, I might be intimidated by the opulence of his wealth and the men in seafaring uniforms calling him sir and Mr. Permian-O'Dair.

"I thought your last name was Jenkins," I side-whisper as we climb the stairs to the top deck.

"It is… And it's not."

There's a story there.

"Sit. Eat." He holds out a chair for me to sit at a smartly dressed table set for two with a view of the sunrise and the Gulf of Mexico.

TV show, remember? Next, he'll be whisking me away on a private jet.

Bite my tongue. I don't think I could handle that. Though, the idea of not bumping against other passengers like cattle sounds ideal.

As we're served a breakfast of eggs Benedict, home fries, waffles, pancakes, fresh fruit, coffee, tea, water and an assortment of juices, all served on china and crystal goblets, I lose my train of thought and gawk at the feast in front of us.

"Everything okay, Kitten?"

It's all my favorite foods. Not just breakfast food. My all-time favorite foods, regardless of the meal. Breakfast is perfection any time of day.

"Did you order this food special for me?" It can't be a coincidence.

He shrugs. "I thought you might like options."

Options? There's enough food here to feed me for a week, maybe two if I ration.

The hamburger last night. It's one of my favorite foods too. "Are you trying to woo me with food?" I'm not complaining, really. Shocked is all. Most people don't give me the time of day, much less think enough about what I might want to eat and plan ahead for it.

"Is it working?" His devilish smile is all too confident.

No. I want to say to be obstinate, but, hello, eggs Benedict. "Maybe."

He watches as I cut off a bite of EB. His eyes follow my fork all the way to my mouth, eyes hooded as I lick my lips and chew. He licks his lips in return as if he can still taste me. "Good?"

The silky hollandaise is pure perfection. I'd like a bath in it.

My eyes lock with the hunk of a man sitting across from me. "I might just dip you in this hollandaise."

"Fuck." He stands, pushing the chair back with his massive thighs and rounds the table, his hand cupping my neck and tipping my chin. Thumb grazing my throat, he waits for me to swallow.

Gah, he's hot when he goes all alpha.

I choke down my bite and melt when he braces his other hand on the back of my chair and leans down, licking my lips, then he dives in, sweeping his tongue, groaning at what I would guess is the hollandaise mixed with me and a shit ton of desire.

I'm Jello by the time he pecks my mouth, forehead, and traipses to his seat like he didn't just suck my bite from my mouth, nearly, and the air from my lungs, completely.

Also, I don't miss the bulge in his pants. He's just as messed up over this as I am.

Smiling, I indulge in another bite or a thousand, but who's counting?

Breakfast devoured, Rowdy rolls me to an outside sitting area, covered and decorated like an indoor living room.

It's insane.

Long, white, linking couches covered in plush sky-blue cushions and white throw pillows make a large arc from one side to the other. End tables, chairs, and another outside eating area with a bar cover the other half.

Rowdy takes a seat in the corner and pulls me down beside him, our hands linked, resting on his leg. He scans the horizon, a far-off look in his eye. "I've always loved this place. It's my escape."

Of course it is. "It's incredible."

His smile is only a wisp of what it normally is as he kisses my temple. "If we had more time, I'd take you out for a few days."

That would be something. I've never been on the water. Even if I had, it wouldn't compare to this. "Another time then."

"It's a date."

Lost in our own thoughts, I rest my head on his shoulder as the boat slips through the water. The sun farther in the sky shines like gold and the promise of a beautiful day.

"He always hated me," he speaks over me, resting his head on mine.

"Who?"

"Drake."

"He doesn't seem to like anybody."

Rowdy laughs and wraps an arm around me, situating us so I'm practically lying on his reclined form.

"He's a sour puss most of the time. I don't know how he even makes it through the day being such an ass all the time."

"Sounds miserable," I agree.

Silence for a beat. "He used to beat me up. My parents thought I was accident prone. It was no accident. For as long as I can remember he'd show up around a corner or step into a room and hurt me in some way."

Ohmygod. "That's horrible. Why didn't you tell anyone?"

He tips my chin, his sorrowful eyes beckoning me. "Why didn't you?"

Oh, fuck. How did we switch to me? I thought this was his story time, not mine.

Anything he needs.

I sigh into his embrace. "Shame. Embarrassment. Worrying maybe I deserved it," I offer my sad truth.

"Same." He runs a crooked finger down my cheek. "I didn't know any better. I thought all brothers were hellish minions. Till my best friend in fifth grade caught on. He sat me down and told me what my brother did was not normal. He had an older brother, but I never realized until that moment that his brother didn't hurt him the same way, get him into trouble to sit back and watch. Drake's attacks were not like normal sibling bullshit. That's when I started fighting back." Rowdy's hand on my back grips my hip, releases, then traces circles. "I outgrew him two years later. By ninth grade, I was a black belt. He never touched me again. His physical attacks stopped, but the verbal abuse never did. He was always an ass, probably always will be."

The darkness, the rage I sense in Rowdy at times makes sense. How could you not be angry when someone who's supposed to look out for you, show you the ropes, is the one tying you up and making sure you trip on them instead?

I'm so disappointed in his parents for not putting a stop to it. They had to have suspected. A kid can't go his whole childhood being bullied by a sibling and it go unnoticed.

"Shh, Kitten." He sinks lower and pulls me tighter. "It's fine. I didn't mean to upset you." Kiss to my forehead. "I just wanted you to know. I want you to know all of me." Kiss to my lips. "Even the not-so-pleasant parts."

Crack. He burrows further into my heart. At this rate, he'll own every splintered piece of it.

But what would he want with a damaged crazy like me for the long haul? Especially if I ever get up the nerve to tell him my *not-so-pleasant parts.*

Not today.

Today is about him.

Today is the day he buries his mother.

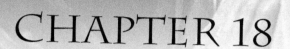

CHAPTER 18

PALLBEARER. I ALWAYS THOUGHT IT WAS pronounced *pole*bearer. Maybe it's the Texan in me. We tend to pronounce things differently. But right here in Mom's program, it says I'm a *pall*bearer.

Learn something new every day, even at Mom's funeral.

Reese keeps squeezing my leg. My hands are clasped in my lap, trying to squelch the urge to curse God for taking my mom.

My Kitten only wants to be sure I'm alright. Which, of course, I'm not. Not by a long shot.

I clasp her hand instead of my own. Her sure, made-for-me fit stills the brewing storm. Doubt it will last.

I need to hit something. Someone. God? Drake?

Drake is probably a better choice. God's a little above my paygrade.

When they found Mom's cancer, it was already too late. The ovarian cancer had consumed her ovaries before moving on to her kidneys, spleen, intestines, and lymph nodes. The brain was probably next, if she'd survived long enough to have treatment. Then survived long enough to make the dismal five-year mark that most stage four ovarian cancer diagnoses don't make.

Mom was a stickler for her yearly checkups. According to Dad, her symptoms led the doctors in so many other directions first. It wasn't until they decided to do a complete hysterectomy that they discovered cancer.

I didn't even know she was having surgery. She never told me. I didn't ask.

It's not something you *ask* in normal conversation. *Hey, Mom, any surgeries this week? No, good. Great news.*

She. Should. Have. Told. Me.

Right there on the operating room table, the surgeon took one look and closed her up. The damage was too extensive. They were going to try chemo to see if it shrank the tumors before attempting surgery again.

That didn't happen.

She rolled over in the middle of the night, grasped Dad's hand, told him, "I love you," and took her last breath.

Her last fucking breath was to give the reassurance of her love to the man she devoted her life to.

Fuck. Me.

Reese squeezes me, leaning in, her head on my shoulder, swiping at her tears.

My Kitten will never know my mom. Not in the way she deserves. Mom would have loved her. I think she already did in the months I talked about my girl.

Mom knew.

It took me a while to get my head out of my ass over Frankie. Mom understood that too. That's why I loved her so damn much.

The vise grip on my chest is crushing my heart and making it hard to breathe.

"Cam," my girl cries into my chest. Does she feel it?

Wrapping her in my arms, I bury my face in her shoulder, gritting my teeth to hold back a sob. Crying is okay, but my grown ass weeping in the middle of Mom's service is not.

Dad squeezes my shoulder from the other side. Next to him is

Taylor. She is sobbing into Drake's chest. Thankfully not being a jerk at the moment, he comforts her with tears looming in his eyes.

He loved Mom too.

Everyone did. There was nothing not to love about her.

Once the church and gravesite services are over, I grab Reese's hand and all but drag her to my car. There's a reception at our house.

Why it's at our house instead of somewhere else is beyond me.

Mourners do not want get-togethers at their home where they have to entertain and clean up. It should be elsewhere so we can show up, make an appearance and get the fuck out.

One and done.

"Do you want me to drive?" Reese tugs on my arm, getting my attention.

Shit. I really am dragging her.

I shake my head and slow my steps. "I got it."

At the car, I open her door but hold her back. "I'm sorry, Kitten." It's a shit day. I'm in a shit mood.

She snakes her hand into my hair, tugging me closer. Nose to nose, she kisses me once. Soft, quick, but a touch of her tongue to my lip has my mood softening.

"You don't need to apologize. You have every right to be upset, out of sorts today." With a pat to my chest, she slips inside the car.

I have permission to feel lousy. I might just take her up on it. Or I might convince her to let me take out my mood on her body.

Nearly home, her hand resting on my forearm on the console between us, she clears her throat, glances at me, her lips stuck between her teeth. "You need to hit something, don't you?"

She's perfect. Made. For. Me. "Yeah, I do."

She nods. "Well, I'm no sparring partner, but you've got quite a home gym. Maybe I could keep you company while you beat the hell out of the punching bag or hold those punching gloves thingies while you whack at my palms."

Damn, she's cute. I crack a smile. "Punching mitts?"

"Yeah." She holds up her hands, weaving in her seat in demonstration.

The idea of taping up my hands and taking swings at *her*, even light jabs, ties my gut in knots. I'd never hurt my girl. I don't know if I'd recover if I flipped her PTSD switch while sparring.

"I could teach you how to throw a punch." I offer an alternative and catch her glower out of the side of my eye. "Some self-defense moves?"

She narrows her gaze. "I know how to defend myself."

Good.

"You think Gabriel would let me live alone if I didn't?"

The baseball bat behind her apartment door comes to mind. "You can try to kick my ass then. Show me what you got, Kitten."

The thing is, she can't stand another man's touch. How can she possibly defend herself if she's in the middle of a PTSD episode? I'm sure Gabriel showed her some moves, and she practiced them on him. But she's not afraid of Gabriel touching her. She's not afraid of me either. Any training she has is useless against anyone who means her harm if they trigger an episode before she can react.

My bad mood just went to defcon one.

Rowdy doesn't take me up on my semi-sparring offer. Or my gawking at him while he works out his frustration on a punching bag.

I won't take it personally. It's his day to be shitty and feel shitty. He gets a pass.

I truly would love to watch him work out. Though, it would be more for my enjoyment than his. I can't really stare at him in the gym at home. It wouldn't be professional. Plus, hella embarrassing.

Leaving the scowling man with his father and sister to mingle with their guests, I search out a bathroom not occupied or with a line.

Finding none on my first couple of tries, I decide heading to Rowdy's wing is probably the quickest bet, though farther away.

I text him so he doesn't worry and take the opportunity to taunt him with a game of pool. How ridiculously big is this place that I'm texting so he doesn't worry about me?

I've seen the billiards room in passing but haven't checked it out. Today seems like a good day for mindless distractions. Plus, it's on the other side of the house, closed off from the reception area.

In the bathroom, I slip off my heels, giving my feet a break. As much as I love the way they make my legs look, I don't wear heels enough to be comfortable in them for more than a few hours.

Is anyone? Really?

Taking a few extra moments, I touch up my barely-there makeup, then bite the bullet and don the torture devices for feet again.

I reply to a few texts from Cap, Gabriel, and Frankie, pausing here and there in the halls so I don't trip or run into a wall. Not getting a reply from Rowdy, I scurry down the outer corridors, avoiding the main rooms where everyone is gathering, and make my way to the billiards room, which is in the opposite wing from Rowdy's.

He might be there.

The room is dimly lit when I enter.

Hmm. Romantic.

And... Empty.

Disappointed, I text him again and mill about, hoping he'll join me.

Footfalls from behind me have me stilling, smirking to myself, excited to play a silly game of pool in the hopes of lightening his mood.

He stills in the entry.

My skin pricks to turn around, but I wait to see what he'll do. Will he hug me from behind and kiss my neck? Or will he pick out a cue, sizing it up, wanting to get right to the game? He's understandably mercurial today. It's hard to know which way he'll go.

The click of the doors closing amps the anticipation.

Unable to resist, I turn.

"Well, if it isn't *Kitten*." My pet name on his lips feels tawdry instead of adoring. "He finally let you off your leash, hmm?"

"What? No."

Drake continues as if I hadn't spoken, "You know…" He saunters closer. I step back, two steps for his one. "My brother and I have been known to share women." He takes a drink of the light liquor in his tumbler. He points his hand holding his drink at me. "One woman in particular comes to mind. Audra." His words are slurred as he spits out her name with distaste.

He steps into me. That same finger used to point lightly touches my hair. "She was quite beautiful."

The buzz that started the second I saw him instead of Rowdy in front of the closed doors ratchets up a notch. Shivering my disgust, I step around him, only to be caught by the arm.

"Now, Kitten, don't be like that." His hold tightens.

"No," I whimper as my vision narrows and darkness descends.

He nuzzles my hair. "Sometimes *no* really means *yes*."

"No." I push against his chest. "No *always* means *no*," I tremble with my last full breath. My knees quake, threatening to give out.

Panic claws at my throat.

This is not happening.

"Oh, but it is."

CHAPTER 19

FIFTEEN MINUTES PASS AND REESE STILL HASN'T returned. I scour the halls around the reception. No luck.

Remembering I have a brain, I pull out my phone to text her, only to find she's already texted me.

Kitten: *No joy on the bathroom situation.*

No joy. My girl's funny.

Kitten: *Heading to our room.*

Love that she calls it *our* room. Setting down my beer, I head that way, continuing to read her texts.

Kitten: *Fancy a game of pool?*

Kitten: *Meet me in the billiards room with the wrench, Professor Plum.*

Damn, I might just love this woman for her texting sense of humor alone.

Love. Well, shit. I lose my mom and fall in love all in the same week.

When one door closes, another one opens, I hear my mom's voice in my head.

Yeah, well, I wouldn't have minded both doors staying open for a while, allowing for a cross breeze and for my girls to meet.

Crushed with a wave of loss, I take a minute in the library to get my bearings. Sitting in Mom's favorite chair that still smells like her, my breath catches and tears break free.

I'm so angry at her for not letting me know she was gravely sick. She stole my choice to tell her goodbye.

If I had known how sick she was, I would have dropped everything to be here. I would've stayed till the end.

You didn't need to see that, her voice echoes in my skull.

"It wasn't your choice," I cry into the empty room.

I died the way I wanted. In my husband's arms, knowing the light of my life was making a life for himself with a girl who could pin his Shadow.

Jesus. I'm losing my mind.

"She's not fucking Tinkerbell."

Wendy. She's your Wendy.

In perfect timing, my phone vibrates with a text.

Kitten: *Miss Scarlett is going to start without you.*

Fuck.

"Sorry, Mom. I gotta go see my Wendy."

Hurry, dear.

I've lost my damn mind. There's no way I'm having an actual conversation with Mom, right?

Nonetheless, I dash out of the room, nearly plowing over my dad, who stops my progress with hand on my chest. He's strong for a little guy at barely 5'10".

"What's the hurry, Son?"

"I'm looking for Reese." Not a lie. Not the whole truth.

"Hmm. I was looking for your brother—"

"Fuck. How long?"

"I don't know, thirty minutes or so. Your sister has had about all of this she can take. I was hoping he'd keep her company, run interference. Better than her being by herself in her misery."

I hurry down the hall, speaking over my shoulder, "I'll send him your way if I find him." Or kill him if he's where I fear he is.

I promised I wouldn't leave her alone with him. I've been too wrapped up in my pain to look out for my girl.

Fuck, I'm an idiot.

Rounding the last corner, my heart skips at the sight of the closed door to the billiards room.

He's dead. Venom courses through my veins.

Seconds before I barrel through the door, I hear my girl's panicked murmur, "No, don't touch me. No!"

Spike through my fucking heart.

I rip the door open, entering without pause for what I'll find on the other side.

Drake has a vise grip on Reese's arms as she beats at his chest, tears streaming down her face, and her desolate cries of "No!" will haunt me for the rest of my life.

"Get your fucking hands off her!" I roar, ripping her from his grasp.

"Now, now, Brother. You never minded sharing before."

"No, please!" my girl screams and resumes her attacking blows, but to my chest instead.

"Reese." I wrap around her like a straitjacket, locking her arms down with my hold, and cup her head to my chest. "Kitten, it's Rowdy," I speak into her ear. "You're safe. I won't let him or anyone harm you." I kiss her head, praying she can hear me. "It's me, baby. You're safe now."

It only takes seconds for her fight to dissipate, her cries to wane into whimpers, and her body to fall slack in my embrace. The entire time I glare over her head to my brother, who hasn't stopped rambling.

"What the fuck are you talking about?" I berate him.

"You just couldn't let me have one thing to myself, could you?" he slurs, red-faced and ridiculously angry. "She was mine!"

"Who?!" I swear, if I didn't need to hold my girl, he'd be laid out unconscious by now.

"Audra! You fucking moron. She was mine!"

I flinch as if he struck me. "The maid?"

"She was mine, and you fucked her!" he bellows. He staggers but manages to catch himself on the pool table.

Jesus. "That was eight years ago. I didn't know you were banging her. She climbed in my bed one night. *She* fucked *me*. I was fifteen, for Christ's sake. I barely knew how my dick worked, much less had the wherewithal or desire to steal a woman from you."

He balks as he pours himself another drink. *Yeah, poison yourself with alcohol, see if I stop you.*

"Is that why you hate me? All this time you've been carrying this anger about a woman I barely remember—who I didn't even know you had feelings for?"

No, that can't be right. He's hated me long before then. Since we were kids, since I was in diapers. He'd walk by me and push me down. Take my toys away or break them if he could. It wasn't long before it turned physical: pinching, scratching, twisting, hitting.

The older he got, the worse it became.

Until I was big enough to hit him back.

Until I was big enough to knock him out.

"God, you really are dense, aren't you?"

Yep, when he couldn't beat me up physically any longer, the mental abuse started. I was *dumb, stupid, retarded.* Any name he could think of, he'd call me that, whisper it behind my back to my friends, to any girl I liked.

His same old repertoire is tiring and gets on my last nerves. He's why I don't come home. Why I rarely did. My parents were blind to his abuse. Avoidance was easier than breaking their hearts by showing them how spiteful he really was.

"Why don't you spell it out for me, Drake? Help a brother out?" Calmer, I lift Reese off her feet and lay her on the couch, sitting next to her, smoothing out her hair and drying her tears. Remarkably, she's asleep in seconds.

"That's just it..." He points a shaking hand in my direction. "You're not my brother."

"You're drunk," I dismiss him, pissing him off more.

He advances, and I stand, a wall between him and Reese.

"I may be drunk, but I'm still Mom and Dad's kid." He points, poking me in the chest. "You, you big bastard, are not."

What. The. Fuck?

"Drake!" my father bellows from the doorway.

We both swing in his direction. Drake stumbles, righting himself once again. I wish he'd just pass out and shut up already.

Steam rises from my father's head as he directs his angry glare at his oldest son. "Drake, go to your room."

"Dad! I'm not a kid." His whine negates his words.

"You're acting like a selfish, spoiled rotten brat." Dad rubs a hand over his brow. "And you're drunk."

Before my asshole brother can comply, I lock on to his arm, swinging him around, and lay him out with a single blow to his cheek. Not as hard as I want, but hard enough to make my point.

He spits some blood. "You mad I called you bastard, bastard?"

"This is about *her*." I lean in. "If you ever lay a hand on my girl again. I will end you. If you even look at her wrong, speak an ill word to her or about her, I will rip off your dick and feed it to you." I push him hard, relishing the fear on his face as he slams into the wall. "You hear me, *brother*?" I consider spitting on him for good measure, but Mom would be disappointed.

A chin nod is all I get before he crumbles to the floor and passes out, finally giving me some peace.

Hitching Reese in my arms, I make for the door.

Dad's sorrowful voice stops me. "Put her to bed, Son. Then meet me in my study. We need to talk."

"I'm not leaving her. If you want to talk, come with me."

Without question, he follows.

CHAPTER 20

I'M JOSTLED FROM UNCONSCIOUSNESS. MY HEAD pounds. I grip at the firm body holding me, taking in his familiar scent. No one smells safe and good like my Shadow, clean with a masculine edge, and yummy-smelling conditioner making me want to delve into his hair and never come out.

Warm lips skim my cheek. "Shh, I got you."

Luxuriating in his hold, I give myself a few more peaceful moments before I have to open my eyes and act like the adult I claim to be.

His brother touched me, and I freaked out in his family home, during his mother's funeral reception.

I'm such a catch. It's no wonder I've never had a boyfriend. My damage flag was flying high.

I squint into the brightness, one eye, then the other.

Clouds.

Clouds?! I jolt forward, blinking till I can focus on the oval window before me. We're on a fucking plane. "Ugh, Rowdy? How the hell did you get me on a plane?"

Sequestered on his lap, in his arms, he tips my chin, presses a kiss to my needy mouth and smiles with sad eyes. "You were lights out,

Kitten." The gravel in his voice makes me want to crawl inside him, find every dark, abandoned corner and kiss it better.

"Why are we on a plane?" *Instead of spending time with your family.* Oh! I bury my head in his chest. "You left because of me, didn't you? Because of Drake—"

"No." He tenderly eases me out of my hiding place, wanting my eyes. "No." He tips a brow. "Though... I would have left for that reason. He had no right to touch you. I'm so sorry."

"Not your fault."

"I promised no one would ever hurt you again. I promised to keep you at my side."

Damn, this man. He knows how to edge inside and stay. But... "I'm not your problem, Cam."

I edge off his lap. Straightening my t-shirt, I notice two things instantly:

ONE: I'm in yoga pants and a t-shirt. The last I looked, I was wearing my dress from the funeral. "Um..." I motion to my body. "How?"

TWO: We're on a private plane. Tan leather seats, two to a side, wide aisle, a couch, flat screen TV, wet bar, and a lady dressed like a flight attendant finger waves at me from the back of the plane. I reticently smile and wave back. Locking on Rowdy, I motion around me. "What the ever-loving fuck happened?"

Panic rises along with whatever is left in my stomach. I swallow hard to keep both down.

He captures my hand and pulls me between his parted legs. "Breathe, Kitten." He squeezes my hips.

Near tears, I fall into the seat across from his—facing him—and close my eyes. I passed out—not merely sleeping. "You undressed me." I'm not upset that *he* did. I'm upset that it could have been *anyone* undressing me.

What if it hadn't been him? It could have been Drake or... Nope. Not going there.

"I assume you packed our bags, carried me out of the house, into a car, and into this plane." I stutter air into my aching lungs. "All while I was completely knocked out and oblivious."

In seconds he's leaning over me, hands on the armrest, eyes burning into mine. "I'd never hurt you. Never, Reese."

I bite my lip, shaking my head. "It's not about that."

He sighs and sits next to me, holding my hands in his so-much-larger ones. "Then what's it about?"

I fight back tears with an ugly grimace, I've no doubt. "My brain wakes up and sees different clothes and freaks, thinking... what if it wasn't you? It could have been—"

"No. Fuck, no. It couldn't and wouldn't have been anyone other than me. I should have realized why that would freak you out, waking up in different clothes. I'm sorry." He picks me up like my 5'8" frame weighs nothing, stalks a few paces and plants us on the couch, then asks the attendant for a few waters and food.

"Whose plane is this?"

"My family's."

Right. TV show. I nearly forgot. "And why are we flying home—that's where we're going, isn't it?"

"Yes."

"Why are we flying home instead of being with your family?" *Please don't say it's because of me and my crazy.*

"Something happened." He buries his fingers in my loose hair. "I'd rather not talk about it."

"Was it me?"

"No!"

"Did you kill Drake?" I'm teasing. But, oh God, did he?

His chuckle is a relief. "No. He deserved it, and I would have been happy to dole out the punishment. But, no. I didn't kill Drake. I punched him and threatened his life. He'll never touch you again." He kisses me softly then sighs on a deep exhale. "Sadly, he lives to pollute another day."

"Okay. I'm sorry for whatever happened to make you leave your dad and sister." I rest my head on his shoulder, feeling him all around me. "I'm here if you want to talk about it."

"I appreciate it." Another kiss. "What about you? Are you okay? Did he hurt you?"

My arms hurt from Drake's hold on me. My hands feel bruised from pulling and hitting him. I'm tired from the adrenaline crash, and my head hurts. "I'm fine."

Rowdy chuffs his discontent, not buying it. His hold tightens, allowing me to rest on him until he rouses me to eat.

When I try to get off his lap to let him eat in peace, he stills me with a brusque "Stay."

He can't be serious.

Reading me like he does, holding my face to his, he reiterates, "Please stay, Kitten."

I acquiesce, letting him feed me bites off the charcuterie board placed in front of us on a table that wasn't there when we sat down.

The magic of TV.

The trouble in his eyes worries me. Me being on his lap is not about him being possessive or protective. It's something else. Whatever happened while I was out is weighing heavy on his soul. He wants me close because *he* needs it.

Whatever he needs, I'm his girl.

I can't bring myself to leave her in her apartment alone. Or drag myself away to be alone in my house.

With little discussion, I drop our bags in her room, undress us for a quick shower, and tuck her into bed in my arms, against my chest, soul to soul, my darkness kept at bay by her nearness and her ability to produce peace where there is none.

She falls asleep long before me, but I'm not restless lying here holding her. Nor am I aroused like I usually am with her near or on my mind.

I'm burdened by what happened with Drake and the revelation from my father that had me accepting a letter from Mom—I haven't read yet—and rushing to pack and get us the fuck out of there as fast as I could without waking up my girl.

Distance is a misnomer. Distance doesn't make the heart grow fonder, and it sure as shit doesn't make the ache in my chest any better.

I can't outrun this news. Instead, I headed right back to the heart of it—only he doesn't know it.

Tomorrow I'll deal.

Tonight, I'm holding my Wendy, loving the lion inside her who believes she's a mouse when really, she's *my Kitten.*

CHAPTER 21

IT'S BEEN A FEW WEEKS SINCE OUR TRIP TO TEXAS. Rowdy's been off ever since. Whatever happened, he's not talking. He's not even coming to the gym. Cap has been understanding, giving him space to work through his grief.

Except, I don't think it's about his mother dying, or at least that's not the whole story.

As for me, I've righted my crazy. I'm back to a normal level of damage. No episodes since his brother.

As for Rowdy and me, that's a whole other ball of wax. Though he's not coming into the gym, even though he's taken me to lunch more times than not, he's not avoiding me. He'll pick me up, but won't come in. Sometimes we eat out. Sometimes he packs a lunch. Those are my favorite times, when we just sit out in the back of his pickup, eat, keep each other company, and watch life happen all around us.

At night, he stays over. He's goes home during the day, works out and does whatever else he does to keep busy. But at night, he's back at my place, meeting me at the door after work. I cook or he brings dinner.

Bedtime is another story too. We cuddle and sleep. There's no making out beyond a few tender kisses.

I don't know if he's lost interest or if whatever is going on in his head is taking a toll on his libido.

He holds my hand and likes to cuddle. If we're together, he's always touching me on the small of my back, holding hands, or has a hand on my neck or thigh. Constant contact.

It's confusing as hell. He wants to be with me. But he doesn't want to be *with me*.

"Reese?" Cap sticks his head out of his office. "Can you come in a sec?"

"Sure." I hit save on a document I'm working on and grab my tablet in case I need to take notes or set up an appointment.

I walk in and smile, noting his desk is still clean and tidy from the decluttering I did yesterday after he left to scout a new fighter.

Noticing my grin, he gifts me with a rare, difficult-to-earn smile in return. "Yes, yes, you did a great job on my desk. And I haven't had trouble finding anything. I don't know how you know where I would look for stuff, but so far you haven't put anything in places I'd never look." He points to a chair in front of his desk. "So, thank you. You're worth every penny and more."

I beam at his compliment. I get Cap. I understand how he thinks. He's gruff and to the point, but I like that about him. I understand grumpy. I appreciate his honesty. And praise from him is high on my list of great moments.

Girls with daddy issues. We're a dime a dozen.

"I want to have your family over for a barbeque next Saturday—a week from tomorrow. I was thinking of including Rowdy, but didn't know if you'd be okay with that."

I start to speak, then stop. Frowning, I contemplate why he's asking. "Why do you think I'd be uncomfortable with Rowdy being included?"

He squeezes the back of his neck, leaning in his chair that no longer squeaks because I put WD40 on it a few days ago. I don't think he's even noticed. "I haven't seen him since he's returned. He's been noncommunicative besides a few texts. I wasn't sure if you were together, and I didn't want to make it uncomfortable by inviting him, only to find out you've broken up."

I see his point, and it's nice he's thinking of my feelings. "Rowdy and I aren't together. I mean… I see him every day, but it's not like we're boyfriend and girlfriend."

Is it? Shit. I have no idea. "So, you can invite him or whoever else you want to invite. It's your house. It's up to you. Have you talked to my mom and Gabriel? Are they available?"

"Yep. They're on board for Saturday around two. Is that okay with you?"

I have no life. No plans. "Sure." I stand, clutching the tablet to my chest, wanting to hide from this awkward *are you in a relationship with Rowdy* discussion. "Anything else?"

"No, that's it."

"I'm going to get back to work." I thumb over my shoulder.

"Reese." He stops me at the door.

"Yeah?"

"I'll leave it to you to invite him or not." The concern in his tone has me thinking I should be worried about my status with Rowdy.

Do I need to label what we are or what we're not? "Yeah, sure."

A few hours later I find myself face to face with the man himself.

"You're here." I was surprised to get his call asking me to come to the gym. I honestly thought it was a joke or he was asking me to come to his home gym.

Yes, he has a home gym. Though I've never seen his house—not many have—I hear it's quite spectacular. Maybe not Texas-mansion spectacular, but in my lived-in-a-trailer-park-most-of-my-life perspective, I've no doubt it's huge and impressive.

"Yeah." He glances over my shoulder before taking my hands. "It was time."

I'm glad to hear it. I'm sure my smile radiates my inner joy. Maybe this means things are back to normal. He'll come back to working out here and do more than just kiss me.

Now that it's been firmly off the table for a while, I realize exactly how much I want Rowdy *that way* too, and not as a friend. I want more than friendship. I feel capable of *more* for the first time in my life, and I'm anxious to get on with it.

In the middle of telling me about his earlier call with his sister, Jonah approaches, his gaze darting between Rowdy and me.

Rowdy squeezes my hands and winks.

"Hey, Reese, do you think you could order me some Black Ops shirts? I've got holes in most of mine." He touches my arm, eyes back on Rowdy. "It's time to replace them."

"Sure. I'll send you the link. Just tell me which ones, size, color, and quantity. If I get the order in today, they should be here by early next week."

"Excellent." A small pat on my shoulder and he walks away.

That was weird.

Rowdy has a dimpled grin, entirely too happy about something.

"What? You need some logo shirts too?"

He shakes his head. "Nah, I'm good. How's your day so far, busy?"

I shrug. "Not bad. Busy is good. Keeps my mind occupied."

His smile disappears, and lines crease his brow. "Occupied from?"

If he only knew how much I think about him in a day, he'd run far away. "Life." And apparently, I need to be worrying about the status of our relationship.

Do we have a relationship?

His frown deepens.

Yeah, me too, buddy. Big frown. I've no idea how to navigate whatever this is between us.

"Yo, Reesie girl!" Walker comes bounding up, bumping my shoulder. "Did the new PT get with you? She needs to order some of those ice packs I like."

"Um, no. But I'll talk to her. She might not realize all orders need to come through me for Cap's approval."

"Thanks. That'd be great." He kisses my cheek in an uncharacteristic move, slaps Rowdy on the shoulder. "It's good to see you, man. We've missed you. Sorry about your mom."

"Thanks, I appreciate that." Rowdy falls somber.

Walker finger-guns me. "You got this?"

I laugh at his cheesiness. "I'll get you your ice packs, you big baby."

"Hey, my body needs what it needs, Reesie."

I'm sure it does.

"Catch ya later." He bounds off the same way he came in—with way too much energy.

"I guess I've got a few things I need to follow up on. Are you working out?"

"Yeah, I'll be done when you're ready to leave." He kisses my forehead and turns.

"Rowdy?"

"Yeah, Kitten?" He moves in close, cupping my hip.

"Cap invited us to his house on Saturday for a barbeque. Gabriel, Frankie, Ox, Mom, you, me. Do you want to go?"

I see the *no* on his face before it leaves his lips. "Can't. Got plans."

No further explanation. He's been with me every day for over three weeks. He never has plans that don't include me, unless I'm at work.

This feels off. "Yeah, okay."

I mean, what can I say?

No, you must spend every waking hour with me?

What kind of plans? Why am I not invited?

Are we in a relationship?

Are we boyfriend/girlfriend?

Though I try not to be disappointed in his brief, no-details answer, a nagging worry takes root.

CHAPTER 22

I RUB AT THE BURN RADIATING FROM INSIDE MY chest. It started the second I lied to Reese. It was a shit move. I wasn't prepared for an invite to Cap's with her family.

I need more time before I'm ready for that.

Coming back to the gym was hard but necessary. I can't spar or effectively train with myself. I've stayed in condition, but I itch to hit someone. I need the release that only happens by fighting a real person, not a fucking sand bag or my Shadow.

It's nice and weird being back with the guys. They're great motivation and annoying as hell. But good people. And they helped me out today.

"So—" Jonah spots me on the bench press, eyeing me upside down. "I think it went well this morning, don't you?"

I chuckle. "Yeah, but you seemed dodgy as hell. You kept side-eyeing me."

"I was nervous, man. I didn't want to set her off. I'd never hurt that girl." He'd never hurt *any* girl, but I know what he means.

The guys hold Reese in a special place in their hearts. Some of them relate more to her condition than others because of their military service. They all know someone with PTSD or have it themselves. The main difference is *why* she has it. We're protective assholes. The idea of someone hurting one of our own, even if we weren't there in their lives to prevent it, doesn't settle easily. The fact that she's a woman and they suspect but don't know for sure that it was her *father* doing the hurting, based on Gabriel's known history, is a thousand times more difficult to swallow.

When I asked Jonah and Walker to help me out this morning, they lapped it up like I offered them sweet pussy. Which I was not. That pussy is mine.

The guys treat her like a stray dog that was traumatized by its previous owner—they want to love the hurt away.

God, I want to do that and so much more.

Since my brother touched her, I've been keeping things PG. Besides all the shit going on in my life, I can't have Reese thinking I only want her for the sex—or sexy *stuff*, since we're not actually doing the deed.

Plus, my head is messed up. I'm not taking her virginity when I don't even know who I am anymore. I was so sure before Mom's funeral. Now, I haven't a clue. I can tell Kitten needs me as much as I need her, but my emotional state is all over the place.

I need to talk to someone, but I don't know who. I'm not the only one impacted by my news. It's not fair to lay it on one person and expect it to stay a secret. It's weighing heavy on me. I don't want to think about the blowback when it becomes common knowledge.

I need to just man up and face it head-on. Talk to the one person who can give me answers.

Or read your mother's fucking letter.

Jeez, that voice sounded like Drake.

First Mom, now Drake is in my head. I'm cracking up. No doubt about it.

Finishing my reps, I come to my feet, searching the room for my fellow Texan. "Cowboy."

His head pops up. "Yeah, man?"

"I need to let off some steam. You game?"

"Fuck yeah!" He's in the ring before I can even finish my first bottled water. He smirks, bouncing on his feet. "I've got a new move. I can't wait to knock you on your ass."

"You can try, young Landry." I spread my arms, egging him on, totally bullshitting him, since we're the same age. "Show me what you got."

"Oh, Lord," Jonah sighs. "I better get the med kit."

Reese drops her purse on the kitchen table. "What the hell happened?"

There was a change of plans. I left before she did.

Deciding I'd better pick up some supplies and dinner before she saw me, I texted her before I left the gym, letting her know I'd meet her at her place.

Her worried gaze scans my face, and she sighs. "You need ice."

I've done that, but I don't tell her. Having her hands on me, taking care of my stupid ass, is next-level heaven.

She takes the food bags from my hands and orders me to sit. I lumber to the couch while she fiddles in the kitchen.

Still glaring, she approaches slowly, as if I don't know how her pussy tastes. "Why are you hesitant?"

Her being unsure around me is not okay.

Close enough to grab, but too far to be sitting on my lap, she stops. "I, uh, don't… I was going to straddle your lap, but you've put this thing between us. I don't know what's appropriate."

The fuck? Appropriate?

I grip her hips and pull her down, sucking the yelp from her lips, claiming what I've obviously been neglecting—her.

Her ass on my thighs and her beautiful pussy hugging my cock, or as she put it, *straddling my lap*, we kiss like we're starving.

Which I am.

I haven't let myself indulge in her body, her fire since the night before the funeral. I couldn't get enough of her then. I can't get enough now.

The frozen ice pack touching my black eye jerks me back. "Fuck. Warning, baby."

She wipes her lips dry.

I'm tempted to wet them again. But the steel in her gaze has me settling into the couch, my hands adhered to her ass. "I'm sorry, Kitten."

Cupping the undamaged side of my face, she gently holds the pack over my banged-up side.

I need to ease her reticence. "I want to tell you what's going on, but I'm not ready. I'm still trying to come to terms with it."

"Is it about your mom's letter?"

"Don't know. Haven't read it."

"Cam," she chastises me, and I love it. My girl is not afraid of speaking her mind—at least to me. Everyone thinks she's such a mouse, but my girl is a lion in hiding.

I see you, Reese.

She continues, her scowl growing, "You can't face your problems if you ignore them. Whatever is going on is obviously big enough to distract you from your friends, your career, from—"

"You," I finish for her, not sure she would've put herself on that list. She should have listed herself first. Her eyes watering reinforces the extent of my fuck-up.

"Kitten." I sink my fingers into her hair on the back of her skull and pull her to me.

She nuzzles into the crook of my neck.

"I'm sorry, baby. I don't want to push for physical stuff when I'm fucked in the head. But me not being in your pants doesn't mean I don't want you."

She nods but stays silent.

"I've always wanted you, Reese. From the first moment I laid eyes on you till this very moment, my want of you only grows. I'm trying to protect you, not push you away. I'm sorry that message got confused. I should have come right out and told you. Talked about it."

"It's okay." Her warm breath teases the skin of my neck and has Cocky getting ideas. "What happened to your face?" Sitting back, she dries her tears on her sleeves, keeping one hand on the ice pack.

"Cowboy went one way. I went another. His new move ended up with his heel in my face."

She frowns, studying my head as if she can spot damage within. "You have a concussion?"

"Nah, I'm good." I kiss her mouth and pat her ass. "I need to eat, though. How about you?"

She jumps up smiling. "I could eat. What did ya bring?"

"Chinese."

"Yummy."

My girl saunters off to the kitchen. I lie back on the couch, closing my eyes for a minute, needing to ease the growing headache.

Fucking Cowboy. Last time I let him try a new move on me without talking it through first. I was anxious for the adrenaline rush and release from fighting.

Turns out, nothing soothes me better than telling my girl how it is: I'm fucked up and need time, but it doesn't mean I don't want her.

We have things to discuss.

But food first.

The last bite of noodles slithers down my throat as I stare at my Shadow. He's clearly lost his damn mind—or I have.

"Just hear me out," he continues, having finished devouring his dinner long before me. "You didn't even notice when Jonah and Walker touched you today."

I noticed. Kinda. "I was distracted."

He hits me with his dimpled smile. My girly parts wave, flagging him in.

"Exactly. You were distracted by *me*."

My brow cocks. "Arrogant much?"

"It's not arrogant if it's true. You feel safe with me." He captures my hand, kisses it before setting our joined hands on his lap. "It means a lot that you do."

"But now that I know, it won't be effective, will it?"

"I don't know, maybe it will. Do you get anxious worrying someone will touch you?"

I let out a big breath. "All the damn time."

"I hate to think of you stressed out and I'm not there. Maybe we work on some of the more common stressful situations. Like walking through crowds or simply shaking people's hands. Does it bother you if you initiate it?"

"Typically no, but I also rarely shake people's hands."

He nods. "Then let's start there. Small steps."

I toy with my bottom lip, pinching it between my fingers. "Okay."

I have a feeling the guys at the gym are going to be casually touching me a lot. But for the first time in… ever, that doesn't scare me.

"What's the goal?"

"The goal is to get you okay with passive touch. That a simple grip of your arm won't send you into a PTSD episode but allow you to assess the situation to determine if it's a friendly touch or an aggressive one you need to put a stop to. We want to reset your instinct to go into self-defense mode rather than PTSD mode.

"If Drake hadn't triggered your fear and dropped you into PTSD shutdown mode, you might have been able to escape the room or simply lay him out with a well-placed strike."

He goes on to discuss my other two triggers: loud sounds and the dark, and his plan for both.

"You're not in this alone. I'll be right there next to you, holding you at first, then slowly I'll give you space but still be near if you need me."

He shrugs. "It's not foolproof, and we might fuck it up, but you've got a whole family ready and willing to support you. Let us."

Sounds like a dream to not be a victim of my trauma, for in the middle of an episode anything could happen, and I'm helpless to stop it.

I've been a captive of my fears, limited my activities, and avoided risky situations, like parties, clubbing, and men. Though that doesn't mean I didn't imagine what it would be like...

"What if it doesn't work?" Will Rowdy still want me after proof that I can't be fixed?

"Then we'll have enjoyed some interesting times together, and we'll go on like we are now."

"Like we are now?" I squeal when he picks me up.

"Except I'll be fucking your brains out by then."

"You will?"

"Yeah, Kitten." He nuzzles the side of my face as he carries me to bed. "I think we should start now."

CHAPTER 23

LAID OUT AND NAKED BEFORE ME, MY KITTEN IS A fucking dream. I'm so revved, I'm not even sure where to start. I want to taste her pussy for dessert, kiss her mouth stupid, and sink my cock balls-deep and then some, nailing her through the bed to the floorboards below.

She's a virgin. Uncharacteristically sensitive, fucking Cocky reminds me.

Looming over my panting girl, she reaches for my hungry cock, tugging it just right. "We don't have to do this," I grunt through the pleasure each stroke sends to my balls. "I want you, but I'm willing to wait until you're ready, Kitten."

Legs spread, her glistening lips advertise just how ready she is—physically. It's her mental readiness I need confirmation of.

"I don't fear your touch." Her gaze falls to my cock. "But your size is a little scary."

Pride swells. I can't help it. I'm a bastard like that.

Cocky beads with precum in anticipation of diving into her fertile haven.

"We'll fit, baby. I promise." I settle between her legs, kissing her slowly.

She opens for me, kissing me back with increasing fervor as Cocky cuddles her pussy lips, doing his own coaxing.

I think a week passes before my girl tugs on my hair, bringing me back to earth, guiding me to suck one tit, then the next.

She's ravenous, near insatiable.

Cocky is chanting *fuck her* and calling to her pretty little kitty, asking her to let him in. It's quite a love story.

But it's her pleas that do me in. "Rowdy, please," and, "Fill me," and my favorite, "Fuck me." For such an innocent thing, she's got a dirty mouth.

I fucking love it.

I fucking love *her*.

With Cocky suited up, I lace our hands over her head and brush kisses over her mouth, moving my hips slowly, stuttering when the head of my cock catches against her opening.

"Please, Cam. I need you." Her blues match her pleas between lazy blinks. "Now, Shadow."

And fuck. I'm done for.

Sucking her tongue, I edge in, just the tip.

My breath catches. *Easy, Cocky.*

I got this. I do this for a living, he reminds me.

She moans like I just licked her from asshole to clit, and I edge a little farther.

Each plunge sends me deeper, grinding our hips together in between shallow pumps.

I stay at this depth, letting her adjust, tempering her walls until they stretch to hug me like a pussy wetsuit.

"Ohmygod, Rowdy. You feel… This is… Oh. My. God." Her whole body tenses, her legs shake, and her pussy locks Cocky in a choke hold.

If I didn't have some clue what was happening, I'd think she was having a seizure. But I've seen my girl come. I wasn't purposely rubbing her G-spot with my shallow, grinding thrusts. I was trying to be gentle, letting her acclimate to my size before going farther.

On a deep groan, my Kitten comes, sucking Cocky so hard I can hear him squeak with each dip in and out. The sounds of our lovemaking enflame my desire as her juices gush.

In the haze of her release, I sink to sea depth, growling to push through her tight muscles still spasming, teasing me with my own release.

Not fucking yet, Cocky.

No way. No fucking way. I just got here. I'm staying.

I kiss across her jaw from one ear to the other, stopping for a little snack on her lips. "Fucking beautiful, Kitten."

Her walls contract each time I whisper in her ear. My girl likes my sweet talk as much as my dirty.

When she finally catches a full breath, blinks up at me and smiles, my heart jumps, knowing she's okay and officially mine.

Mine.

Finally, fucker. Cocky rolls his eyes at me.

Pulling her hands free, she wraps around me, lifting her heels to rub my ass, and swivels her hips.

"Fuck," I exhale into her hair. Her fucking me from below is mind-blowing. Better than her mouth trying to suck my cock down her throat.

So fucking made for me. No doubt about it.

"I want to feel you come, Shadow," she mewls into my ear.

"Keep feeding me your pussy like that, and it won't be long."

Clench. Fuck. Her virginal walls squeeze their approval.

"Don't stop, baby." I suck on her neck. My hips join hers, diving deeper with each thrust.

Her desperation grows as she claws at my shoulders, pulling me closer, edging up her legs, her feet now hugging my sides.

Deeper I sink.

Holy God.

"Jesus, Kitten." I'm gonna have a heart attack or pass out if I don't come soon.

She squeezes and lifts her hips, moaning her pleasure, amping up mine, igniting an inferno.

She bucks and I grind.

I growl and she shivers.

I fuck her mouth with my tongue. She fucks me back.

She cries out her need, her pleasure, gripping me like she needs me under her skin, not just inside her.

I drive into the sweetest pussy I've ever known, attached to the kindest woman who's a lion no longer acting like a mouse.

I fall over the edge just as hard as I've fallen for her. Calling her name, begging her to never dim the lights on the path she's burned inside of me.

A path that leads to my cock, but more importantly, it leads to my heart.

It's lit for her, so she's not scared.

It's lit for me because that's what she is.

She's my light in the darkness within.

She's my Wendy, and she just fucking pinned my shadow to my foot.

He came. And ohmygod, I felt it. He pulsed inside me. Warmth filled the condom. I wish he'd bathed my walls in his cum.

I shiver at the thought and ache with the need to come again, but I don't want to be selfish. I mean… Right?

He doesn't stop, his monster cock touching every internal erogenous zone I never knew existed.

He palms my breasts. "Fucking love these."

Pinching and pulling on my nipples, he kisses me stupid, hot, and needy.

I buck below him.

"Fuck, Kitten," he chuffs.

Tingles skitter along my skin.

He can't still be hard, can he?

"Not stopping, baby. Gonna fuck you until we both come again."

Thank God.

"You're gonna be sore."

Don't care. "Don't stop."

"Never, Kitten. I'm in this, Reese. I'm all in. Never gonna stop fucking you."

His words do crazy things to my body. It's like my vagina needs him and tries to prevent his escape, his words only feeding its hunger, my desire.

"Rowdy, please."

"Yeah, baby. I got you."

He slips his hand between us, flat on my stomach, his thumb grazing my clit with each thrust.

"Ohmygod."

He groans, "Fucking love the way you feel. Fucking love you."

His words of love trip a wire, flinging me to the finish line. "Oh, fuck—" *I'm coming.*

He growls his approval, nipping at my neck, fucking into my pussy, teasing a nipple, rubbing my clit.

It's an all-engines overload. He takes me into overdrive, burning out my accelerator and lubing my engine with each thrust.

"Oh, God."

He doesn't stop. He drills hard, deeper. His entire body works, undulating into me in wave after wave of full body thrusts. He's fucking beautiful.

He's relentless.

He's tireless.

He's The Pussy Whisperer.

He's going to kill me with orgasms.

"I'm coming, Kitten." He bites my mouth. "Fucking come with me."

Oh, dear God. I can't.

"Ohmyfuckinggod." I can.

I do.

"Cameron!" I bow off the bed, my head exploding as sheer pleasure rips through me, starting at my calves.

His growl is animalistic as he comes, riding me like a bucking bronco, lashing me with words of praise as I come, and come, and come.

"Fucking love you, Reese!" he barks over my cries.

Latched to my mouth, he kisses me through our release and eases me back from sex euphoria.

I didn't know it was a place. But it is. And now I've been there, thanks to my Shadow and the monster between his legs.

Before I drift off, buried in his arms, I whisper across his chest, "I love you too."

CHAPTER 24

GRIPPING HER HIPS, I PUSH INTO HER FROM behind.

She hisses.

The fucker inside me preens, knowing I'm the reason my kitten is sore. She fucking let me touch her. I'm the first. I'm proud and humbled by her trust.

"Sorry, baby." Not really. Sorry for her discomfort. Not sorry for the reason.

"Don't be. It's perfect." She groans into the pillow, gripping the sheets.

I grow harder.

Her responsiveness and the sight of my cock slipping in and out of her pussy, my shaft so wet it drips down my balls, has my jaw tightening, fighting to stay in control.

Fuck. I could drink her juices in my coffee as creamer.

The thought pushes me deeper, relishing her cry as I bottom out.

I tried to lay off her after we fell asleep with words of love swirling in the air coated in the musk of sex.

But she wasn't having it. My Kitten is greedy. I woke to her stroking my granite-hard cock, slipping on a condom before I could remind her she'll be sore. Cocky buried deep and happy as a clam, she started riding me like a rodeo star, hard and dirty.

This morning, I woke her with my face between her legs, her coming on my tongue before she even opened her eyes. She then flipped over and asked me to ride her from behind.

I swear. She asked.

I wouldn't have broached doggie style so soon after losing her virginity. Some positions take working up to, especially when the woman I'm fucking owns my heart, and I want to be sure she knows I'm not taking her from behind because I want to pretend she's someone else.

There is no one else.

Ever.

She's it.

I might have fucked other woman in this position pretending it was Reese.

Maybe.

More than likely.

Okay. I did. Often.

But not since I got serious about pursuing her. I haven't touched a woman in months. Before Ox was born.

"Fuck." I slap Reese's ass when she pushes back on me. "Don't rush me."

"I need it," she pouts.

Jesus. I swear she's going to kill me. Who would have ever thought sweet, innocent Reese would be a vixen in the bedroom?

I fill her deep and hold, pulling her to her knees, her back hitting my chest. I cup her neck and lick up to her ear, kiss her jaw, then mouth. My other hand teases her nipples, giving a little twist.

"Ohmygod," she cries.

Short thrusts, hitting her G-spot, has her legs shaking, her hands grasping my butt and latching on to my wrist of the hand around her neck.

"Touch your clit, Kitten. I want to feel you squeeze the life out of my cock when you come."

"Oh, fuck." My girl does as directed.

I regret not being able to see her. Next time, we do this in front of the mirror.

I grip her arm not rubbing her clit and use her hip as a handle to drill into her, leaning back to change the angle.

Two seconds later she's lighting up the room with her explosive orgasm, deafening me with her chants for more, and driving me to release as she bucks into me so hard, I'm sure my pelvis would be bruised if it wasn't for her cushiony, delicious ass.

"Morning, Kitten." I kiss her head, tucking her back into bed, then dispose of the condom and traipse naked to the kitchen to make breakfast.

The smell of bacon and syrup tease me into the kitchen where I find Rowdy flipping pancakes on the griddle.

I tug my robe tighter to keep from mounting him right here. He is naked, after all. It would be warranted. Maybe even expected.

I snag a slice of bacon, popping a piece into my mouth before holding it up for him to bite.

I sneak a peek as his half-hard cock, long on this thigh, well-manicured, and looking like a delicious morning treat.

Good god he's hung.

"Don't burn the pancakes," I order as I drop to my knees and lick him from tip to base.

"Oh, fuck," he hisses.

"Pass me the syrup." I lift my hand, taking my time rimming his crown. He's got a beautiful cock. It deserves special treatment—like syrup.

"Kitten." His growl sends shivers down my spine.

I ignore him, snap my fingers, my hand still waiting for the syrup, and suck deeper until he complies.

Who knew pancakes were such a turn on?

"You're a naughty kitten." I lick her seam, taking a deep breath and relishing the smell of her sweet sex.

"You enjoyed it, right?" Her confidence from earlier wavers slightly.

She's delusional if she thinks any man wouldn't enjoy his woman dropping to her knees and sucking on his cock like it's providing oxygen for her lungs.

"Of course I did. Just as you'll enjoy this." I run my finger over her plate, coating it with left over syrup. Using my shoulders to hold her open, I rub the gooey goodness on her heavenly lips, paying special attention to her clit. Something so beautiful deserves a little something extra.

My kitten whimpers and shimmies her hips. She's turned on but sore.

"I'm gonna lick your tenderness away, Kitten. Make you all better."

Or so turned on she won't care when I fuck her on the couch, the floor, the kitchen table, or the bathtub.

Who knew falling in love would make me this horny?

"We need to talk." His tone is troubled.

Is this where he tells me he's had enough? We've had sex. Now he's ready to move on.

I simply nod and follow him to the bathroom. I'm shocked when I see a bath drawn, bubbles shimmering and popping on the surface.

He urges me forward. "I know you're sore, Kitten." He unties my robe and lets it waft to the floor. "Get in."

Using his arm for balance to ensure my entrance is as graceful as possible, I step into the tub.

Still naked, he kneels next to it and dips a washcloth in the water and begins wetting my shoulders. "Next time, we'll go to my place. I've got a bathtub that'll fit both of us."

His place? "That would be nice."

Soaping up the rag, he begins to wash me. He's gentle and extra cautious where I'm tender.

"I should have taken you there sooner. I'm not trying to hide anything from you. In my experience, money can make people uncomfortable."

"You mean the fact that you have so much and most of us don't?"

His lips tip. "Yeah, Kitten. Namely that." He kisses my shoulder. "But you've seen where I grew up. My place is nothing like that, but it's not a one-bedroom apartment either."

Not like where I live.

"I want you to be comfortable there, feel like it's yours. That's why I've waited."

He tips my chin and brushes his mouth across mine. His tender gaze caresses my face. "I love you, Reese. I don't want to scare you, but I've fallen hard. And I'm not one to take things slow."

I capture his face and pull him closer. "I've been falling for you with every breath I've taken since we met. Being loved by you doesn't scare me, Cameron. *Not* being loved by you does."

"Fuck, Kitten." He secures me around my back and under my legs and lifts me out of the tub, splashing water everywhere. "Then we're good. 'Cause I love the fuck out of you."

CHAPTER 25

I T'S BEEN A WEEK TODAY SINCE I GAVE ROWDY MY virginity. He didn't *take* it. I didn't *lose* it. I wouldn't necessarily say it was a *gift*. And it wasn't a *burden*. Well, maybe it was.

My virginity was a symbol of my fear. I'd never let—wanted—anyone close enough. *Let* is misleading too. I hadn't been sure if I even wanted sex... If I *could* be touched so intimately. I voluntarily let go of it. I gave it to him. Just like I gave him my heart. He awakens things in me I never thought I could have, was capable of, or even knew existed.

Before him, the idea of a man's penis in my mouth would send ripples of terror down my spine. I'd seen what a man can do with his penis. I wasn't interested. It was a weapon used to hurt, control, and punish.

Yet Rowdy's cock is the most glorious thing I've ever seen. Having it in my hand, mouth, or between my legs is freedom from my past, from my demons, from the dark that nips at my heels. He makes me feel *good*. He's freedom from my fear.

"Kitten?" The concern in his voice breaks my unfocused gaze on the lake to find his eyes on me, his brow raised. "You're thinking too hard. What's wrong?"

"Nothing's wrong." I take the last bite of shrimp salad I can muster. It's so good—he keeps me in constant supply now. He first brought it for one of our picnic lunches a few weeks ago. It was meant to be a side, not the main dish. But I couldn't stop eating it. I still can't. My stomach, however, believes a third serving is too much. Quitter.

His fierce glare has me smiling. Not the intended reaction, I'm sure.

I bump his shoulder. "Don't glower at me." I set my plate down and turn toward him, hitching my leg up so only one is hanging off the tailgate. "If you must know, I was thinking how your monster cock set me free."

"Jesus. Fuck." He hops off the truck. Running his hand through his loose hair, he takes two strides away then stalks back, gripping my thighs and pulling me to the edge so he can stand between them. "You can't say shit like that, Kitten." He glides his hand up my arm, over my neck and into my hair.

I shiver, nipples harden, goosebumps erupt, and lust crackles in the air.

"It's hard enough not bending you over every hard surface we come across."

"I wouldn't mind." I wouldn't, truly.

"Reese," he warns in his *I'm in charge* voice.

Fine. I'll behave. Party pooper.

His forehead lands on mine. One hand grips my hip. "You test me, woman."

I smirk. "Someone needs to. You can't always be the king of the roost."

"No?" he teases.

"It's okay to not always be in control." The second my lips touch his, a loud horn sounds. I sink further into his chest. "What was that—"

It happens again.

I arch away from the sound coming from behind.

He wraps me in his arms and kisses my head. "It's just an air horn. You're safe."

Scowling, I peek around the side of the truck but don't see anything. "Where'd it come from?"

He motions to over the hill. "From there, I think."

I still, waiting for it to sound again, my eyes on the lake, not really seeing it.

After a few more seconds, my Shadow tips my face to his. "You didn't get scared."

"Huh." I didn't. It surprised me but didn't trigger my PTSD. Wait. "Did you do this?"

"Maybe." His smile gives the gloating ass away.

I smack his chest. "You did, didn't you?"

He holds my face in the palm of this hands. "You didn't have an episode. You didn't check out. *That's* what matters."

"I guess it is."

He holds me against his chest, murmuring his approval of my progress. I don't know if it's progress or not. I'm in his arms. Not much gets past the bubble of his gravitational pull. But it seems like a good sign.

I want him with me tomorrow. "Will you reconsider coming with me to Caps?" I don't want to go without him. Mom, Gabriel, Frankie, and my nephew, Ox, will be there. It'll be fine. But I've gotten used to Rowdy being around, at my side. I want to experience my family with him now that we're together. I'm no longer the silly, unrequited crushing girl who can't stop looking at him, fantasizing about him.

He's mine now. I want to show him off.

His face hardens.

I've ruined the moment. My heart sinks. I'm still that silly girl, I guess. "Never mind." Pushing him back, I climb off his truck, dusting crumbs off my lap, and start packing everything up.

"Reese."

He's sorry. I know. He's going through stuff. Stuff that I know nothing about. Stuff he's not ready to talk about. Even with me.

You haven't told him your secrets either.

True. But he knows my damage, even if he doesn't know the details. He'll never look at me the same if I tell him. Once he knows, I can never take it back.

His silence isn't the same. He knows my drama. I don't know what his drama is even related to. It's not the same. I'm vulnerable with him every second of the day, working through my issues *with him*. He's not even giving me a chance to help him, to support him, to love him through whatever's going on.

It's a silent ride to the gym. I don't know if he's staying or heading out. He has plans for tomorrow I know nothing about. Maybe they start tonight.

I drop out of the cab before he can even turn off the engine—if he's staying, that is. "Thanks for lunch." I slam the door and walk inside.

I don't stop to see his reaction or if he follows. I'm a silly girl. I've gotten my feelings hurt. Now I'd like to pout and lick my wounds in private.

He doesn't come after me. He doesn't call.

The pain in my chest worsens, and the worry that I'm losing him only grows.

I get a text a few hours later.

My Shadow: *Come to my place tonight.*

He's placating me. It's the first time he's invited me to his home since mentioning it the day after we had sex for the first time. I've wanted to see his space so bad. I should go. I won't.

He's got plans. I need space.

I'm willing to give him everything. He's holding back.

Do I have a right to ask for more, for full disclosure? Probably not. He's still not ready.

I'm still feeling bitchy.

Me: *Thanks, but can't. I've got plans.*

Right away three dots dance on my screen. I smile as I wait on his reply.

"Hey, Reese." AJ, the new physical therapist Cap hired to help Frankie out through her pregnancy and now her maternity leave, leans a hip on my desk. "I was hoping you might be available for that drink we've been talking about getting. I could use a night out. TGIF and all." She rolls her hazel eyes and twirls her strawberry blonde hair around her finger.

"Yeah, sure." Now I really do have plans.

My phone pings with Rowdy's response. I don't look. It'd be rude to AJ.

"Excellent." She stands, twisting her lips. "You wanna go from here? Or do you need to go home first?"

"I'm good to go from here." It's not like I'm getting all dolled up for a real date.

"Yay." She claps. "I'll see you at five, then."

"Sounds good."

I wait until she disappears down the hall before reading Rowdy's text.

My Shadow: *What kind of plans? You didn't mention it before.*

My Shadow: *Are you mad about tomorrow?*

My Shadow: *Come on, Kitten. Don't ignore me.*

My Shadow: *???*

I let him stew for ten more minutes before answering.

Me: *Why do you assume I can't have plans that don't include you?*

My Shadow: *I don't assume. I know.*

The sad fact is, he does know me, and if AJ hadn't shown up, he'd be right. I am mad about tomorrow. I want him there. I want to be more important to him than whatever it is he has planned. I want to be important enough for him to want to tell me what's going on—what his big secret is.

How can we share a life with secrets between us?

But as I said, I'm feeling bitchy, and my feelings are hurt.

Me: *Well, know this. I have plans tonight. I have plans tomorrow. I'm free on Sunday. Otherwise, I'll see you at the gym next week.*

My Shadow: *Fine.*

I don't answer.

He's being childish.

So am I.

We're quite a pair.

CHAPTER 26

SATURDAY MORNING COMES TOO EARLY AFTER way too many beers with AJ. I don't go out often. It's never been my thing. But I had a good time, except now I remember why I don't drink all that often. It's fun while you're doing it, but the hangover is for the birds. I groan, rolling over to see who's texting me so early.

My Shadow: *Good morning, Kitten. Still mad at me?*

Someone appears to be in a better mood. It's certainly not me.

Me: *If I wasn't before, I am now for waking me up.*

My Shadow: *Can I take you to breakfast?*

No matter how much I want to say *yes*, I can't. He has plans today, and seeing him this morning and then having to separate to do our own thing will just put me in an even fouler mood.

It's not the fact that he has plans. It's the fact that he's holding back from me. Not just his plans, but whatever *thing* he's going through, he's shutting me out of, like a stranger.

I don't need the reminder I'm low on his priority list. He doesn't need me like I need him.

Me: *Can't. Busy dying.*

Pulling the covers over my head, I considering turning off my phone. My shit mood is going to cause problems if I keep texting him. Sometimes silence is the best policy.

Before I can make a decision my phone beeps.

My Shadow: *Want me to kiss it and make it better?*

Me: *No.*

Guilt hits me as soon as I hit send.
I'm being a bitch.

Me: *I can't today. Sorry.*

I don't know if that soothes the sting. I turn my phone off and fall back asleep.

When I wake hours later, feeling more like myself, I turn my phone back on. If my brother or mom try to contact me, they'll only panic if I don't answer. After I toss it on the bed to boot up while I pursue bathroom needs, it starts chiming before I've barely crossed the threshold.

Ignore it.

A quick shower, hair semi-dried and in a messy bun, I pull on some cutoff shorts, a loose t-shirt and my favorite pair of pink, tie-dyed, high-top Chucks.

I juice a berry kale protein shake to give me a boost of energy and replace the electrolytes and nutrients I drank away last night.

We didn't even eat. So stupid.

A few of the guys were at the bar last night. They flirted hard with

AJ. She ate it up. I just watched and drank my sorrows, numb. Also stupid.

Thankfully Jess was on his way out when we were ready to leave. He gave us rides home, but that means I either need to take an Uber to Cap's or to Hannigan's to get my car.

Hannigan's is the better choice. I can run some errands before the BBQ, and I won't have to worry about picking it up later.

Finishing my shake, I order a car, brush my teeth, and then sit on the stoop, waiting.

I give in and check the text I know Rowdy sent, the notification taunting me since I unlocked my phone to open the Uber app.

My Shadow: *Breakfast tomorrow, then. Don't say no. I'll be there early.*

Early? Sounds horrible.

Me: *Fine.*

My Shadow: *Don't be mad at me all day, beautiful.*

I sigh and roll my eyes. Of course, he's all sweet when I want to stay upset. Instead of being a total bitch, I reply with my main fear.

Me: *If you're going on a date, I will rip off your balls, fry them up and feed them to you.*

Okay, maybe I didn't hit the don't-be-a-total-bitch marker, but it's true all the same.

Just as the Uber arrives, my phone rings. I answer as I climb in.

"Kitten." The tender regard in his voice makes my eyes sting. "Is that what you really think I'm up to?"

I give the driver a tentative smile, then turn to hide in the window. "Maybe. I wouldn't know. You're not saying. Secrets are the devil's playground." And my brain has been playing on the merry-go-round all damn night, imagining what's so important he can't hang with the people he loves—including me.

His heavy sigh fills my ear. "I'm not going on a date. I'm not going anywhere. I just… can't go today."

"So, she's coming to you then?" I prod the beast. Not my proudest moment. Let's check off this whole morning as an utter failure and start again.

"Kitten," he growls, sending chills down my back. "I think you need to come over so I can remind you there's only one woman in my bed, riding my cock."

"If you're referring to me, I've never been in your bed."

"Not true. You were in my bed in Texas."

"We're not in Texas, and I'm still not in *your* bed."

I catch the driver's eye in the rearview mirror. He winks. Embarrassed, I tuck further into the door and focus out the window.

"You would be if you'd come over last night."

"I had plans."

"With AJ."

How'd he know? Oh, Jess probably told him. Traitor. "Yes." No point in denying it.

"You didn't tell me."

"You didn't tell me about your plans today." Ohmygod, I'm a pouty fish.

Another heavy sigh practically blows my hair back. "I'll make it up to you tomorrow, Kitten. I promise."

"Okay." I don't want to fight with him. I know he's going through stuff I don't want to force him to tell me before he's ready. But… I'm too insecure about *us* to not let it affect me.

"Okay?"

"Yeah, whatever. I gotta go." We pull into Hannigan's parking lot. "I'll see ya tomorrow." I hang up before he can reply.

He sends another text.

My Shadow: *Enjoy your day with your family, Kitten. Remember, I love you.*

Gah, way to make me feel like a heel and confused as ever. He loves me, yet he's still holding back, keeping his secret from me, not wanting to socialize with me and my family.

Me: *I'm not happy, but I love you too.*

My Shadow: *I'll make it better. Promise.*

If only he could. If only I wasn't so inexperienced with this whole boyfriend thing, I might have handled this roadblock with more finesse.

Truth is, I am who I am, and right now I'm unsure of where we stand because of what's holding him back.

CHAPTER 27

PULLING UP TO CAP'S HAS MY HEART RACING. His house butts up to the land his new state-of-the-art gym resides on—but I can't see it from here. I've no idea where Cap gets his money, but he obviously comes from it, made some really good investments, or Black Ops MMA is bringing in the dough.

He started building out here months before they all moved back from California. The small-town idea was good, but he says they need to be where the action is. He keeps the flagship gym in town for beginners and offers classes to the public. It's more of a storefront to the serious contender's gym he built here. It's out of town, not too far, but far enough to escape the craziness of Vegas and feel like you're in the country on a lake. Most of the guys live close by. Gabriel built a house just down the road. My apartment is only ten minutes away, and somewhere around here is Rowdy's home.

I park next to my brother's Hummer. I don't spot my mom's car, but that doesn't mean she's not already here. Gabriel could have picked her up, though it would have been out of the way since she refused to move closer to us. She wants to keep the house Gabriel bought her when he started making money. I'm not sure if it's sentimentality or just plain stubbornness. Either way, she's not big on driving, so having her closer would be more convenient—for us.

Maybe I should have offered to pick her up. It didn't even cross my mind. Normally, I let Gabriel deal with all things Mom-related. She prefers him anyway.

It's no secret I'm not her favorite person, much less favorite child. She loves me. It's just that my father drove a wedge between us—it's probably more of a wall that neither of us cares to look over or investigate too deeply.

Another lingering gift from dear old Dad.

I shudder with goosebumps. Thoughts of Dad are never good.

Grabbing my purse, I make my way to the door. Before I even knock, it flies open, and I'm greeted by Gabriel's smiling face. "Hey, Ree."

"Hey."

He pulls me into an awkward hug as I try to avoid squeezing a sleeping Maddox riding my brother's chest in a baby carrier contraption.

"Hi, Ox." I kiss his head and breathe in his baby scent. It's like crack. Seriously. Like puppy breath. Just can't get enough.

"Everyone's in the kitchen."

"Okay." I set my purse on the entry table. "You gonna hold him or put him down?"

He pats Ox's rump with a little bounce to his step. "Nah, he had a rough night. Tummy upset or something. He'll sleep better on me." He couldn't look prouder or more confident. And happy.

"Fatherhood looks good on you."

His smile cracks the seriousness his features usually carry. "Who would have thought?"

"I did." He was more a father to me than our own.

His smile fades when he frowns, his eyes studying me a little too intently. "You okay?"

"Yeah." I swallow around the tightness in my throat and blink away the threatening water works.

"You sure? Where's Rowdy?"

Shit. I forgot to tell them he wasn't coming. "He, uh, had plans."

My brother's eyes narrow. "Plans?"

"Yep," my reply's a little too high with forced perkiness.

His glare intensifies. "Hmm," he rumbles more than speaks.

Note to self: avoid Gabriel today.

"I'm going to say hello." I point in the direction of the kitchen, turn quickly to escape his glower, and start to walk that way.

Hugs and hellos all around, I sigh with relief when I get the questions about Rowdy joining us out of the way.

Done. Handled. No more Rowdy questions. Except, I don't miss the hurt in Frankie's eyes, the empathy in them too.

She's disappointed. I know she loves my brother more than life itself, but right now she's hurt Rowdy didn't show for me—not just herself.

"You okay?" I lean on the counter next to her and snag a raw carrot.

Her head pops up, her eyes searching out Gabriel before coming back to me. "Yeah, I'm good. I was hoping Rowdy would come. It's been a while since we've seen him."

Probably not since we've been back from Texas. I guess he's kinda been avoiding everyone—except me. Except today his avoidance includes me.

He asked you out for breakfast.

I'm an idiot. Coming back to the gym was a big move. Maybe coming to a social gathering was just too much right now after his mom's passing.

Him not being here doesn't have to be a reflection on how he feels about me. Or her. "Losing his mom was hard. He's not really himself right now."

"Yeah." She nods. "I get it. I do. I just wish he'd open up to me about it. We were so close… But then—"

"You chose Gabriel." Oops, did I say that out loud?

"It wasn't like that." Her back straightens.

"Maybe not for you."

"He didn't—"

"Maybe he did."

She looks horrified. She had to have considered how he'd feel watching the woman he proposed to marry someone else, have someone else's kid.

"It might not have been love for you, Frankie, but maybe it was for him."

She shakes her head, tears looming in her eyes. "He loves me. We have a special connection. He was there for me when I needed him most. But he's not in love with me."

"Maybe not now. But the hurt could still be there. You having Maddox and his mom dying could have reopened old wounds." I dip a carrot in dressing and take a bite. "Maybe him not being here has nothing to do with you at all."

Gah, harsh much?

"I'm just saying, don't read too much into it. I think he needs a little grace right now." I need to take my own advice. "I was thinking he's not here because of me."

Her eyes widen.

"We can't both be right. We could both be wrong too." I shrug, not having a clue but hoping it has nothing to do with either of us.

She squeezes my hand. "You think he didn't come because of you?"

"He... We..." Shit. I won't cry.

I. Will. Not. Cry.

I clear my throat and grab a bottled water from the cooler at our feet. "He's been different since the funeral. Something happened after his brother... Never mind."

"His brother what?" The concern on her face is not good. I can't have her saying anything to Gabriel. He'll handle it worse than Rowdy did.

Let's pretend I didn't say that. "His dad told Rowdy something that upset him. But he's not saying. Whatever it is must be big." I hate to suggest it, but, "You should call him. Maybe you're who he needs to talk to about this."

It stings to admit they have a bond he and I don't share.

"Let's eat!" Cap comes in from grilling with a massive plate of food, saving me from having to talk about this anymore.

CHAPTER 28

I AVOIDED GABRIEL AND MY MOM FOR MOST OF the day, but Gabriel finds me sitting in Cap's porch swing around the back of the house. He's sans baby. We ate. It must be Ox's turn.

"You doing okay, Ree?" He sits down next to me. The wood creaks from his weight, and he messes up my swinging.

"Why's everyone keep asking me that?"

"Who's asking?" He stops the swing, pushing back and holding. "The people who care about you hiding out avoiding us?" He lets go, lifting his legs as we swing forward and back.

He used to take me to the park when we were kids. He taught me how to pump my legs to swing faster, how to go down the slide on my tummy, and he soothed the sting when I faceplanted in the dirt my first try. He was only three years older than me, but he always seemed so much bigger, tougher, smarter than me or any other kids I knew.

He was like a god. Bigger than life. He could do no wrong in my eyes.

He still can't.

"You know me. Never the life of the party."

He captures my hand and holds it tight between his massive paws.

"You've been doing good, though. I heard the sound test didn't freak you out."

I groan. "Lord, does everyone know my business?"

His smile is indulgent. "They care. They want to help. It seems Rowdy's been able to accomplish more than any of those asshole shrinks you've seen over the years. More than me or Mom. I can't be mad at that. So maybe give them a break, and let your big brother worry over you a minute."

"One minute."

He stills the swing. "So, you and Rowdy, huh?"

I shrug. He can't possibly want to know the biggest hurdle Rowdy helped me overcome—intimacy. Or that with Rowdy, it didn't seem like a hurdle at all. It was all too easy and natural to spread my legs and take him inside, not just physically but emotionally too. Every fear I've had, Rowdy has smashed through with ease, which is why him shutting me out is so hard.

"What happened in Texas with Rowdy's brother?"

"Drake? Phfft." I stand and walk to the railing and gaze out over the lake. The same lake Rowdy and I have shared a lunch around more times than I can count. "He's an asshole. Especially to Rowdy." I turn, crossing my arms over my chest.

"Did he hurt you?"

"N-no."

Gabriel comes to stand beside me, facing me as I face the house, counting bricks.

"Did he touch you?"

I shrug, unable to lie.

"Fuck." He scrubs a hand over his face. "Did you have an episode?"

I nod.

"Goddammit."

Turning toward him, I hold up my hand. "Don't ask if I'm okay. I'm here. *I'm okay.*"

"Why's Rowdy not here?"

161

"You'd have to ask him that."

"Okay."

"Okay?"

He smiles and wraps his arm around my shoulder, guiding me around the porch. "Let's have some cake."

"Ooooh, cake. Yes, please!"

I swing open the door and groan. "This can't be good." I step back, waving the big asshole in.

"How are you, Rowdy?" He pins me with his brows. "Really?"

I shut the door and walk past him to the living room, plopping down on the couch, grabbing my half-full beer. "Beer's in the fridge."

"Nah, I'm driving precious cargo."

Ah, yes, his gorgeous wife and new baby—that family could've been mine.

Fuck. I set down my beer. I've had too much to drink if I've stirred up that old crock of shit. I don't love Frankie. I love her, but I'm not *in love* with her. I don't want *her*. I love the idea of a wife and kids. That's what I'm pining over, not this big asshole's blessings. But it's not about Frankie.

I love *Reese*.

Worry hits me hard. "Why aren't you at Cap's? Everything alright?" Is Reese okay?

He sits on the edge of the couch, hands clasped between his knees. "Tell me what happed with Drake."

"Fuck. She told you?"

He shakes his head. "Not really. She let it slip when she was trying to explain why you weren't at Cap's. We'll get to that. First, tell me what happened with your asshole brother."

"He's just that. An asshole. Always has been. Always will be. He tried to hurt me through Reese. I stopped him, but not before he triggered her PTSD. *Deliberately.*" A wave of guilt hits hard.

"He didn't hurt her?"

"No. She was more rattled than anything. He held her by the arms, but that was it, physically. Believe me. He won't be doing that again." I take my beer to the kitchen, pour out the contents, and recycle the bottle. "Not that he'll get the opportunity again."

I grab two waters from the fridge and hand Gabriel one as he leans against the nearest kitchen counter.

He pops the lid and the drink's half gone before he pins me with his familiar scowl. "I'm really sorry about your mom, Cam."

Fuck. I clench my jaw, fighting the emotions his sincerity unleashes. When it seems like it's a losing battle, I turn my back. I won't cry in front of him. I haven't cried except with Reese. She's my sanctuary.

His strong hand grips my shoulder, his chest pressed to my back, his other hand clutching the opposite arm. "She must have been a good woman if you loved her this much."

"She was the best." It hurts with the tightness in my throat. I swipe at my eyes. "Except she wasn't perfect, apparently."

Shit. Am I going to tell him?

Is Gabriel the person I need to confide in?

"No one is." He squeezes then releases me, stepping back. "What happened? What did you find out that's fucked up your world?"

I turn, unashamed by the red of my eyes. This is Gabriel. I've seen him cry over Frankie when she was in the hospital after tumbling down the stairs. I've seen the fear and loss in his eyes. It made him no less of a man.

"How'd you know?"

"I recognize the pain. You love your mom, but something else happened. Tell me. Let me help."

"Yep." I finger two shot glasses and the whiskey and sit at the kitchen table.

"Fuck. The hard stuff, huh?" He takes out his phone and sends a text. "Cap will take Frankie and Maddox home. I'll Uber or walk."

As he sits cattycorner to me, his phone lying on the table next to him lights up with a message. "Angel says you'd better call her tomorrow or your ass is grass." He smirks.

I fill the shot glasses, pick one, and wait for him to take the other before clinking mine with his. "May she forgive me once I bare my soul to you."

He laughs. "God help me."

We throw back the shots. I pour us a second.

He waits. Fingers laced, full shot glass at the ready.

I take a deep breath and blow it out. "My dad is not my dad."

"Fuck."

"Exactly."

We toss back our shots.

Gabriel pours another.

CHAPTER 29

W E SWAY ON THE DOORSTEP. AT THIS POINT, I'm not sure who's holding up whom, our arms swung around each other's shoulders.

Gabriel bangs on the door. "Open up, old man!"

"Shh, you're gonna wake the neighborhood."

Gabriel whirls around, taking me with him, and his arm swings wide. "I don't see no fucking neighbors from here."

True. But neither he nor I live that far way. So, there are neighbors, even if we can't see them.

"Maybe this was a bad idea," I try to whisper, but I don't think I succeed.

"Jesus. Tell me you two are not drunk on my front porch at this time of night?" Cap's bark has us swinging around to face him.

"My family get home okay?" Gabriel stops our progress with a hand on the doorframe.

Cap looks embarrassed for a half-second before his stoic demeanor slams into place. "Frankie and Ox have been home for hours, which is where you should be, Gabriel."

Gabriel pats my chest. "Cam needed me."

Snitch.

"He did, did he?" Cap's gaze pings between the two of us. Then he steps back. "Come on in before you fall over."

We stumble over the threshold but right ourselves. I'm sure I'm not this ungraceful. It's got to be Gabriel bringing me down. I push off, standing on my own.

"Whoa." Cap seizes my arm. "Maybe we should sit."

I nod. "Good idea."

Gabriel pats Cap on the cheek. "I'm just going to lie down." He points at me. "You got this, bro." He sways his way to the couch and falls face first. "Wake me when you're ready to leave. I'm here for you."

Two seconds later he's snoring.

"He's not going to puke, is he?"

I chuckle. "Nah, he's good. He's a god. Gods don't puke."

"If you say so." Cap laughs, urging me into the kitchen. "I'd offer you something to drink, but it's obvious you've had enough."

I blink through the eye-stabbing brightness when he turns on the light. "Coffee." I take a seat. "Coffee would be good."

"Have you eaten, son?"

Son. Fuck.

"Nope. Well, I ate breakfast. I think." Did I? Or was that yesterday? "What day is it?"

"Lord, Rowdy. What's got you so fucked up? It's Saturday night around eleven p.m."

"That's right. You had Reese and her family over."

"Yeah, and you didn't show up. Frankie and Reese were disappointed."

"They were?"

He sets a piece of chocolate cake on the table in front of me. "Eat. Coffee will be ready in a minute."

"I shouldn't eat sugar. I'm in training." I cram a forkful in my mouth and die as the sinful goodness coats my tongue. Reese would love this. I need to take a piece to her.

"You shouldn't be drinking either. You've fucked that up, so a little sugar won't kill ya. I can make you a sandwich if you want."

"Yes, and more cake. I need to take some to Reese. She loves chocolate." I take another bite and mumble, "I luf chocate too."

"She does. She had a piece earlier."

"She did?" Sadness hits me square in the chest. "I should have been here."

"Yep, you should have. Why weren't you?"

He sets down two cups of coffee and a bottle of water before joining me.

I break open the water and guzzle it.

"You," I say, setting my water down and forking another bite. I shake my head, the drunk fog lifting a tad.

"Me?" Cap stirs creamer and sugar into his coffee, then switches it with the cup in front of me. I guess he was stirring it in *my* coffee.

How's he know how I take it?

"You take your coffee just like me." He repeats the creamer-sugar maneuver, then takes a tentative taste. "Why am I the reason you didn't come?"

It takes a second for me to realize he answered my coffee question I didn't know I'd said out loud.

Hello? Drunk.

"Rowdy?"

"Yeah?"

"Why didn't you come today?"

"Did you know a Vera Orlena Permian-O'Dair?"

Cap chokes on his coffee, spitting it all over the table. "Fuck." He snatches a napkin and wipes at his face and table. Once he's composed and able to speak, he squares his jaw and asks, "How do you know that name?"

"She was my mother."

"W-what?" He stands so fast the chair bangs on the floor behind him. But he's oblivious. Hands digging in his hair, he paces the kitchen two turns and then stops, pinning me with his fiery scrutiny. "Vera was your mom?"

"Yes."

His gaze takes in each of my features before he nods. His chin hits his chest, and his hand covers his mouth as a groan like he's dying escapes.

I stagger to my feet, approaching him slowly. "Did you love her?" I'm not sure if I want him to say *yes* or *no*. Which will hurt less?

He falls against the counter. His sorrowful, teary eyes lock on me. His mind races. I can see every painful thought as it floats to the surface.

I repeat, "Did you love my mom?"

He grips the counter. "I didn't mean to, but God help me, I did."

I should stop there. Give the man a chance to digest the news that a woman he loved—or loves—is dead.

That's the kind thing to do.

I stalk to the table and take a long drink of coffee. It's cooled enough that it's easy to drink. I need the caffeine if I'm going to drive Gabriel and myself home.

"That's why you didn't come? Because you found out I knew your mom?"

I freeze.

He steps toward me. "Rowdy?"

Don't make me say it.

I shake my head. It'll hurt more.

"Rowdy." He steps toward me, a plea in his eyes. He wants the truth.

It's still gonna hurt.

"No, that's not why I didn't come tonight."

Growing closer, almost chest to chest, he says, "Tell me."

Am I doing this?

Possibly.

Our eyes lock, his green to my pale blue, nose to nose. I tell him the terrible secret neither of us knew, "I didn't come because I found out my dad is not my dad. You are."

CHAPTER 30

I T'S A SHIT SHOW TO SEE A GROWN-ASS MAN YOU admire fall to his knees and cry. It's a deal breaker for the hold I've had on my emotions for the past few weeks.

"I'm sorry, Cap." I sniffle and wipe at my eyes. "I wish there was an easier way to tell you. I wish we'd known."

I slide down the cabinet till my ass hits the floor beside him. Bending my knees, I place what I hope is a comforting hand on his back.

Until this moment, I was pissed at the world.

I was pissed at my parents—particularly my mom.

I was mad as hell at Cap.

But seeing him now, busted up over hearing what could have been the love of his life, for all I know, is dead, all anger leaves with every tear that streams down my cheeks and every racking sob that leaves Cap's body.

He's lost more than just a person he loved.

He lost the opportunity to be a father to me... "Uh, Cap. I don't mean to make this worse, but I feel I should tell you the rest. Not drag it out." And prolong his agony.

"Fuck, there's more?" He dries his face and fights to get a full breath. His eyes meet mine over his shoulder. "Cameron…" He freezes and sits back. "Jesus."

He searches my face like he's seeing me for the first time.

"What?"

"Your name. Cameron is my middle name." He punches out a few breaths.

I'd forgotten that detail from Mom's letter. "They named me after you."

"So they did." He cocks his head. "What's the rest of the news?"

"You've got a daughter. My younger sister. Taylor is yours too."

His head hits the cabinet, eyes falling closed. If Cap were an older man, I'd worry for his heart, but he's only twenty years older than me. He would've been a young dad, if given the chance.

His head falls to the side, his eyes opening. "I'm sorry, Rowdy. I just need a minute here."

"No." I shake my head. "I get it. I've known for weeks, and I'm still fucked up over it." I stand and pull him to his feet.

"I don't expect anything from you, Cap. You've already done a lot for me. But this was a secret I could no longer carry. I'm sorry for dumping it on you like this."

He clasps my arm, pulling me till we're head to head. "You did right by telling me. We'll figure this out." He shakes his head. "I just need a minute."

"Yep." I look up to see a red-eyed Gabriel staring at us from the kitchen entry. I guess he wasn't as out as we thought. "I should get Gabriel home to his family."

Cap gives Gabriel a curt nod. "Thanks for getting him over here, Gabriel."

"Sure, Cap." Gabriel steps up and hauls my father into a hug and then hooks me behind the neck and pulls me in, heads on shoulders, arms around each other in a three-way embrace.

"This is y'all's business." Gabriel's gruff voice reflects the emotions surrounding us. "Frankie and I are here for whatever you need. But don't think for one second this isn't a blessing in disguise."

He pulls back, locking his hands on our shoulders. "Rowdy, you just lost your mom but gained a father."

A chin nod and grunt are all I can manage.

"Cap, you're like the father Frankie and I never had. You're a good, kind-hearted man, who should've been a father all along. Turns out you were—you just didn't know it. Take whatever time you need. But know the guys will support you all the way if y'all decide to let it be known."

After another embrace, more grunting and eye swipes, I leave Cap at his door holding an envelope with a letter from my mom. She enclosed it in mine.

I don't know what he'll do with the information or how he feels about gaining two kids—real blood-of-my-blood kind of kids.

But no matter what he decides, I feel lighter than I have since hearing Mom had cancer.

It's time to see my girl.

I've been pacing, checking the window since Gabriel called to tell me Rowdy was on his way to see me. He wouldn't tell me why. Just that my *man* needed me.

My. Man.

The way Gabriel said it, I knew he approved of my relationship with Rowdy. I thought for sure he'd fight me on getting involved with a fighter.

Turns out I was wrong.

I jumped out of bed as soon as I hung up with Gabriel, brushed my teeth, and didn't bother getting dressed. I'm hoping once Rowdy gets here, I won't have my sleep shorts and tank top on long.

A girl's gotta have dreams, right?

As soon as his truck pulls into the parking lot, I'm waiting at my open door. When the elevator door opens and my Shadow steps out, I run, leaping for him.

He catches me midair with a grunt, pulling me into his body. I wrap around him, arms and legs holding tight.

"Kitten," he breathes into my neck.

"Whatever it is, Shadow, I got you."

"Thank fuck. 'Cause I need you, baby."

My heart pounds and soars at the same time. He needs me. "I needed to hear that so bad, Cam. You have no idea."

His fingers pull on my hair as he walks in my apartment and kicks the door shut with his foot, capturing my eyes. "I never stopped needing you, Kitten. I'm just a little fucked up. I didn't want to burden you with my news. But I'm ready now if you're willing to listen."

"One million times, yes."

He squeezes my ass. "Maybe I could love on you first?"

I trace the shadows around his glassy eyes. He's been crying. "I've got what you need."

He smiles his dimpled grin and the sadness falls away. "You do, don't you?" His mouth claims mine in a tender kiss. "I love you, Kitten. Don't ever forget that."

"Never." I kiss him back. "I love you. Don't forget it either."

"Never, baby. Never."

CHAPTER 31

BEING INSIDE MY GIRL HAS NEVER FELT SO RIGHT. I rock into her and savor the visual of her arching back, moaning my name, clawing at my arms, begging me to go deeper, faster, harder. But not this time.

This time I'm loving my kitten with steady strokes, deviously slow kisses with deep tongue and grinding hips.

Her gasps are my fuel.

Her sighs are my exhales.

Her beating heart thudding in time with mine is my lifeblood.

Twining her legs around my ass, I thrust deeper, grind harder, tweak her nipples, bite her neck, and suck her sweet lips until her bed creaks and her body starts to shake.

"That's it, Kitten." I coax her into giving me what I crave—the feel of her coming around my cock, gripping the life out of me with every pulse of my release.

"I'm, uh…"

"Yes, baby, take it."

Goosebumps break out across her skin as she tenses, pulling at me with every inch of her body touching mine.

Thrust deep. Hard grind. Dirty talk. The formula to my girl's pleasure.

"I need to feel you come on my cock, Kitten."

Moan and clench.

"Your tight pussy squeezing me is… Fuck… So good."

Gasps and shakes.

"You're gonna make me come, baby." That's not just talk. Her grinding into me, squeezing me with her wet heat are going to be my undoing.

"Rowdy."

"I'm never gonna stop fucking you, Kitten."

"Ohmygod."

"You. Are. Mine," I growl in her ear.

The magic words she needed to hear send my girl skyrocketing, calling my name, seizing in tremors and locking onto my cock so hard, I can't do anything else but explode with her.

"Goddamnkitten!" I roar. My release is so intense, my balls quake, and streams of mini orgasms wrack my body with each pump of my cock inside her heaven.

Panting, we lay there, a mass of arms and legs, entwined and lifeless.

"I think I died," she murmurs, her voice rough from her screams.

"I knew you felt like heaven."

She giggles and kisses my cheek. "You're amazing, my Shadow. I never imagined it could be like this."

Cocky twitches, preening at her praise, hardening for round two.

I slowly pull out of my favorite place to rest beside her. It's time for talking, not fucking. But first… "I'll be right back." I slip out of bed, dispose of the condom, and grab us some water.

Her eyes eat me up as I stalk back to bed. "Drink this to cool the heat in your eyes, Kitten."

She bites her lip, rubbing her thighs together. She has no idea how hot she is.

"You're killing me." I kneel over her, press my mouth to hers, soft, no tongue. "We need to talk." I cup her between the legs. "Then I'll take care of this."

Moaning, she parts her legs. My fingers glide through her folds. "So fucking wet."

She clenches around my fingers when I push inside her, a small tremor taking us both by surprise.

"You need more, dontcha, Kitten?"

"Yes." She bows off the bed, her breasts high and tight, begging for my mouth.

"Fuck." I latch onto her nipple, sucking and teasing with my tongue and teeth, my fingers moving inside her, the sound driving me insane.

Before she can come, I pull away, standing, and offer my hand. "Come 'ere."

Without hesitation she takes my hand. I tug her from the bed and into the bathroom. She blushes when I turn on the light.

"I want to watch. I want to see you fall apart."

"Oh." Her blush spreads across her chest, her nipples hardening.

I press her to the counter, facing the mirror, kissing along her shoulder and neck. "Hands on the counter."

She obeys without question.

"Good girl," I chuff my approval.

Pulling back on her hips, I push down on her back till she's bending over. "Don't forget to brace yourself."

I steal a kiss before moving behind her. I massage up her back and over her shoulders, around her sides to squeeze each breast. All the while my Kitten pushes her glorious ass against me, rubbing my cock, making it harder.

One look in the mirror has me ready to plunder. Her back is arched, her tits forward, my hands teasing her nipples, her mouth open on a long moan with each exhale.

"So fucking hot, Kitten."

I push Cocky between her legs, rubbing him through her arousal, testing her entrance.

Her head falls forward as she groans, "Please."

My girl is aching for me. "Tell me what you need."

She looks back, her glazed eyes meeting mine as she flexes her pelvis. "You."

Perfect answer. I bend over, kissing up her back, gripping her shoulder. "You've got me, baby."

I push into her slowly, swallowing our moans in a bruising kiss before standing, holding on to her hips and diving in hard. "I'm. All. Yours."

Her hand slaps against the mirror. Her eyes fall shut, and a silent plea coats her lips. As I drive into her, my balls lift, and my nipples tighten at the sight of the two of us.

"Open your eyes, Kitten. Watch me love you."

"Fuck," she whispers as her eyes lock on my reflection.

That's right, baby. Watch.

She fights to keep her eyes open with each thrust. I, on the other hand, can't take my eyes off her. The sway of her tits, the flexing of her fingers on the counter and mirror, the stream of noises coming from her mouth and echoing around us only drive my thunderous plunges and chest-beating growls.

"You're gonna come for me, aren't you, Kitten?"

She nods over and over again, her face morphed in pleasure. "Yes. Yes... Oh God, yes!" She smacks the counter and throws her head back as her whole body shakes with her release.

"Fuck, yes." I continue to drill into her, fighting each time to push through her vise grip on my cock.

Not fucking coming yet, Cocky.

Make her come again, he says. He always has the best ideas.

I grip her around the shoulder and ease her up until her back hits my chest. I wrap my hand around her neck and jaw to capture her mouth. "I need you to do that again."

She moans her consent into our kiss, licking, and sucking my tongue like it's my cock.

I cup her mound, rubbing her clit, feeling my cock drive into her, her wetness coating my shaft and my hand. "I'm gonna come so hard. Fill you up."

"Yes." She latches on to my wrist holding her neck and grips my ass, squeezing and kneading. "Come for me, Cam."

She moves her hand to play with her breasts, squeezing and pinching her nipples. "Come so hard, I'll be tasting you for a week."

"Fuck, my Kitten has a dirty mouth." And I love it.

I press harder against her mound, each thrust rubbing her clit against my hand, my fingers grazing my shaft, sending a whole new sensation to my balls.

"Come, baby," I bark seconds before I shoot into her, filling her up just as she comes again, squeezing and prolonging my release to mix with hers.

"Fuck." I push her down, her chest flat on the counter, and grip her hips. "Not done."

I grind and drill her until she comes so hard, she gushes her release down our legs, sending me into an uncontrolled hammering frenzy of need.

When I come again, I fill her so damn much I'm convinced she'll get pregnant a year from now.

And damn if Cocky doesn't harden at the idea.

CHAPTER 32

HE CARRIED ME TO THE SHOWER TO CLEAN US up. After coming I don't know how many times, I'm deliciously spent and completely boneless. How he managed to stand, much less carry me, is beyond comprehension.

Oh, that's right. He's The Pussy Whisperer.

Mad skills, I tell you. Mad. Skills.

Only now we're cuddled on my couch, snack consumed, him in his black boxer briefs and me in his t-shirt that smells like him—I don't ever want to take it off—my mouth opening and shutting like a fish out of water.

I try to suck in air.

It takes a few attempts.

His sheepish gaze washes over me, patiently waiting for my reaction. "I can't... You... Wow." My mind is blown.

I can't sit. Hopping up, I round the living room as I mull his news over. "Cap is your dad—your real dad."

"Yep."

"Your mom and Cap... you know." My eyes nearly bug out of my head.

"Turns out." His lips twitch. I'm glad he can find humor as I'm freaking the fuck out.

"Cap is also your uncle because he's your dad's—the one you thought was your dad for the past twenty-three years—half-brother."

"Yes."

"Which makes your dad—who's no longer your real dad—your actual uncle."

He scowls. "And stepdad, I think, since he's married to my mom but not my father by blood. Well, except the blood he shares with Cap."

I hold up my hand. "Holy... And Drake is your half-brother but also your cousin?" I rub my eyes. "Can that be right?"

"Shit, Kitten. I never got beyond the idea that Cap is my father. You've taken it to a whole other level of complicated. But I—" he leans forward, his head in his hands, then looks up at me, "I guess you're right.

"Cap is my uncle and my father.

"Barrett, who I thought was my father, is actually my stepfather and my uncle.

"Drake is my half-brother and my cousin.

"Taylor is my sister—nothing changed—except Cap is our dad."

"Hold the fort." I kneel in front of him, hands on his knees. "Regardless of Cap being your dad, how did you not know Cap was related, or how did he not know who you were? I'm confused by all the different names too."

"Cap and Barrett have different fathers, so they have different last names. Barrett is *O'Dair* after his father, and Cap is *Durant* after his father. I don't know the details of their mom's marriage situation. Since Cap is younger than my dad—Barrett—I assume she divorced Barrett's dad and married Cap's dad. Or maybe, like me and Taylor, he was the outcome of an affair. I just know I'd never heard of a James Cameron Durant, or Cap or Jimmy—whatever you want to call him—until my mom suggested I move to California and hook up with the gym there with the hopes of getting on Cap's radar. She had a plan all along to send me to him. We just didn't know it was for a different reason than his coaching skills."

I crawl into his lap and cup his face. "I know this sucks for you, so many lies and secrets. But poor Cap, he's been a father all this time, and he didn't know it." Tears spring to my eyes. "He's a good man, Rowdy. He would've made a great father. I know shitty dads, and he wouldn't have been one of them. I'm sad for you and for him for missing out on that."

He pulls me in tight, head buried in my neck. "Yeah, Kitten. He would've made a great dad. I doubt Drake would have gotten away with half the shit he did."

I chuckle at that. "No, Cap would have put Drake in his place and made him see his worth is not a reflection of you being in his life."

"God, Kitten. Don't ever fucking leave me."

"Not going anywhere. I'm here for as long as you want me."

He presses me back. "For however long I want you?" He glowers. "Reese, I'm in this for the long haul. If you don't want that, you need to speak up now. 'Cause we're past the point of return here, darlin.'"

"Darlin'?" I can't hide my smile.

"Kitten," he growls, and my insides liquefy with want.

"I love it when the Texan comes out in you."

He narrows his eyes and stands, holding me against him by my ass. "You're about to get a whole lot of Texas inside you, *Darlin'*. So, if you don't want me for the long haul, you need to tell me. Now."

Gah, long haul or not, who could turn down that offer? But... "I want you now, tomorrow, and always. Whether you're an O'Dair, a Durant, or a Jenkins." I frown. "Hey, why is your name Jenkins and not Permian-O'Dair like Drake and Taylor?"

"It was. But when I decided to become a professional fighter, I wanted to separate myself from my family's influence. Jenkins was my best friend's last name. He died in a car accident our senior year of high school. I took his name to honor him and give myself a new start in California, and now Vegas."

My forehead hits his shoulder. "This is making my head hurt."

He kisses my neck, rubbing my back as he turns off the lights, then checks to be sure the front door is locked. "I'm gonna kiss it and make it all better," he promises on the way to my bedroom.

"No more secrets?" Except the truth of my past.

"No more secrets, Kitten." He falls backward on the bed, securing me across his thighs, and spreads his arms and legs wide. "I'm an open book. Open me up and have a read."

I shimmy on his groin. "And a taste?"

"A taste. A bite. A lick. A fuck. I'm all yours, baby."

"I don't know how I'll manage—" I wiggle his underwear down and lick his shaft. "But I'll try."

"Fuck, my girl is insatiable."

"Not insatiable, Rowdy. Just set free."

CHAPTER 33

WAKING WITH MY GIRL SLUNG ACROSS MY body, cozy and warm, has to be the best way to wake up. Except maybe her mouth diving for cock or my mouth lapping at her pretty little kitty.

Okay, this has to be the *third* best way to wake up.

I check the time and inwardly groan. I feel like I've been run over both physically and mentally—or maybe that's emotionally. All are probably accurate and true.

Stretching, I try not to rouse her from sleep as I gradually make my way out of bed and inch her off me and onto the mattress. She grumbles her discontent but doesn't open her eyes.

When the cool air hits me, I eye the wet spot on my thigh and marvel at our joined juices sliding down my leg. Before it can hit the carpet, I jump into the shower.

Bare, skin-to-skin is the best sex ever.

It didn't take any convincing. I get tested regularly, and I've never had sex without a condom. She's never had sex before me—so we're good. Plus, she's on birth control.

Wham, bam, out the condoms go, and *hello* riding bareback.

Best invention ever. Wet spot and all. A reminder of how turned on she gets and how hot sex is with my girl. And the fact that it was inside her before dipping out to land on my leg while she slept on me is caveman-worthy.

Before Cocky can take over my thoughts, I turn the water cooler and soap up. It's not like I haven't had enough sex in the last twelve hours. I've essentially drilled my dick's imprint in her pretty little kitty.

I'm sure she needs a break.

You sure? I can be tender, Cocky chimes in.

Down, boy. I'm sure.

Exiting the bathroom with just a towel on, I find Reese sitting up in bed, pensively checking her phone.

"You good, Kitten?"

Her head snaps to attention. "Gabriel is just checking in. He says he's never drinking with you again."

"Yeah, tell him *me too.*"

"You went drinking with Gabriel last night?"

"No, he came over while you were at Cap's. I assume you were still there. He wanted to know what happened with Drake and what the hell's going on with me. We shared some shots, and I confided in him. We then drove to Cap's and, well, you know the rest."

"You told Gabriel about Cap before you told me?" Her face falls.

Shit. She's hurt. Rightly so.

"It wasn't intentional. I'd already had a few beers before he showed up. It was an impulsive decision based on timing and the fact that he needed to know I wasn't trying to fuck things up with you." I sit next to her and cup her cheek. "I've been messed up about this, Kitten. I didn't want to keep it from you, but I also didn't feel like it was totally my secret to tell. You work for Cap—everyone in my life *here*—works for Cap. I didn't want to fuck it all up, my relationship with you, my friendships, my career. It was all on the line."

Her gaze softens. "I don't know if there is a right way to handle this type of news, but I get it. You needed time. And Gabriel was the hammer that forced you through the round hole."

Square peg. Round hole. She gets me. Totally fucking made for me.

"Are we okay?" Do I need to fuck the hurt out of your eyes?

"We're good." She turns and kisses my palm.

I lean in and steal a kiss for myself. "I love you."

"Love you back."

Having slept and mulled over Rowdy's family drama, it feels more settled today.

He feels more settled. Like he can breathe without his secret weighing him down.

He's been giddy all morning, which was cracking me up, until we got a call from Cap.

Now, he's nervous and keeps glancing my direction from the driver's seat as we drive to his house. "We don't have to stay if you don't like it."

"I'm sure I'll love it." I love him. How could I not love his home?

"If you don't have everything you need, I can run back to the store. Shit. Did you get garlic?"

"Yep."

He had me pack a bag with everything I might need and clothes for work tomorrow. We also went grocery shopping for dinner. I'm cooking in his kitchen. Should be interesting considering I don't even know his set up. But if I can cook in my tiny kitchen, I've no doubt I can make his work.

"You sure about this? I can call Cap back and tell him today's not a good day. Or I could just run over to talk to him for a bit."

I squeeze his hand. "Shadow, we're good. You'll show me your house. We'll hang for a bit. Then I'll make dinner for the three of us. If you and Cap want privacy, I can give it to you. But I'm happy to sit by your side and support you in whatever way you need."

He lets out a relieved sigh. "I want you there with me."

"Then I'm there."

The one thing I wasn't prepared for was him handing me his mom's letter as soon as we drop my stuff off in his massive bedroom suite.

He pulls me into his lap.

"Are you sure? You can just tell me the gist if it's too private."

"No more secrets, Kitten."

I lean back, my head resting on his shoulder, his arms banded around my waist, and read his mom's words:

Dear Cameron,

I'm sorry I didn't tell you about my cancer sooner. There wasn't much to be done. I promised to try for your dad's sake. But I felt in my gut my time was up.

I've always been so proud of you for following your dream, forging your own path, and not giving in to your father's wishes to join the family business.

If I'd been braver and had as much passion as you, I would have pursued my own interests too. But I didn't, so I stayed the path that made my parents happy and worked to grow the family business.

But you won't suffer for not having done the same.

I've ensured your financial security. You will want for nothing other than pursuing your dreams and making your Wendy happy.

I stutter over the name *Wendy*, reading it again. "Who's Wendy?" *Am I going to have to fight her for you?*

He kisses my cheek. "It's you."

"What?" I frown my disbelief.

He grins. "It's like Wendy from *Peter Pan*. Keep reading. I promise I'll explain."

Wendy. Hmm, should be interesting.

I continue reading:

Don't feel guilty for not being here. You know I'm not one for teary good-byes and saying goodbye to the light of my life would have surely been harder than giving birth to your massive head. I know. Too much detail.

You were where I wanted you to be, in Vegas with Cap, pursuing your dreams and finding love. You finding Reese couldn't have come at a better time.

Remember, always make her feel heard, cherished, and respected. Your time and attention are more important than any gift you could give her. Listen to your heart. You will know how she needs to be loved. And if in doubt, ask her, then be quiet and listen to her words.

I'm sorry for this next part:

I pray Reese is by your side as you read this. If not, call her, go to her, let her help you cope and find peace with this news…

I didn't suggest you go to California or Captain Jimmy Durant by fluke or research as I led you to believe. I knew Jimmy as a young girl. He was my first love. Maybe my forever love. Don't get me wrong. I love your father. I've loved our life together. But Jimmy was a different sort than your father. Full of passion and dreams.

He's also your father's half-brother. They have different fathers—same mother—your Grandma Jean.

I fell in love with Jimmy (Cap) when your father was away in business school. It was wrong, maybe forbidden, but I can't for the life of me regret a single second I had with him. When he joined the Marine Corps, I was devastated and heartbroken.

I soon married Barrett. A move that would drive a wedge between the two brothers who never truly got along in the first place.

Cap was a career soldier, and my place was in my family business, beside a man like your father, who could lead and eventually take over for my father.

That is why you never knew Jimmy, why Barrett never talked about him in front of you or your brother or sister. But that's not the entire truth.

Jimmy came home on leave the year after Drake was born. I was lonely, a new mom, and married to a man who was home less and less. I had an affair with Jimmy that lasted until he deployed again. But from that beautiful moment in time came you.

Jimmy—Cap—is your true father.

Barrett knows the truth. He's always known and chose to love you as his own. But he also knows the time has come to tell you the truth.

Cap is your father, and he doesn't know. It's a shameful secret we never should have kept from him or you. I will regret and carry that burden to the grave.

Okay, one more...

He is Taylor's father too.

That is a story I will let Cap tell you, if he so chooses. Or if Taylor chooses to tell you (I'm also writing her a letter for your father, Barrett, to give her when the time is right).

I know this news on top of losing me is a shitty thing to do. But I could not bear to taint my last moments with you knowing you'd be hurt and angry.

We waited too long to tell you—all of you—and then it was too late for me.

This is me trying to do the right thing, make amends as best I can.

The only thing I ask of you is not to be mad at Cap. He has no idea about you or Taylor. I'm enclosing a letter for him. Please give it to him when you are ready.

He loved me with all his heart. I'm the one who chose your father (Barrett), but selfishly stole moments with Jimmy over the years. It wasn't fair to Cap or to Barrett.

I was a selfish woman, and I loved them both.

I will leave you with this, my sweet boy...

You can't help who you love, but you can help what you do with that love.

Take my word for it. If Reese is the woman I believe her to be, then love her with all your heart and don't let a second go by that she doesn't know it—doesn't feel it.

Life is too short for regrets. Don't let Reese be one of them.

I love you, my son, my heart, my fighter by choice, my champion by birth.

Mom

"Rowdy." I crumble into him, unable to hold back my sobs, my heart breaking for the woman who wrote this letter with her dying breath, who loved one man she felt she couldn't have while loving another she could.

"I've got you, Kitten. I've always got you."

CHAPTER 34

I HOLD MY KITTEN TIGHT, SOOTHE HER TEARS and lay waste to the demons dogging me since my dad burdened me with the news of their betrayal.

Secrets are terribly destructive, not only to those in the dark, but those holding the lie. This secret was eating me up inside, the hole growing each day I suffered in silence.

No more.

My girl knows my truth.

Cap knows his new truth.

We move forward. I don't know what that looks like. The ball is in Cap's hands to determine if he'll play or sit on the sidelines. Either way, no judgment. The man has gone over twenty years believing he had no kids. I thought it was a life choice, now, maybe it was a choice his heart made when my mom married his half-brother.

Some cuts leave scars too big to hide—to forget.

I hope Cap can.

"Do you want Cap to claim you publicly as his son?"

Claim. It's an important word. Possessive. Protective.

Nuzzling into her rose-scented hair, I think about it for a moment before I reply, "What's the point of knowing if he doesn't? But I also don't expect him to take out an ad advertising it either. Cap's a good man. I'm sure he'll need a while to reconcile what he thought to be true with the actual truth. A twenty-three-year deception based on an affair that left him brokenhearted without his family—can't be easy to come to terms with."

"How do you think Drake found out?"

"I assume he overheard them talking. He was just a baby when I was conceived. There's no way he can remember it firsthand." I brush my lips across her temple, relishing the softness of her skin. "I don't think he knows about Taylor. He's never really been mean to her—not in the I-hate-that-you-exist way he is to me."

A comfortable silence surrounds us. She slowly plays with the hair at the back of my neck and burrows in deeper with a sigh.

"You okay, Kitten?"

"Yeah." She kisses my neck, and I will Cocky to ignore the tingles. "It's just sad." She sits up swiping her face with her palms. "Nothing against your dad... Barrett." She cringes. "I hate having to make that distinction."

"Me too."

"It sounds like your mom really loved Cap. I imagine she downplayed their relationship, wanting to give you only the pertinent details in her letter." Her tender gaze hits mine. "Do you think she's why Cap never married? Never had kids—at least that he knew about?"

"I don't know. It would make sense." I toy with her hair before sinking into it, pulling her closer. "My mom called you *Wendy* because she thought you could be the one to tack my shadow to my feet. Help me tame my dark."

Be my shadow whisperer, Kitten. Be my Wendy.

She hugs my neck so tight, it's hard to breathe, but I'd never ask her to let up. "I thought we were slaying my demons." Her voice is soft, unsure.

"I don't know about slaying, but give me your dark, and it can dwell inside me, and together we'll rule our shadows. Ride or die, Kitten."

"Ride. Always ride."

"That's my girl."

I ease my nerves with cooking. Cap should be here any minute. Rowdy stepped outside to talk to his dad, Barrett, who just called a few minutes ago.

I'm plum worn out from crying today and the endless sex with Rowdy last night—not complaining—just exhausted. But nervous energy keeps me going as I check the roast and stir the pots on the stove.

Rowdy's kitchen is a dream. I had nothing to worry about. Should have known he'd have a chef's kitchen with a six-burner range with a double griddle, side-by-side double ovens with a warming drawer, and a walk-in pantry I could simply move into and be perfectly content.

"It smells amazing in here." Rowdy wraps his arms around my waist, kissing my neck.

"It smells the same as it did when you were here five minutes ago."

He releases me and leans against the counter. "I guess coming in from outside amplified the smell."

"I hope Cap likes roast."

A lone finger traces my jaw and tips my chin. "Kitten, it's beef. Cap is a meat and potatoes man. He'll love it."

"Let's hope." I point to the rolls. "Could you put those on a cookie sheet?"

"Abso—"

A knock on the door has us both freezing. Our locked gaze keeps me captive.

"Do you want me to get it?" I offer.

"Uh, no. I got it." He kisses my forehead on his way past.

I opt to stay in the kitchen, setting the table instead of greeting Cap. They may want—need—a minute to themselves.

A moment later Rowdy enters the kitchen with his newly discovered father on his heels.

"Hey, Reesie." He's taken to calling me by Walker's nickname as of late. I don't mind. I find it endearing and only hope he feels closer to me than just an employee-boss relationship.

"Cap." I rush over, overwhelmed with the need to comfort and hug him much harder than he anticipated—or at all—by the fact it takes some coaxing by Rowdy to get Cap to hug me back.

"You can hug her. She initiated..." Rowdy encourages, and I realize how casually I initiated contact with Cap.

His embrace is sure and comforting, his hand moving up and down my back. I don't freak out.

"Sorry," Cap whispers. "I didn't want to—"

I pull back and tap his chest. "It's fine. I appreciate your thoughtfulness." I shrug. "You never know with me." Especially lately, my ability to touch and be touched is growing by leaps and bounds, all thanks to the man who pulls me into his side and kisses my head.

"It smells amazing in here." Cap takes in the state of the kitchen. "Anything I can help with?"

"I got the rolls, Kitten."

"Maybe putting the salad together?" I direct Cap to the large bowl and set out the lettuce and veggies I cut up earlier but kept separate for the sake of freshness.

"On it."

As we all work side by side, I slip out to turn on some music. When I step back into the kitchen, I freeze at the sight of Cap and Rowdy hugging. I bite my lip and blink back tears.

Don't cry. Don't cry. Dammit, do not cry.

I wipe a disobedient tear away before it can grab anyone's attention.

This is not fatherly behavior I recognize, but I know it exists. I've seen it on TV. I've seen Rowdy's dad, Barrett, hug him. So, it's not completely foreign to me. But the impact of these two finding peace, or making peace in each other's embrace, sets my heart fluttering and my cheeks burning.

I know, in this moment, no matter what obstacles they face in finding their way as father and son, they will face them together.

When they pull back, each clasping the other's shoulder in the same manner, staring eye to eye, I see something I hadn't before. Rowdy's long dirty-blond hair to Cap's short light brown with a little gray, Rowdy's light blue to Cap's piercing green eyes, they are the same height, same build, same profile, and when Cap's smile is bigger than normal, for the first time I see his dimples.

Holy shit. I never saw the resemblance before, but now it's irrefutable.

Cap is Rowdy's father by blood.

Now we have to wait and see if he's his dad by choice.

CHAPTER 35

"ARE YOU GOOD FOR YOUR FIGHT IN TWO weeks?" Jonah taps on his clipboard. It's been a few hours, but the news of Cap being my dad has thrown off the mojo in the gym.

When Reese and I arrived this morning, Cap had everyone in the gym waiting for us. Frankie and Gabriel even came in for the meeting.

My nerves simmered. Reese squeezed my hand, reading the situation the same as me.

Without much fanfare, he got right to the point. "This is a family." Cap looked all of us in the eyes. "I picked each and every one of you to be a part of my team, but you all made it a family, because our commitment runs deeper than blood. It's a family by choice, not birth."

He locked on me. "Rowdy lost his mom, who I just found out was also someone I once loved very much."

Gasps of questions flew around the room.

Cap held up his hand. "My past is long and messy. It's also not up for discussion unless Rowdy or I initiate it. But with the news of his mother came the surprising blessing that he's also my son."

"What the fuck?"

"No way?"

A hundred other exclamations of surprise rang out that I couldn't make out for the rush of blood pounding in my head.

"I know it's a shock. Neither of us knew. So, I ask you to give us the grace to find our way, figure out our new normal as we digest this news. I also want you to know it doesn't change who each of you are to me." His eyes lock on Frankie, who's fighting back tears. "You *are* and *always* will be my family. It just means Rowdy is a permanent member, whether he wants to be or not." I got a quick smile and a nod in my direction.

And there you go, no more secret.

The only one remaining is about Taylor, but the guys don't know her, and based on my discussion with Dad—Barrett—she doesn't know. He hasn't even told her about me. He confirmed Drake found out years ago, and it was the fuel for his misplaced animosity.

Asshole.

Frankie barreled into me the second Cap finished spilling my deep dark secret. She wasn't upset about her standing with Cap as I feared. She was concerned for me.

"I can't believe you told Gabriel before telling me," Frankie chastised.

"Get in line." My Kitten squeezed in beside me.

I tucked Reese under my arm. "It wasn't intentional, promise." I'm not sure I would've wanted it to play out any differently. Gabriel forced me to confront the situation head-on. The girls wouldn't have been as forceful. Though, Reese did tell me to read my mom's letter as soon as she found out about it.

Now, hours later, I wipe the sweat from my face and nod. "Yeah, Jonah, I'm good."

The guys knowing wasn't as unsettling as I thought. Though, it will take a while for the dust to settle and the news to be no big deal.

Personally, I can't imagine it ever not being a big deal. Time will tell.

"Good, because unless Hammer is planning on disparaging Reese, we need to work on your concentration. We can't plan on a KO on the first strike."

A bit prideful and defiant, I smile. "I don't know, Jonah, I wouldn't mind being known as the KO King."

He chuckles. "Yeah. Keep dreaming." He pats my shoulder. "In the meantime, every day I need you here, focused, and ready to go."

"Not a problem."

He studies me speculatively. He has doubts.

I'll just have to show him.

Cap's announcement has my head bouncing in a million directions. It wasn't totally unexpected. We discussed last night at dinner the idea of him sharing the news with the team. Rowdy left it up to him to tell the guys or not; he'd follow Cap's lead.

Apparently, Cap decided it had been a secret long enough.

I agree.

Hours later, I've managed to get some decent work done, despite my brain fog.

A shadow out of the corner of my eye has me whipping around to find Gabriel hovering, freshly showered from working out. "I thought you went home."

"Nah, needed to work out with the guys."

He's been staying home with Frankie as much as he can, but I know he missed his daily workouts and camaraderie with the other fighters.

"You okay, Ree?" Gabriel's scowl no longer unsettles me. It's his resting bitch face.

"Yeah, I'm good. You? Frankie?"

His hands dig deeper into his jean pockets. "We're good." He eyes me from under his heavy brow, motions to the door. "Do you think we could talk a sec in the conference room?"

"Umm…" I check the calendar on my phone. "Yeah, Cap doesn't need it for a few more hours."

My worry grows with each step as I follow him into the room. The click of the door has me spinning around and hugging myself, watching him pensively.

"Is this about Rowdy?" I need a second to prepare if he's going to try to dissuade me from seeing him.

"No." Not elaborating, he points to the chair. "Sit."

Gabriel has always been a man of few words. At least for me. I've seen him talk Frankie's ear off, but never before her.

I remain standing. "I'm good."

His scowl deepens, his eyes searching the room as if he'd rather be anywhere else but here. When he finally lands on me, he pulls out two chairs. "Please sit."

This can't be good.

When I finally take a seat, he takes the one next to me, turning to face me. "There's no easy way to say this…"

"It can't be this bad. Spit it out." It's not like him to be so cautious.

"It's Dad." The bite in his tone tells me he'd rather be talking about anyone else other than him.

Me too. I shake my head and stand. "Nope. I'm not wasting a single breath on him." I've wasted entirely too much time fearing him in my mind. I'm not actively inviting him into my conversation.

Gabriel seizes my wrist.

For the first time in as long as I can remember, I jerk back. "Don't." Fear coats my voice, clouds my vision.

Releasing me, shock morphs his face. "Ree, I'm sorry." He stands, holding up his hands. "I would never—"

It's Gabriel. Not our father. My synapses start firing again. "Fuck." Dropping into the seat, I cover my face. "I know." I hate this. I hate being a slave to my fear. "I know. It's… He's—"

Gabriel sits closer this time, tentatively touching my shoulder. "I get it."

No, he doesn't. He has no clue.

"He's the last person I want to talk about. But you have a right to know, Ree. I don't want to take this choice from you."

My head pops up. "Choice? Like whether I'd kill him myself or let you or Rowdy do it?" Anger taints my humanity when it comes to my father.

I swipe my sweaty palms on my jeans, rocking back and forth.

Would I really kill him if given the chance? Probably.

God, I'm going to hell.

He smirks. "If you wanted to, I'd let you kill him, Ree. But it seems God has beaten us to it."

"He's dead?" Relief floods me. The man who was supposed to protect me instead of cause me harm is dead. Tears prick my eyes. I take a deep breath. I've forgotten how to breathe.

"No. Nearly. But not yet."

Fuck. My heart thumps and trips over itself. "What are you telling me?" I'm legit going to have a heart attack.

"He's been in prison the last couple of years—"

"Prison?! All this time I've been worried, and he's been locked up?" All this time I've feared him showing up, running into him on the street, finding him hiding in my apartment. So much energy wasted on *him*.

He's not dead. He's in prison. I'm going to be sick.

Gabriel squeezes my knee. "I didn't know, Reese. Swear. If I had known, I would've told you."

I wave him on to continue.

"He's dying of pancreatic cancer. They think he has less than a month to live."

"A month too long." *Shit.* I shouldn't have said that.

He chuckles, patting my hand resting on the table. "I couldn't agree more. You need to decide if you want to see him. Say goodbye. Tell him to fuck off. Get whatever kind of closure you need. This is your chance."

"See him?" Is my brother insane? I never want to see that man again.

Gabriel's brow furrows. "I know. You don't really want to, but do you *need* to?"

Do I need to? "Do you?" I honestly can't believe Gabriel's suggesting this. There's no way I want to see him. Ever.

He slumps in the chair, gripping the back of his neck. "That's the thing, right? I want to kill him for everything he's done. I never wanted to see his face again. But the opportunity to rub my happiness in his face and tell him *fuck you* one more time." He screws up his mouth. "It's tempting. I'm considering it."

Could I?

"Think about it, but don't take too long. We have to request special dispensation from the Warden to see him since he's in the medical ward. They might not even approve it. But if you think you might want to see him, then it wouldn't hurt to get the ball rolling. We can always not show up. It would serve him right."

"Does he want to see *us?*"

A stiff chin nod, his nostrils flare. "He asked to see us. His lawyer called me this morning. We have to reply in the next day or so. They said a month at the most. He could have weeks."

The buzz starts soft, like a mosquito near my ear.

I've got it under control. I can swat the panic away like that damn mosquito.

Deep, steady breaths. In. Out.

Focus on that crack on the wall. In. Out.

It's okay, he's not here.

In. Out.

It's okay, he's not here.

In. Out.

He's not here...

"Ree?"

It's okay, he's not...

I can't breathe.
The buzzing intensifies.
My hands are clammy.
Sweat dots my forehead.
The room slants.
I'm going to be sick.
It's okay.
But it's not...
"Reese!"

CHAPTER 36

"WHAT THE FUCK HAPPENED?" I WAS coming to find Reese when I heard Gabriel hollering her name. I all but broke down the conference room door to find him on the floor with her slumped in his arms, crying and mumbling incoherently.

"I had to tell her, Cam. She deserved to know." Gabriel panicked is not a good thing.

"Know what?" I gently lift her into my arms and sit. "I got you, Kitten." She clings to me, hiding in my chest.

Gabriel stands, washing his face with his hands. "Our dad is in prison, and he's dying—cancer. He wants to see us. She needs to decide if seeing him will give her closure."

"Fuck." I stare daggers at him. "I should have been here."

He pulls at his short hair, the same color as my Kitten's. "Yeah, sorry. I'm still getting used to the idea of you two. I'm usually her go-to person."

"I'm her person now, Gabriel," I growl. "Look what you did!"

He eyes us cautiously. "I see that. And I never meant to upset her."

"No more dad talks without me around. Got me?"

"Yeah." He wipes his mouth. "Yeah." He holds out his hand. "Give me your keys. I'll pull your car around back. Take her home. Or I can drop you home and get one of the guys to help me drop your car off later."

"Second option. I'm not letting her go." Before he makes it out the door, I add, "*My* home."

Gabriel glares over his shoulder, grumbling, "Yeah, alright."

He may not be overjoyed about Reese choosing me. I imagine it stings being replaced as the sole person who could bring her comfort.

He has a family now. Frankie and Maddox are his priority.

He needs to let Reese be mine.

The throbbing in my head wakes me, or maybe it was movement from the strong man wrapped around me. The gentle rise and fall of his chest lulled me into dreamland once again.

The second I remember *why* I'm in bed during the day, I need to get up from my prone position. I'm too vulnerable lying down.

"Hey," his sleepy voice tickles my ear. "You're alright, Kitten. I've got you."

It's then I realize I'm in his house, in his bed, his hard body pressed to mine, spooning me.

"How?"

"Your brother dropped us off." He props up, looking me over. "You remember what happened?"

Rolling over, I nod. "Wish I didn't."

"You want to talk about it?"

"Not really. Maybe later." I stretch and sit up, eye him over my shoulder. "I'm hungry."

"Same." A boyish smile breaks free. "Let me feed you." He hops up and grabs my hand, pulling me out of bed and toward the kitchen.

Growing up, the kitchen was a scary place. A place where my dad did despicable things. As an adult I took the kitchen back when I started cooking, finding solace in the preparation, in the tools that could so easily become weapons. Here in Rowdy's kitchen, when he brushes against me, I don't flinch. I don't slink away, praying I'm invisible. In his kitchen, I'm safe. I'm free to glide my hand along his back or his firm, irresistible ass and relish the fact that I can—and I *want* to.

My man makes a mean roast beef sandwich from the leftover roast.

Plopped down on his couch, I dig in as he pulls up the latest show we started binge watching when we're together: *The Witcher.*

Once it's playing, he eases the coffee table closer so I can put my feet up and eat in comfort.

"You good, Kitten?"

"Yep." As I chew, I lean my head against his arm, his muscles twitching as he takes a monumental bite and groans at his own masterpiece.

"So good."

"Really is. You're the official sandwich-maker in this relationship."

His smile is radiant as he swallows then kisses my head. "Deal." His eyes linger on me for a moment before returning to the show.

A full belly and two episodes later, sleepiness creeps in.

He tucks me into his side and adjusts so we're practically lying on his sectional, my feet on the couch, his on the table. "Sleep, baby."

When he switches to the sports channel, I stop fighting and give in to the food coma.

I leave Reese sleeping on the couch to get in a run on the treadmill. It's not ideal. I prefer to run outside, but I refuse to leave her alone. I need to be near in case she wakes in a panic.

My need to keep her close is not only about her. Knowing she's near takes the edge off. I'm amped about my coming fight. Maybe nervous. Not about my skills or my ability to win. The obstacle facing me is focus.

Can I focus on training and not allow my worry over Reese to derail my fight? Should I cancel and let another fighter duke it out with The Hammer? Reese would not be happy if I sacrificed for her. I'd cancel in a heartbeat, but it's not just myself I'd be disappointing. Cap and the team have time and money invested in this match—in me. Earlier, I committed to Jonah that I'd be there, focused and ready to fight daily. I'm already fucking that up to be home with Reese.

I don't regret it, but my choices impact others.

I run harder, faster, chasing down the elusive runner's high, working to beat the guilt and worry out with each footfall, concentrating on elongating my strides, reaching farther.

Smooth. Controlled.

When my quads burn, I push harder.

When sweat drips in my eyes, I run blind.

When I hear a rustling at the door, I hold my breath until she comes into view.

Then I'm running to her, for her, because of her.

Her hair is mussed from sleep, t-shirt barely touching her thighs, nipples screaming *suck me*.

"You're beautiful," she says on a sigh, her eyes eating me up.

I want to tackle her to the floor and pound the worry out of her and my love into her. "There's only one beauty in this room, Kitten, and I'm looking at her."

Her blush is innocently seductive.

I reduce my speed with the intention of consuming her right here.

But she holds up her hand. "Don't stop. Do your thing." She plays with the hem of her shirt. "I'm going to start dinner. If that's alright."

"Sure." I pull my t-shirt over my head and swipe it across my face. I savor her hungry gaze. "You never have to ask. What's mine is yours." I'm yours.

Her sheepish smile has me wanting to swallow her whole, tuck her in close, and keep her there for the rest of my days.

"Okay." She backs to the door, turns, pauses and looks over her shoulder. "I love you, my Shadow."

Then she slips away like she didn't just rock my world, like she isn't my Wendy, pinning my shadow in place every fucking day.

CHAPTER 37

WHEN CAP CAME OVER FOR DINNER THE other night it was awkward for a few minutes, from the space of time it took to open the door, welcome him in, walk into the kitchen, and Reese to give us tasks to busy ourselves with. I was nervous as hell until he slammed me with a hug and said, "I couldn't have asked for a better son... Son."

His eyes shimmered with looming tears, and I fought to beat mine back.

We just stood there embracing like he wasn't my boss, my mentor, the head of my family-by-choice. He wasn't any of those things, yet he was all of them at once. Then add on the father-by-blood, and I was done. I choked back my sobs.

In that small space we inhabited in the world, in that very moment, I felt like I finally belonged. I wasn't the looming giant among my Texas family. I wasn't the dark son who needed to fight to stay sane. In this world, where Cap lives, I am more light than dark. My thirst to inflict damage, overpower, and reign supreme in the ring is the norm. Not an anomaly.

In Cap's world, I belong. Finally.

I felt it before. The settling at the edge of my darkness as soon as I followed Cap and Frankie from Max's Gym on their rounds to scout Cowboy and other fighters. It was instant. I thought it was Frankie that settled me, and in many ways she does. But in this embrace—father to true son—I understand it was always him. His influence and acceptance of Frankie and her need to have me near when she and Gabriel broke up. It was in his acceptance and influence over me.

I don't even think he realized the impact he has on the lives of those he draws near. The ones he welcomes into his fold—his family-by-choice.

He gripped my shoulders, looked me square in the eye. "I loved your mother with everything I had. I want you to know that. If we had made different life choices, I would have been the one raising you. I'm sorry I wasn't. But please don't hate your mom and Barrett. I was on a different life path. One I'd set out on long before I fell in love, before she chose Barrett, before you were conceived. I didn't fit in Vera's world. I knew it. She knew it. Barrett and I were like oil and water, which made him the perfect fit for her."

He stepped back, releasing me.

I still felt his embrace, his strength, his determination.

"I regret not knowing about you and Taylor. But I'm here now. I want to be involved in your life as much as you want me to be, in whatever capacity you're comfortable with."

The wash of calm was instant. In this man's eyes, I'm not a disappointment. I'm not a reminder of my mom loving another man. I'm not another man's child. I am Cap's son, the apple that didn't fall far from his tree.

His way of life is mine. His family-by-choice is mine.

"I'd like that. I want you to be my dad, not just my boss."

He clapped my shoulder and looked over at Reese watching us from the doorway. "Then that's what I'll be."

That was that. So simple.

Now, days later, he stalks toward me in the gym. I stop lifting to watch him move.

It's so familiar, I don't know how I didn't see the resemblance before. I'm a younger version of him.

He's only twenty years older than me at forty-three, young enough to have a wife and young kids. But he surrounds himself with grown misfits he deems his family. Someday, I'll ask him why he never married and had kids—ones he purposefully conceived and raised.

But today, he's pensive—on a mission.

"Hey, Cap." I don't call him Dad. I'm nowhere ready for that. Does he expect it?

"Son." His brow is tight, gaze, pointed.

I don't read into his choice of address. He's called me *son* way before he knew I really was his son.

"Have a minute?"

"Sure." I grab my towel and water.

A few turns later, I find myself outside, around back near the picnic benches with a view of the lake. But he's the one who holds my attention.

"It's Reese." The sternness in his voice a minute ago softens with worry.

"Can you be more specific?"

"She's not herself." He starts walking toward the lake. I fall into step beside him. "She's jumpy, timid even. Reminds me of when I first met her, years ago. She's not the confident woman she was just a few days ago."

"This thing with her dad is messing with her head," I agree. All the progress we'd made with touch and sounds have fallen by the wayside.

Jonah touched her arm yesterday. She jumped back like he burned her. She apologized profusely, as did he. I'm not sure which of them is more hurt by that interaction.

I dropped a glass this morning, and she nearly came out of her skin. She didn't have an episode, but she cowered into herself, shaking. I held her until the trembling stopped, until she pulled away saying she was *fine*.

She's far from *fine*.

"Do you think I should give her some time off? Send her home?"

I stop and stare out over the water. "Is she not able to perform her job? Is that why you're bringing it up?"

"Fuck no." He comes back to stand next to me. "I'm worried about her, is all. I don't want her being here around the guys, and the loudness of the gym making things harder on her."

"She says being here is good for her." I sigh and scrub my face with my hands. "Honestly, I think it's taking everything she has to keep it together. Logically she knows her dad is locked up and can't get to her. But the weight of seeing him again is fucking with her."

"So, she's decided?"

"No. Not yet. Gabriel texted her this morning asking if she'd made a decision." I shrug. "She didn't reply."

"She's always welcome here, Rowdy. I'm not sending her home or saying she's not doing a good job. Her work isn't suffering. But she is. I only mention it as I don't want her being here to make her PTSD worse."

"I'll talk to her."

"Don't upset her." His protectiveness makes me smile.

"Never my intent, Cap." Never.

He studies me for a moment.

I stand there and let him. I've nothing to hide.

"You doing alright with all of this?"

By *this*, I assume he means finding out he's my father. "I still haven't talked to my dad... err, Barrett, or Taylor. Focusing on my fight and Reese is about all I can handle right now. Maybe after my fight..." I don't really know how to finish that sentence. Maybe I'll talk to my dad, forgive him, tell Taylor, tell Drake he was right. The list is endless.

Before he can respond, I get a text. "Sorry, I just want to see if it's Reese."

"No worries."

It's a group text to Gabriel and me from Reese.

Kitten: *Gabriel, okay. I'll meet with him. Set it up.*

"Fuck." I shove my phone back in my pocket.

"What?"

"She agreed to meet with her father."

He squeezes my shoulder, keeping his hand there. "Whatever you need. I'm there."

"Thanks. When I figure out what that is, I'll let you know." In the meantime, the only thing I do know is I need my girl, but she's working. She's keeping her shit together as best she can.

I need to do the same.

Focus on my fight.

Be what she needs.

Kick some ass.

Love the hell out of hers.

CHAPTER 38

I THINK A STRONG WIND COULD KNOCK ME down. I'm anxious and feeling all too fragile after agreeing to meet with Dad.

Germain. I should start calling him Germain. Not Dad. There is nothing Dad-like about him.

A part of me prays to be like Rowdy, finding out the man I thought was my father turns out not to be. I'd love for any other middle-aged man in the world to be my dad. Anyone. Anyone other than *him.*

I finished what needed to get done and left work shortly after lunch. Cap had already suggested I knock off early. I guess he was with Rowdy when I sent my text, so he knew what I had agreed to.

Is it a mistake?

Gabriel will be there. Rowdy will be there, won't he?

Nothing bad could possibly happen.

He's in prison, for Christ's sake.

What could go wrong?

Everything.

Nothing.

You got this. You will face down the spawn of Satan and tell him to fuck himself.

That's what I'll do, I keep telling myself as I start dinner, losing myself in the mindless task of chopping veggies. It's stir-fry night. A dish I learned from Gabriel.

I'm not the only one with the cooking bug from Mom.

Mindless chopping and preparing.

Waiting for my Shadow to get home. Though, I'm not at his home. I'm back at mine. I need the familiarity of my stuff, my place, my security blanket. The home I built from nothing but a few boxes of clothes and a hand-me-down couch.

Mindless.

Chop.

Chop.

Chop.

The lock rattles. I drop the knife and still.

Breathe. Listen. Am I hearing things?

Seconds pass before his strong arms band around me. "Kitten." Rowdy presses into my neck.

Thank God it's him. I sigh on a shaky exhale.

I should have grabbed my bat. But no. I froze. Quaking in my bare feet, I didn't even keep the knife in my hand. "I need you to teach me self-defense."

He turns, frowning, leans on the counter and snags a peapod out of the bowl of veggies. "You know self-defense."

I pick up the knife and obliterate an onion. "I need practice. I'm rusty."

His head bobs, face lost in concentration. "How would you feel about Cowboy working with you?"

"Landry? Not you?" Not Gabriel?

"I think you need practice on someone other than the two people you're okay with touching you. Plus, he taught some self-defense classes back home. He'd be good."

"My mom can touch me."

"Do you want to spar with her?"

I laugh. "Hardly. That woman couldn't break a carrot if she tried." That's entirely sad and true. "Cap?" I offer. Why am I avoiding Landry?

"You're too comfortable with Cap too. Besides, do you really want to hit your boss?"

Sometimes. "No?"

That gets a chuckle. "You're comfortable with Landry, but not too comfortable."

"Jonah?"

"He's training me with Coach. Plus, I think if you went PTSD on him, he might cry. He's still recovering from the last time he touched you."

Poor Jonah. "True."

Rowdy grabs a handful of carrots. He unapologetically smirks when I side-eye him.

Swatting his hand when he goes back for more, I turn on the wok and whisk the sauce until the pan is hot, then swirl in a little oil and dump in the sliced steak.

"Damn, that smells good," he groans when the smell of charred meat scents the air.

We both like our beef on the rare side, so it doesn't take long. Scooping out the meat. I add the veggies in batches, starting with the ones that take the longest.

Rowdy sets the table as I finish the vegetables, slide the meat back in, and stir in the sauce to finish and coat everything in flavor town.

Quick. Easy. And oh so tasty.

Plate piled high with rice and beef and vegetable stir-fry, Rowdy sits. I grab the egg rolls I made earlier out of the oven and join him.

"Damn, Kitten, everything tastes even better than it looks. So fucking good." He bites off half an eggroll and groans like I just sucked his cock into my mouth.

Heat creeps up my cheeks from his appraisal.

I can't help but enjoy feeding him. He's so appreciative. I've never made anything he didn't rave over and ask for again.

Besides, he cleans up when we're done. "You cook. I clean. That's the deal." He ushers me out of the kitchen with a kiss on the cheek and soft pat on my butt. "Go relax."

I consider watching him clean. Any chance to openly gawk at him should be heavily considered. "I'm going to take a shower."

Walking away, I don't miss the heat in his eyes or the feel of his gaze on my ass as I slip into my room.

Leftovers put away, kitchen spick-and-span, I toe off my shoes by the door and make my way to her room. It's early yet, but I'd rather spend the rest of the night loving my Kitten than watching TV.

She was skittish when I arrived. I think she'd forgotten she'd given me a key to her place. Usually we're together so I don't need to use it. But she texted me earlier she was leaving work and to come for dinner at her apartment.

I was disappointed she didn't go to my house where we've spent the majority of our time since the whole Cap-is-my-dad revelation. I don't mind her place. I just want her to feel at home in mine too.

Someday it's going to be hers—ours. Sooner rather than later, if I have my way.

Finding her sitting on the bed, legs outstretched, ankles crossed, soft music playing, my chest aches for the beauty before me. No makeup, hair in a messy bun—like mine, wide-necked t-shirt hanging off one shoulder, she's fucking gorgeous.

She kneels on the bed, bites her lower lip before releasing it. "Get naked, my Shadow."

"Done."

She giggles as I pull off my shirt rather unceremoniously, wriggle out of my jeans and socks while hopping toward her.

She didn't say strip-tease. She said *naked*. There's a finesse to one and an urgency to the other. I took the urgent route.

In only my boxer briefs, I tip her chin and kiss her shower-warmed lips. Between kissing her mouth and nipping at her neck, I murmur what I want to do to her once we're both naked, which can't be soon enough for me. "Your turn."

I stand back, grip my cock to remind Cocky who's in control, and drool as she slips her t-shirt over her head, revealing the best set of tits I've ever seen. More than a handful with perfect dusky nipples always begging for my attention—or so I tell myself. I swallow around the lump in my throat to find her completely naked, no panties to remove.

"Fuck, Kitten. You're trying to kill me, aren't you? Waiting here panty-less for me to find and fuck you."

She shivers, her hands on her thighs, arms bracketing her breasts, and her back arches before she settles back on her haunches, legs spread enough to tease me stupid.

"That's right." I pull out Cocky, giving him a good tug, swipe my thumb over the glistening head. "I'm gonna fuck you so good, baby."

I step closer, running a finger down her chest. "Lie down."

She hesitates for a second, but when I step back, she complies.

"Open those sweet thighs, Kitten." I stroke up and down my raging erection. "Let me see what's mine."

Her knees fall open.

Her little kitten gleams with want. "Fuck, you're beautiful." I tug harder. "Touch yourself."

She sucks in a breath. Her eyes glaze over. She shakes, but doesn't move.

"I want your mouth." One. Two passes over my cock thinking of her mouth fucking me down her throat, I practically growl, "Do you want me to touch you?"

Her breathing shallows, her face pales. "No," she whispers. Wrapping her arms around herself, she squeezes her knees together.

"Reese?" I release my cock, hold up my hands. "What just happened?"

"No, please." She shrinks back on the bed, trying to cover herself with the sheet.

Fuck. It's not me she's seeing. The realization of *who* she thinks I am has my dinner threatening to make a reappearance.

I quickly cover up, throw my t-shirt on and approach the bed slowly. My heart is pounding so hard against my ribs, I swear she can see it. "Kitten. It's me. Rowdy."

She groans like she's in pain.

"It's okay, Reese. I won't hurt you. It's me, Rowdy."

As I step closer, she doesn't cower. She blinks up at me. "Rowdy?"

I let out a whoosh of air. "Yeah, Kitten. It's me. Can I touch you? Hold you?"

"C-cucumber." She backs away, averting her gaze. "Can…" She swallows and sucks in air. "Can you leave?"

Oh, fuck. This is bad. She safe-worded me, and I haven't even touched her. "Kitten."

"I…" She stutters in a breath. "Please," she begs.

I'm gutted. My girl is begging me to leave.

Begging. Me.

I step back, toss her t-shirt to her. "Put that on. I'll call Gabriel. Okay?"

She nods, pulls the shirt over her head and disappears below the covers until only her eyes up are visible.

"I'm going to wait by the door until Gabriel gets here. I won't come back in unless you call to me."

"Mmm'k," her child-scared reply pierces my heart.

She's scared of me.

Me.

Fuck.

I snatch my clothes and rush to her apartment door, pulling on my jeans before dialing her brother. I take a few cleansing breaths and hit *call.*

He answers quickly. "This better be good," his gruff ass barks at me.

"She needs you." I die a little inside at the implication she no longer finds me *safe*.

I hear commotion in the background. "It's Reese. I'll be back," a muffled remark to Frankie, I'm sure.

A moment later his engine roars to life. "Where are you?"

"Her apartment."

"What happened?"

A dying animal noise rumbles up my chest. "She had an episode and thought I was *him*."

"Fuck. I'm on my way. Don't hang up."

I was smug.

I thought I had this.

I thought I had *her*.

I would be all she needed.

Life shit on me and proved me wrong for that arrogance.

"It's not you, Cam. You have to know that. It's the fucked-up situation with my dad. It's bringing it all up. Cap said she's been on edge at work. This has been building since I told her about Dad. Then her deciding today to see him. It has to be it. She loves you, man. Don't give up on her."

"She begged me to leave."

"Frankie told me to leave, and it was the last thing she wanted. It was the last thing *I* wanted. Sometimes you have to leave to find your way back."

Fuck. Fuck. Fuck. "I don't want to leave her like this."

I want to fix it.

I want to fix her.

I want to kill her father.

"I know, man. I may not be much better. She just needs a minute to get her head on straight. Give her a minute."

"I'll give her forever."

CHAPTER 39

GABRIEL'S SAD EYES ARE MORE THAN I CAN BEAR. I turn away. "Can you give me a minute?"

He hesitates and then stands. "Sure."

Once I'm alone, I throw off the covers and pull on some clothes.

My ever-protective brother showed up a few hours ago. I heard the front door shut once he stepped into my bedroom. I assume it was Rowdy leaving.

My heart aches at my fuck up. My damage was shining bright tonight. The pain I saw on Rowdy's face is not something I'll soon forget.

It's not his fault. It was just the way he moved, the stroking of his monster cock, and the words coming out of his mouth set off a memory I couldn't escape. I didn't get totally consumed by it, but it was enough to taint what was happening between my Shadow and me. I don't ever want to connect my intimacy with Rowdy with the sick deeds of my dad. So, I asked Rowdy to leave.

Teethed brushed, dressed, and a bag packed, I enter the living room, interrupting Gabriel on the phone.

He eyes me and the bag slung over my shoulder. "I'll call you back." He pockets his phone. "Going somewhere?"

"I'm not afraid of him—Rowdy. You need to know that."

His scowl deepens. "I didn't think you were."

"Good." I grab my purse and keys. "Will you drop me off at his place?" I'd prefer not to drive. I'm shaky and fighting the adrenaline crash that always comes.

"Sure." He relieves me of my bag and purse. "I'll get the elevator."

I wasn't sleeping when Gabriel texted he was bringing Reese to me. I was in the gym beating the hell out of a punching bag, frustration dripping off me in torrents of sweat. I immediately unwrapped my hands and headed for the shower.

My girl is coming to me. Was it his idea or hers?

Do you really give a fuck? Cocky perks up. He's been pouting since leaving her place.

You stay out of this. This is all your fault.

Let me kiss it and make it better.

Shut the fuck up.

But, maybe…

I'm on the front porch when Gabriel's Hummer pulls to a stop. I'm down the stairs in a flash.

My girl pops open the passenger door and flings herself at me. Her arms, legs have a stranglehold on me. "Rowdy, I'm sorry—"

"Shh, Kitten. You're here now." I lift my head to catch her brother's eyes on us. "Thank you."

He nods and hands me her bag and purse. "Don't forget these."

She slips from my body and rushes to her brother, hitting him with a hug he wasn't expecting, judging by the shock on his face.

"I'm sorry for ruining your night." Her murmured words barely reach me.

He holds her tight, dipping his head. "You don't ever apologize for needing me." He kisses her temple before releasing her. "I'm here for you. Always." His eyes meet mine. "But I think Rowdy has a handle on what you need, Ree."

My chest tightens at his endorsement.

I can't see her face as he backs toward me. Is she smiling or frowning at his words?

"Tell Frankie sor—"

"Nope. No apologies." He waves her off and lifts his chin to me. "See ya tomorrow."

One final goodbye and my girl places her hand in mine.

Silently, we enter my house.

Once the door is closed and locked, I scoop her into my arms and hastily climb the stairs. "You need a drink or anything?"

"No. Rowdy, I—"

"Nope. I'm with Gabriel. No apologizing." I set her down next to the bed. "I just need to hold you, Kitten."

I need to know you're alright. That *we're* alright.

"I need you to do more than hold me, Shadow. I need you to love the darkness away."

Her eyes brimming with tears stab at my heart. "Kitten."

"I need you to hear me." She slips off her shoes and starts to undress. "I didn't really want you to leave." Her shirt hits the floor.

Fuck. Look at her eyes.

"I wasn't afraid of *you*, Rowdy." She wipes a tear that managed to escape. "Once I realized it was you, I wasn't afraid." Her hand hits my chest. "I was embarrassed."

"Reese—"

"I love you. I'm not *afraid* of you." She palms my hardening cock. "I'm not afraid of your monster."

Jesus. "You don't play fair."

"I'm not playing." She slinks out of her shorts.

When she turns to crawl on the bed, my eyes fasten to her gorgeous ass, completely visible since she's, once again, not wearing any panties.

Dead.

I'm fucking dead.

She slips out of her bra and kneels before me, tugging at my shirt. "If you don't want me, that's one thing. If you're afraid I'm going to go mental on you—then don't. I'm here. I know it's you." She fists my shirt and pulls me down. "I want you."

"Fuck, baby." I squeeze her ass and whisper across her mouth. "Leaving you was the hardest thing I've ever done."

"Then don't ever leave me again. Stay and fight through it with me."

I wanted to.

When she used her safe word, I should have just left the bedroom—not the apartment. I let her fear rule my actions. It won't happen again.

"Lie down, Kitten."

She pushes the covers down and lies back, her eyes shining with want, not fear.

Stripping this time is faster. I only have a t-shirt and gray sweatpants to contend with.

"Commando?" She smirks.

"Just like my girl." I climb over her, not stopping to stroke my cock. Not taking any chances on setting off whatever trigger I tripped last time.

We need to talk, but right now she needs me as much as I need her.

I need her to not be afraid of me, Cocky chimes in.

She's not afraid of you.

"Fuck," I groan when she parts her legs, and I sink inside her wet heat. I didn't intend to go right in. I meant to tease her entrance.

No, this is perfect. Little kitty needed me. Cocky nudges and rubs his head inside her, making peace.

Little kitty squeezes in return.

"Fucking perfect," Cocky and I groan in unison.

"I need your dirty mouth." My girl sets her fingers in my hair, tugging me closer.

I don't make her wait. I can't.

Our mouths collide. It sounds rough, but it's the perfect union of luscious softness with quantum need. Tongues joining, dancing, sparing. Dipping in and out as Cocky slides in and out.

Wrapped around her, touching from head to toe, my pace is slow and deep.

Her cries spur me on.

Hips grind, ensuring maximum clit contact.

Slow and easy.

Sweet kitty, Cocky coos, loving her like she's the one and only.

She is the only one.

Shut the fuck up, I'm working here.

When her sex sounds spear my concentration, instinct kicks in, thoughts go out the window, and I ride the wave of her body undulating under me, with me.

"Rowdy." She arches and claws at me. My lion awakened.

"I've got you, Kitten." I've always got you.

I lift her legs until I'm hitting that sweet spot inside her, and she begs me not to stop or move. But what she means is *keep fucking moving just like that.*

I got it. I speak fluent Reese.

Her moans and sighs morph into one long chorus.

She cries out. I growl.

I push in. She raises to meet me.

Cocky pulls out. Little kitty sucks him back in.

She squeezes and trembles like the perfection she is, made for me.

Made. Fucking. For. Me.

When I slide my hand under her ass, gripping and kneading, my middle finger rubbing her tight rosebud, she catapults over the edge, moaning my name, taking me with her like a siren song to my balls to let it rip.

I do. Deep and endless, I fill her, praising my Kitten the entire time.

CHAPTER 40

"OH, FUCK. THAT HAD TO HURT." COWBOY wipes at the blood on his lip, bouncing around me.

His kick to my ribs *did* hurt. Like a motherfucker.

"I'm sorry, man."

I stand, shaking it off. "Quit fucking apologizing."

"Get your head in the game, and I won't keep landing strikes and having to apologize. Reese is gonna be pissed if I fuck you up. She chewed me out for the black eye I gave you last time."

My girl is protective as fuck. Love it. Love her.

"Don't give me that evil grin, Rowdy. I didn't say shit about your girl." He backs up as I charge.

He dips and sways.

I miss, but he ends up in the path of my jab, taking it square on the jaw.

Damn that felt good.

"Fuck," he hisses and stumbles back. "I need to find a girl to get all pissy over."

He has no idea the drive Reese inspires in me. He didn't say anything wrong. But the idea of her sets a fire off in my gut.

The instinct to kill and protect takes over, fueling me until I can't lose.

I go at him again.

And again.

He's practically running from me by the time Jonah warns time is up, and Gabriel enters the gym.

I immediately notice the fire in his eyes and the clench of his jaw.

Without looking back, I say to Cowboy and Jonah, "Thanks. See y'all tomorrow." I jump the ropes, landing feet away from Gabriel, who's holding up a towel and my water.

"I have news."

The edge to his tone gets my hackles up. "I can see that. Can we talk while I shower?"

A stiff nod is all I get.

"You're worse than a fucking girl." Gabriel sighs as I condition and clip my hair up.

I'd already washed it—twice. Now I soap up my body while my hair conditions. "What do you expect? My hair is no different than any woman's. If you had any, you'd know that."

He scrubs his inch-long black spikes. "If I had long hair, I'd still only wash it once and not condition it."

"Then you'd have a tangled mess and wouldn't have long hair for long." I rinse off, talking over my shoulder. "You think Frankie wants to get her hands stuck in a rat's nest?"

He scowls.

"Yeah, you'd condition the fuck out of your hair because your woman would love the feel of it, and you'd love the feel of her hands on you. Trust me."

He grumbles and sits on the nearest bench while I rinse my hair.

Towel slung around my hips, I towel-dry my hair, brush, and man-bun it before Gabriel can give me more shit about being a *girl* about my hair.

"What are you going to do?" he asks.

I pull on boxer briefs. "It's not even a question. I go with y'all. I'm not leaving her to deal with this alone."

"I'll be there, asshole. *I'm* not leaving her to deal with *him* on her own, either."

It's been over a week since Reese decided to meet with her dad. Gabriel heard news today they have the okay to see him on Saturday.

The day of my fight.

"You'd cancel your fight for her?"

It's my turn to scowl and growl, "Not. Even. A. Question."

He scrubs his face. "Yeah. I hear you. She won't like it."

"She won't have a choice." I pull on my jeans, t-shirt, socks, and boots.

"She won't like that either." He says it like he doesn't agree with me.

"If it were Frankie facing down her father, what would you do?"

He stands, pinning me with his fierce gaze. "I'd say screw my fight. Screw her dad. And screw her until she forgot all about it."

I shove my stuff in my bag, pocket my keys, phone, and wallet. "Then what would you really do?"

He huffs, "I go with her and be there for her. I wouldn't let her tell me *no.*"

"We're on the same page then?"

"Same. Fucking. Page."

"Good." I head for the door. "Meet at my house? Say one hour?"

"You cooking?"

"No. That's your and Reese's territory. I know not to step on those toes."

"Damn straight."

Ass. "See you."

He follows me out of the locker room. "Yep. I'll bring steaks to cook."

I nod and turn the other way as he exits. I need to get my girl.

She's not going to like this one fucking bit.

"What is it about babies that makes you so delicious to smell and to kissy, kissy, kissy on?" I bury my nose in Maddox's neck. I'm just trying to get more of his scent in my nose. He thinks I'm trying to tickle him.

He screams, grips my hair in his meaty little paws, and giggles like he isn't the cutest baby already. His beautiful blue eyes stare back at me, lighter than his daddy's and mine, but not gray like his mommy's. Ox's are somewhere in between, and they shine with the innocence of youthful laughter.

I can't resist. I pull up his shirt and blow raspberries across his chubby baby belly.

He screeches and giggles. I join right in, laughing at his joyousness.

"Baby looks good on you, Kitten." Rowdy's heated gaze stalks me from where the kitchen and the den meet.

"I think if he could, he'd get me pregnant from over there, Ox," I stage whisper, holding his hands as he squeezes my thumbs.

"Don't temp me." Rowdy swoops in and steals my little man right out of my arms, holding him against his chest. "I would, Ox-man. I'll knock up your aunt as soon as she'll let me."

Ox screams his delight like he has some idea what his crazy godfather is saying to him.

My blushing admiration of my man is interrupted by my brother clearing his throat, taking up too much space in the doorway Rowdy just came through. "Can you not talk about getting my baby sister pregnant in my presence?"

"Just sayin'." Rowdy bounces Ox gently in his arms. "I wouldn't mind." His eyes land on me, but his smile fades. "Kitten?"

He's at my side before I can wrap my brain around what he's saying. I thought he was joking. "You want babies with me?"

"Loads. Oodles." He says it so easily, like I'm not broken-mommy material.

"Oodles?"

He presses his head to mine. "As many as you'll give me. As soon as you're ready."

"Christ. You're still a kid yourself." Gabriel snags Ox and steps back. "Don't listen to them, Maddox. You need to be married before you have babies."

"Right, because that's how his daddy did it." Frankie joins us, amusement dancing in her eyes.

"I want to teach him right, Angel." He takes a second to scan us. "None of us had the best parenting situation." He shrugs at Rowdy. "Sorry, Cam, no offense."

"None taken." Rowdy pulls me into his side. "Then marry me, Kitten. Let's do this right."

"The fuck?" Gabriel growls. "You can't ask her like that, you ass."

Rowdy smirks at my brother. "Really? You're an expert on proposals now?"

Gabriel sheepishly looks to his wife and smiles. "I think I did pretty good once I figured out what I wanted. Didn't I, babe?"

Sauntering over to her husband, Frankie kisses a squealing Ox before kissing Gabriel's cheek. "You did perfect, Big Man. You give me everything I need, just the way I need it."

"Aaah no, that's a visual I didn't need." I shudder, and my man pulls me into his chest.

"In the not-too-distant future I'll ask you officially, Kitten. I just need you to be ready."

I shudder again for a whole other reason.

"Ree, we need to talk about Dad."

Leave it to my big brother to bring the mood down a level or a thousand.

Turning in Rowdy's arms, I face my brother, keeping Rowdy at my back. I wait.

Gabriel hands off Ox to Frankie and steps closer. "I heard from his lawyer. We've been approved to see Dad."

I sink into Rowdy. He tightens his hold around my waist. His breath tickles my ear when he says, "I got you."

"Th-that's good news. I guess. I was kinda hoping they'd turn us down."

"Truthfully, me too." Gabriel moves closer. "The thing is, Dad's gotten worse. We've been approved to see him on Saturday. It'll probably be our only chance."

No. "*This* Saturday?"

His eyes meet Rowdy's over my head. "Yeah, *this* Saturday."

I turn and catch Rowdy's gaze already on me. "Your—"

"I'm going with you," he says with such certainty and not an ounce of shock or disappointment.

I step out of his arms and back up from the two of them. "You already knew. You two discussed this already."

Frankie shakes her head from behind them, sitting on the couch with Ox on her lap, nursing.

Rowdy moves forward, his hand out to touch me, but I back up. He stops. "Gabriel gave me a heads-up."

Shooting daggers at my brother, I huff. "He's *my* dad. You should have come to me first or told us at the same time. Now I feel ganged up on like you two already decided how this would play out behind my back."

"Told ya," Frankie mumbles from the couch.

She knew too?

"Angel," Gabriel warns, but softens his stance when they share a silent exchange.

"Reese, I want to be there for you. Supporting you is more important than any fight will ever be." My Shadow looms over me, so close he'd touch me if he thought I'd let him.

I want his touch, but… "I don't want you to throw your fight. My dad is not worth it."

He cups my cheek, pulling me in. "*You* are worth it." His possessive growl is a promise, laden with sacrifice and determination.

"I need to think about this." I don't want to make a rash decision or say something stupid because I'm caught off guard and angry.

"There's nothing to think about. I'm coming. I'll call Cap. He'll understand. He'll even support my decision." He grazes my lips with his thumb. "Every one of those guys, including Cap, would be there for you if you let them. Let me do this for you—for us."

"So, just like that. No discussion. I don't get a say?"

"We're discussing it now."

I step back. "No, we're not. You've already decided because you had time to think about it, digest the information."

"I didn't need time to think about it, Reese!" Rowdy grips his neck and looks to Frankie and Gabriel, trying to find his calm, I suppose. "My response was instantaneous. I'm going. End of discussion." So much for *calm*. He found his caveman instead.

"Nope. I'm not doing this." I grab my purse and keys off the table in the foyer.

"What the fuck are you doing?" Rowdy is hot on my heels as I head for the front door.

"Doing what you did. Making a decision without you."

He crosses his arms. "And what decision is that?"

"I'm going home. If you follow me, I will break up with you. If you don't fight on Saturday, I'm breaking up with you."

"The fuck?" Gabriel's impatience is no match for how I'm feeling.

I point between the two of them. "You two don't get to make decisions for me that concern me. I know you're trying to protect me. But I have a say in how that happens."

"Kitten." The defeat in Rowdy's voice nearly topples my righteous determination.

"I'm serious, Cameron. You and I are done until after your fight on Saturday." I poke his chest. "Don't test me, Shadow. My dark is just as devastating as yours."

Probably worse.

Definitely worse.

229

I turn on my heel and wave over my head as I stomp out the door, thankful my car is here. "Bye, Frankie and Ox. Love you."

"Reese, please, don't do this." My man's pain is palpable.

"I'm not doing anything, Rowdy. You fight on Saturday. I'll see my dad on Saturday. I'll see you after. If you want to be with me, then show me you trust me to do what needs to be done. I'm not as weak as you think. I can do this."

God, please help me do this.

"Don't make me look like a weak ass bitch by forfeiting your fight to hold my hand."

I got this.

And if I don't. I only have myself to blame.

Making it to my car, I stop, then march back to him, lean up and kiss him hard on the lips. "You say I'm a lion and not a mouse. Well, let me prove it."

Three days.

I have to make it three days.

CHAPTER 41

THE SECOND MY KITTEN DRIVES OFF, I WANT TO hit something so hard, I'll still be feeling it next week, next month, next year.

"That went well." Snarky McSnarky Pants, better known as Frankie, glares at me from the den.

I'm too angry to reply. Stalking to the kitchen, I pull down a low-ball glass and the whiskey.

Gabriel's hand wraps around mine, stopping my pour. "That's not what you need."

I let him pull the bottle and glass from my hands. "What I need just walked out my fucking door."

He nods. "She did. Other than her, what do you need?"

"I need to hit something—someone." I squeeze my head, trying to stop my racing thoughts of doom and how much I fucked up. "I need to fight."

"Good thing you have one of those coming up—and someone to show you how to win it."

Prick. I grin.

"Angel, we're leaving," he hollers to the other room. "Give me ten minutes to get her home and settled. I'll meet you at the gym."

My brows shoot up. "You're going to what? Spar with me?"

A wicked smile slides into place. "No, Cam. I'm going to fight you."

Bring it the fuck on.

Fifteen minutes later I'm at the gym, wrapping my hands when Gabriel enters. He tosses down his bag and tugs his shirt off. He fiddles on his phone until "Bodies" by Drowning Pool pours from the speakers.

Fuck yes.

We finish our prep, warm up, and square off on the mats in lieu of the ring. I need the space to breathe and spread my wings, frustration rolling off me in waves as the adrenaline surges.

The only rule he threw out in addition to our normal sparring rules is wearing protective headgear. We'll be in a world of trouble from Cap and our women if we end up looking like we got in a street fight. I grumbled, really wanting to land a few jabs to his face, but in the end agreed.

In all this time, I've never sparred with Gabriel. I work out beside him. I've seen him spar. I've watched his fights. Standing before the devil of a man should be intimidating, but fuck if all I want to do is laugh and give him a hug. I know he'd rather be home with family. Instead, he's giving me this.

"Are we gonna do Pilates or fucking fight?"

"Fight." Absolutely fight.

He moves and jabs, nothing lands.

His intense focus penetrates my soul. He's here. One hundred percent in this with me. But he's waiting.

Waiting for me to decide.

Waiting for me to come at him.

Waiting for me to decide if a fight is really what I want or just a workout.

I need both.

He blocks my right hook. Evades my leg kick. But my straight jab hits him squarely in the chest. My arm zings from the impact. He simply grunts, smiles, and waves me on.

When I land a jab-hook combo, he does the same. The sting warms my blood and drives me forward.

On a kick out I take him off his feet, but I don't follow him to the mat.

I need to move, and the last thing I want is to get locked in a chokehold by No Mercy Stone.

He hops up, and in the next second, I'm on my back. Same fucking move.

Evade.

Jab.

Kick.

Punch.

Roundhouse kick.

Uppercut.

Flying knee.

Superman punch.

We go on and on. Landing as much as we're taking.

The heavy beat of music fills the room.

The smell of sweat and testosterone swirl in the air.

When our limbs are like noodles, we're panting to suck in air, and sweat is dripping off us in torrents, making the mat slippery, we take each other down with a body slam I initiate but he finishes.

We hit hard, roll off each other and lay there staring at the ceiling.

"You went easy on me." I grab a towel and throw one to him before collapsing back to the ground.

"Not much. I'm worn out, same as you." He nudges my fist with his.

I nudge him back. "But you let me land more hits than you ever would in a real match."

He chuckles. "Possibly." His head lolls to the side, his scowl softened to a satisfied smirk. "I'm not sure I'd want to fight you in the octagon, Darkboy. I wasn't the only one holding back. I felt the rage inside you. Thanks for keeping it in check."

"Thanks for this. I needed it. I feel like I can actually breathe now."

"It's only three days. Give her that. You fight. I'll take her to see our dad. Then don't ever let her walk away again."

"Never."

"Good man." He groans getting to his feet and offers me a hand.

On our feet, we down our waters and stagger to our discarded clothes and gym bags.

"Do you think we could get Cowboy to come drive us home?" His gruff voice is too loud once he stops the music.

"I was thinking of sleeping here." Not serious, but kinda am.

Our gear in hand, he swings an arm around my shoulder. "Come on. I'll help you to your car."

"Thanks again. You're a good brother and friend."

"You'd do the same."

"In a heartbeat."

We say our goodbyes, driving home the same direction, until his turn off for his house. I stay straight ahead, determined not to head to Reese's apartment.

She says we're broken up until Saturday.

I don't think so.

I'll give her the time she needs to find the lion she's gonna need to face her asshole of a father.

But she's still fucking mine.

Morning came entirely too quickly, as it always does when I can't sleep. I tossed and turned, second-guessing my ultimatum. I don't want Rowdy to throw his fight. I also don't want to lose him.

Anger made me say it was one or the other.

Was it a wrong move?

I have no idea.

As I yawn into my second cup of coffee, Cap looms over me, reading the copy of a new brochure I'm working on.

"It's good." He pats my arm. "It's really good, Reese."

I tip my chin to him. "Let me fix those two items, then I'll print it out for you to proof before sending to the promoter."

"Sounds good."

It only takes a few minutes to make the changes and print a color copy for Cap's review. Setting it in his To-Do bin on his desk, I come out and stop at the sight of Rowdy holding up the wall.

I didn't expect to *not* see him, but the heat in his eyes steals my breath and shakes my resolve.

"Kitten," he growls low as he pushes off the wall. "I'd like to take you to lunch."

Shake it off.

I round my desk, needing a barrier between us. "I'll see you on Sunday, if you're still interested in sharing a meal."

"Sharing a meal? Sunday?" He prowls, reducing the space between us. "That doesn't work for me." Twining my hair around his finger, he leans in.

I hold my breath, my heart beating out of my chest.

He presses a kiss to the corner of my mouth, forcing me to bite back a whimper and fight the desire to take a real kiss.

He smirks, fully aware of my struggle. "Saturday after my fight, I'll be at your place."

Stepping back, his arm stays outstretched until my hair falls from his grasp. "We'll be sharing a hell of a lot more than a *meal*, Kitten."

Air doesn't fill my lungs until he disappears around the corner.

I sink into my chair, my head falling into my hands.

Way to show him your lion.

Fuck. I need to get it together.

Two days.

I can do this.

When Gabriel shows up an hour later with food, I couldn't be happier to see him. Though, as much as I try, I can't focus on much other than Rowdy.

The want in his eyes ate me alive with every look, every unrealized touch. If he's trying to turn me on and distract me from the idea of seeing my dad, it's working.

A little too well.

CHAPTER 42

"YOU GOT THIS."

"Yep." I so don't.

Gabriel pulls me to a stop in front of the prison gates. It's scary to think of how much evil resides inside those walls, how many bad choices, bad men, are confined inside the gates we're willingly entering. I'm sure there are innocent, wrongly convicted men in there as well, but they aren't the ones I'm worried about. They aren't my father. There's not an innocent cell in my father's body. If there ever was, he's replaced every one with dark matter and endless voids.

This is insane.

"Breathe for me, Ree." He cups my face. "You can do this. I'm with you every step of the way."

He's not asking if I *want* to do this.

Yesterday, I made him promise no matter how much I beg him, don't let me chicken out.

I *have* to do this. I know it. He knows it.

But it doesn't make it any easier or any less scary.

I'm terrified of the son of Satan.

If Gabriel knew all Dad had done, he'd never have agreed to this.

ROWDY

"I'm good." Maybe the more I lie, the more I'll believe it.

He shakes his head in disbelief but doesn't call me out. Instead, he captures my hand, and we begin walking again.

Inside, it's paperwork and formalities, which is a bit more my forte than Gabriel's. I push my nerves aside to accomplish what we need in order to see our dad and get the hell out of here.

Having never visited a prison before, we're unfamiliar with how much of the red tape is protocol and what's additional due to visiting a prisoner in the medical ward.

We're asked to wait. Someone will escort us to the medical facility shortly.

The wait is long enough for my nerves to reappear and to amp up when a guard approaches, asking, "Mr. and Mrs. Stone?"

"Yes." Gabriel doesn't even flinch at the assumption we're husband and wife.

If the guy had read the paperwork, he'd know we're brother and sister. As concerning as it is that he didn't read the paperwork, I've no time to correct or consider the implications before Gabriel presses his hand to my back, and we follow the guard down a maze of corridors separated by gates we have to be let through before the next one opens and closes behind us.

I flinch and close my eyes every time a gate clangs closed and the buzzer sounds when the next gate unlocks. Gabriel presses me closer to his side. His hand, tight on my hip, will probably leave a bruise. A visual reminder of today's visit. But the contact, the minute bite of pain serves to calm my nerves ever so slightly.

"You got this," he whispers every few minutes.

Does he ever get nervous?

Does he want to double over with anxiety and the need to puke?

I don't remember a time when Gabriel was afraid of our father. In my memories, if Gabriel was home, he always stood between me and Dad. He got hit more times than I care to remember for doing so, especially if he came between Dad and Mom.

Those were always the worst beatings.

I'd like to say I'd do the same, but I'm not sure I could or would.

Past a large metal door, we step into what has to be the medical unit. The hospital smell is unmistakable, and the employees are wearing scrubs.

The guard pauses outside another door, motioning us to go inside. Gabriel grips my hand. "You ready?"

Nope. Not even a little.

Here in the Vegas arena, the crowd has been going crazy as the matches before mine begin and end. It feels like an eternity before it's my turn. Hammer and I are the second-to-last fight. The bigger ticket gets the last match of the night. Someday, that'll be me.

But for tonight, I'm second-last and it can't come soon enough. I should be focused on my match, but all I can think about is Reese and how it went with her father. The drive to the prison is about an hour each way. Depending on how long they stayed, it's possible she's home or on her way there.

Gabriel offered to bring her here. But I figured dealing with a large crowd is the last thing Reese needs after facing her biggest fear—her father. Plus, having her here and not having time to talk to her beforehand would only sidetrack my focus more than it already is.

Especially if she looks upset.

"Hey." Jonah slaps my cheek. "Focus. Be here."

I shake off the sting. "Yeah, yeah, I'm here."

"You sure? You seem anywhere but *here*. If you're lost in your head, be lost thinking about Hammer and not about Reese. She's fine. Gabriel will be sure of it."

"I know." I do. It just doesn't feel right. It feels selfish being here, furthering my career when my girl is facing down her asshole father.

She might have been fine with me not being there for her, but *I'm* not.

When you love someone, you sacrifice for them. You put their needs before your own.

I tried. She wouldn't let me.

She sacrificed for me, and I let her.

I'm a selfish fuck.

Damn.

"It's time." Cap sticks his head in the door.

Jonah and Coach bump fists with me.

"You got this." Coach grabs my wrists. "This your match to win or lose." He steps back. "Don't fucking lose." As he exits, he grumbles about Hammer being an idiot who couldn't tie his own shoelaces.

Smirking at Coach, Jonah slaps my back as we walk out. "Fight for her."

I'm not sure if he means fight for my relationship or actually get in the octagon and fight for my girl. I'm assuming he means the latter.

I get a nod from Cap before he heads for his seat with the guys. He's been giving me space this week. He doesn't want to cloud my thoughts. Honestly, I've been so wrapped up in Reese, I hadn't even thought of my situation with Cap.

Fuck. Now I am.

Landry saunters over as I bounce on my feet. He holds up his hands, allowing me to punch them, giving me something to focus on. "Listen, you have a lot going on with your mom, Cap, Reese, her dad."

I punch his palms harder.

"Fuck." He shakes out his left hand before holding them up again. "Use your anger, frustration over all of it. Direct it toward Hammer. Make him feel every last inch of your wrath."

A growl reverberates up my chest. I double punch for good measure, and when my entrance song starts to play, I feel the raw beat of "Wolf Totem" in my soul.

Together we make our way into the arena. The crowd is on their feet, their chants matching the tribal sound of my warrior's anthem.

My blood pumps with adrenaline.

My sights narrow.

I'm ready to kill and conquer.

CHAPTER 43

I DON'T KNOW WHAT I THOUGHT I'D SEE WHEN Gabriel opened the door to Dad's hospital room, but it wasn't the sallow, fragile man before me. He looks so small in the bed, not at all like the towering man I remember. IV in his arm. Oxygen tubing in his nose. I can hear him fighting to breathe from here. The stench of death is hard to ignore.

Gabriel's hand flexes on my back as our father's dark, heartless gaze lands on us. He blinks a few times before his lips twitch in what I assume is a smile, or maybe he's having a stroke.

I pray for stroke. I'm ready to leave.

"I was wondering if you'd come." The grate of Dad's voice is rougher than I remember but still sends prickles up my spine.

Gabriel's hand slips into mine. "You got this," he whispers so only I can hear.

"We came." Gabriel's stone-cold glare seems to have the desired effect on the man in the hospital bed, who shrinks into himself.

"You look horrible," the words escape before I can think twice.

Our old man chuckles. "Cancer will do that to a man."

"Not having a soul or a heart could do it too," my brave brother bites back.

Dad winces when he tries to sit up. He gives up when his pillow is half off the bed and his upper body leans to one side.

Neither of us make a move to help. Not touching him with a ten-foot pole.

Maybe a cattle prod.

He could fall on the floor, and I wouldn't lend a hand. It might make me a horrible person, but I can't for the life of me feel bad about it.

Karma's a bitch. You get what you give, and me not beating him to death is my gift to him.

He motions to the chairs next to the bed. "Sit. Let me get a good look at my children."

"Don't act like you had anything to do with how we've grown up or the people we've become."

"I'd say, by the anger in your voice, I've had a lot to do with the man you've become, Gabriel." He manages a full smile this time, showing off his yellow teeth and pale gums.

"Death. It's coming for him," I say under my breath.

"Not soon enough," Gabriel replies, taking one step forward, pulling me with him to stand at the end of the bed.

"Daughter, won't you sit? Let me get a better look at you."

Gabriel tightens his grip. "We're fine where we are."

I'm thankful for his protectiveness, but the more I stare at the old man in front of me, the less I fear him. He's not the monster I remember. He's a mere shadow of the behemoth he used to be. Though, I've no doubt evil still resides where his soul should be.

Dad nods, accepting our refusal. "At least pull the chairs to you, Son. Don't make your sister stand the whole time."

His words sound kind, but there's no kindness to me in his tone. He wants to bend Gabriel to his will, even if it's just moving a few chairs and sitting at the foot of his deathbed. Gabriel's hatred for the old man battles his consideration for my comfort. *Don't stand down, Brother. I'm fine.*

Surprisingly, Gabriel relents. Releasing his hold on me, he grabs the chairs by the back and sets them at the end of the bed—side by side.

241

Again, my amazing big brother put my comfort over his pride.

Gabriel nods for me to sit when I remain standing. I can flee faster if I'm on my feet.

With a harrumph and his bitch-face scowl, he sits.

Uncomfortable silence surrounds us.

As the minutes tick by, I shuffle on my feet, wishing I'd taken a seat, but now it seems like a *thing*—my refusal to sit. So, my stubborn ass has to remain standing.

"If you have something to say, Germain, you should say it. We both have better places to be." Gabriel leans forward, his arms resting on his wide-spread knees.

"Germain?" Dad's cackle sets me on edge.

I sidestep behind the chair meant for me. I can throw it at him if need be, if he's faking this frailty and not really dying.

Sure looks like he is, though.

"Like father, like son. A hard-ass through and through." Dad sounds all too proud.

"He's nothing like you," I bite. "Gabriel is a good man. He's made a great life for himself and his family. Something you'd know nothing about."

Gabriel's gaze meets mine over his shoulder, his brow raised in surprise, but settles into acceptance.

Dad's eyes widen. "Seems my girl's got some balls after all."

"I'm not your—"

"She's not your girl," Gabriel speaks over me.

The ass in the bed smiles and nods. "You're protective over each other. That's good." His eyes land on me. "Gabriel always *tried* to protect you… He thought he saved you, didn't he? But we know the truth, don't we, beautiful?"

"What?" Gabriel pushes to his feet. "What are you saying, old man?"

Dad's gaze remains locked on me. "You didn't tell him?"

Tell him? My mind races with all the things Gabriel doesn't know. All the terrible things he'd hate himself for, if he knew.

"Tell me what?"

"Fourth of July." Dad glowers at me, only… I have no idea what that means.

"Independence Day?" Is it some kind of code?

Dad motions to Gabriel. "Before he got big enough to kick me out, I got what I wanted, didn't I?" His hard laugh turns into a fit of coughing.

Gabriel glances at me as my mind spins to figure out which Fourth of July and what incident he's referring to. Which time he hurt me that I tried to hide from Gabriel. I don't remember dates, but holidays usually stood out, even in our crazy house.

"You never told him? I thought that was why he kicked me out."

"I kicked you out for hurting Mom. I kicked you out for looking at your daughter in a way a father never should. There, I said it, you sick fuck."

The evil Dad may have been trying to hide now blazes in his eyes and devilish leer. "I did more than *look*, Gabriel. You didn't watch her 24-7. I got mine. I took what I wanted. What was *mine* to take."

"No." Backing up, my knees start to quake as I search for the door. The room begins to close in. How could he say this to Gabriel?!

"Take? What did you take, you miserable piece of shit?" Looking bigger and meaner than I've ever seen him, Gabriel looms over our father.

My back hits the wall when my father's eyes land on me. "You never forget your first, do you, girl? I bet you think of me every time some guy fucks you like the whore you are. Just like your mother—"

"You son of—"

"Gabriel," I scream when he lunges at Satan incarnate.

My knees give out, and I crumple to the floor.

The buzz in my ears drowns out all other sounds.

The last sight I see is the guard pulling Gabriel off our dad.

Then nothing but darkness.

We circle each other like caged lions.

Lion. My kitten. Is she home? Is she okay? Did Gabriel call Cowboy like I asked him to once they were home?

Wham. Fuck. Hammer's fist hits me square in the eye. As I try to shake it off and focus on him instead of thoughts of Reese, he kicks my legs out from under me.

"The fuck?" Jonah exclaims from the sidelines.

I hop up faster than Hammer anticipates and charge with two swift kicks to his inner thigh, followed by a feint and a superman punch straight to the face just as the bell sounds.

Blood dripping in my eye, I make my way to my corner and a frowning Jonah and Coach.

"Where's your head at, son?" Coach barks.

"If you're going to think about Reese, then at least think of Hammer as her father, and beat the hell out of him." Jonah sighs as the cutman works on the laceration above my eye.

I don't even feel it. "Fix it up. I'm not losing the fight over some blood." When you're so full of scar tissue, doesn't take much to open old cuts that bleed like stuck pigs. They mostly hurt your score—making it look like your opponent's done more damage than they really have.

Pressure and a medicated cotton swabs stop the bleeding. A quick check by the doctor determines I'm good to go.

As everyone steps away, Jonah leans in, pointing across the ring. "See that fucker right there? He's keeping you from getting home to Reese. Finish this, and let's get the fuck out of here."

Third round. I've let this fuck keep me going for two rounds. I've never had a fight go to the last round. I'm undefeated, and this fucker just put his fist in my face. Reese won't be happy when she sees me.

Reese.

I need to get the fuck out of here.

The bell sounds.

Hammer smirks like he's got this in the bag.

No. Fucking. Way.

"Time to go home," I growl. My girl needs me, and I'm dicking around with *this* asshole?

He swings. I duck, punching him in the gut. When he folds over, trying to catch his breath, I land a hammerfist punch coming straight down on the trapezius muscle between his shoulder and neck, dropping him to his knees.

I take him to the ground in a rear naked choke, falling on my back, wrapping my legs around his torso, squeezing his belly like a boa constrictor.

Holding.

He's like a fish out of water, squirming, trying to break free, but soon he's going to pass out if he doesn't tap out.

Holding.

Holding.

It takes a few seconds more before I feel that invigorating tap on my forearm, and the referee jumping in to confirm.

Releasing Hammer, I'm on my feet, arm in the air, and then I'm declared the winner by submission.

About fucking time.

CHAPTER 44

"REE, WE NEED TO TALK ABOUT THIS." Gabriel looks like a dejected puppy, standing in my living room, hands in his pockets, his chin nearly hitting his chest.

"There's nothing to talk about." I'm not having this discussion with him.

"Fuck if there isn't." He's understandably upset.

I'm more upset. "I don't remember!" That's the honest truth. I have no recollection of the night my dad was referring to. The fact that he would even bring up something like that makes me want to puke.

I told Rowdy I was a virgin. I *thought* I was a virgin.

My stomach clenches.

If I don't remember *that* horrible detail, what else have I locked away?

This isn't happening.

I was a virgin until Rowdy.

I was a virgin.

I was a virgin.

Wasn't I?

"You need to go. I need time to think." My calm is all show. The second he's gone I can fall apart, but until then, *keep it together.*

I woke up in the back of Gabriel's hummer, laid out on the seat. I didn't ask what happened. How I got there. He obviously carried my PTSD ass out of the prison and to his car. I'm such a sad sack of a sister.

I thought I could do it. I truly did, but the minute the evil side of Dad appeared, his true nature, I was done.

I'm relieved to be away from the man who claims to be our father but never showed a morsel of parental concern.

"I don't want to leave you. I'll stay until Rowdy gets here."

Shit. Rowdy.

"I'm meeting him at his place," the lie rolls off my tongue with disgusting ease.

"Then I'll drop you there." He pockets his phone and pulls out his keys.

"No. I need my car." I push at his chest, backing him to the door, knowing full well I couldn't move him an inch if he didn't let me. "Go home. Kiss your wife. Kiss your son. Forget today ever happened. And if you can't, we'll talk tomorrow or the day after. But not tonight."

Not ever if I have my way. "I need some time."

He reluctantly agrees, making me promise to call him when I wake up.

I hate to lie or break my promises, but that's not going to happen.

The second the door shuts, instead of falling to my knees and sobbing, I drag myself to the bedroom, pack a bag for a few days, and slip out of my apartment before Rowdy shows up.

Where I'm going, I have no idea.

I can't face him knowing what my father so cruelly shared with us. His intent I'm sure. His sadistic way of getting to us one more time.

Was he telling the truth?

I pray for the millionth time that that man is not really my father. I can't accept that the evil running through his blood is part of me, a part of Gabriel. I shudder at the thought, wanting to claw my skin off to remove any hint of him from my body.

I took what I wanted. What was mine to take, my dad's voice plays in my head.

My virginity.

All this time, I didn't remember. I still don't.

I sure as shit don't want to.

How could I not?

I don't put lying past my father, but he seems so sure, so gloatingly happy and triumphant. It's hard not to believe it's true—or at least he believes it's true.

But even if it's true, there are some memories you don't want.

The road is dark and rainy, making it hard to see, especially with the waterworks. Swiping at my tears, I pull in at the first motel I see, making it barely five miles from home.

Some runaway I am.

I can't stay home knowing Rowdy is coming by, but maybe I can stay here. At least for tonight.

Tomorrow I'll figure out what I'm going to do.

How I'm going to sever myself from Rowdy. The man I thought I'd given my virginity to.

Turns out it wasn't mine to give.

My calls to Reese and Gabriel go unanswered. I push my truck a little harder to get to her place a few seconds faster. Concern crawls across my spine.

A gray Honda gets my attention as I zip by. For a split second I thought it was Reese's car, but there are a million gray cars. What are the odds it's her, heading in the opposite direction?

I call her number on repeat. Right before reaching her apartment, I leave a voicemail, "Call me, Kitten. You've got me worried. I'm almost to your place."

I hang up and call right back.

Any high I felt from winning my fight slips away when she doesn't answer her door. It must have been worse than I thought.

Why the fuck wouldn't Gabriel warn me?

Using my key, I enter, finding the place dark and silent. Her scent inundates me immediately, but I don't fell her presence.

To cover my bases, I walk through her apartment looking for signs of where she might be, where she went. Was she even here?

I call Gabriel again. When he doesn't answer, I call Frankie.

"Hey, Darkboy. Congrats on your win." Her words are chipper, but her voice is not.

"What happened? They aren't answering their phones." I don't need to specify who. She knows. "Where is Reese?"

"Sh-she's not at her apartment?"

"No. I'm standing in her bedroom, and there's no sign she was even here." As she mumbles something about getting Gabriel, I head for the door.

There's no point in staying here. I'll go crazy waiting. I have to find her.

Muffled voices come over the line before I hear, "What do you mean she's not at her apartment?" Gabriel sounds like he's been eating razor blades. Not a good sign.

"I mean she's not fucking here." I'm losing my patience. "What happened, Gabriel?"

"Fuck. I left her in her apartment, not an hour ago. She... uh, wanted time alone."

"I swear to God if you don't tell me what happened, I'll..." My eyes land on the door, the corner behind the door, to be precise. "Her bat." I turn in circles looking for it. I open the hall closet, shoving stuff out of my way. "It's not here."

"What?"

I rush back to her bedroom closet and scan her clothes. I can't see anything missing. Her suitcase is still on the top shelf.

"Her fucking bat is gone."

Gabriel lets out a heavy sigh. "I can't swear to it, but I'm pretty sure it was there when I left. I'd notice if it was missing. It's always a punch to the gut when I see it."

Same.

"Well, it's not here now. I don't see any clothes missing, but that doesn't really mean much. Her suitcase is here."

"Her duffle. I noticed it earlier when I picked her up. It was sitting on the chair in her room. I figured she was taking stuff over to your place."

"It's not there." I stare at the empty chair, glance around her room and stop back to the closet. "It's not here. Fuck." I walk through her apartment looking for the bag.

"I'm coming over."

"There's no point. Stay there in case she comes to you. I'm going out looking. But first, you're gonna tell me what the fuck happened."

CHAPTER 45

THE SOUND THAT LEFT ME THE MOMENT MY dad told me Mom died doesn't compare to the agony leaving my body over Gabriel's words.

He raped her.

When she was only twelve years old, the person who is supposed to protect her from the world ended up being the greatest darkness she would ever face.

He raped her.

Gabriel's emotional emission leveled me.

I sank to the floor and broke. I openly wept, and if it wasn't for my own sobs, I could have sworn I heard Gabriel's heart breaking too.

He didn't know. He thought he'd protected her. Kept her safe. The guilt he feels is not a burden I'd want to carry. My own for not knowing her back then—not being able to save her—is unreasonable, but his…

It's *not* his fault. He was only a kid himself.

But still—guilt is not a reasonable, logical beast. For him. Or me.

"I gotta find her." I sniff and drag my t-shirt across my face. Pull it together. She's out there alone and hurting. "I gotta fucking find her." I tumble to my feet, leaning on the door till I can suck in a full breath.

"I'm coming with you." Gabriel's voice breaks, fighting to keep his emotions in check. I get it.

"No, when I find her, she's won't want you there. She loves you, man. You know that. But this. She asked you for space, right? Give me this. Let me find her. If I don't in the next hour, we'll call in the cavalry and track her down."

"Find her," he pleads like a man on his last leg.

"I will." I take one last look at her place. Leaving a few lights on, I lock and close her door. "I'll call you in an hour."

The clock is ticking.

Reese is a creature of habit. She doesn't like to stray into the unknown. She doesn't like crowds. She packed a bag, which means she didn't plan on coming home tonight. The fact that she took Slugger, her trusty bat, means she wasn't planning on staying someplace familiar where she'd feel safe.

Gabriel's and my house are out.

She wouldn't go to her mom's. There's too much baggage there—especially after this.

Cap's? Maybe, but I doubt it. He's her boss first and foremost. She'd want to keep this news from the workplace.

Unless she went to someone else's house like Jonah or Landry's, or even AJ's. I'm betting she found a little hotel not far away to hide out at until she can get her mind around what's happened.

I understand the feeling—the need to escape all that's familiar so you can think.

I did the same when I found out Cap is my dad, except I ran to her, keeping her as close as I could without revealing my secret.

But given this news is of a sexual nature, it makes sense she'd run from me—fearing what I'd think.

I couldn't give a flying fuck about her past.

I race to the place where I thought I saw her car. It might have been her after all.

Maybe God is on my side and wants me to find her.

I'm coming, Kitten. Hold on.

Sadness wraps around me like a vise. It's not comforting. It's stifling. Finding it harder and harder to breathe, the room feeling too big, too unfamiliar, I slip off the bed to the floor, crawling until I hit the corner between the wall and the dresser, hidden from the door.

I curl into myself, Slugger at my side, trying to remember why I thought it was a good idea to leave the safety of my home.

Rowdy.

Why I forced Gabriel to leave.

My father.

My father.

My father.

All roads lead back to him.

He can't die soon enough. If he thinks I'll come to his funeral, he's sorely mistaken. I'd be shocked if anyone showed—if anyone cared.

How many people did he hurt in his lifetime? His evil depravity couldn't have been limited to Mom, Gabriel, and me. He was in jail for a reason, and it didn't have anything to do with the three of us.

I didn't ask. I don't want to know.

I want to forget the man ever existed.

I want to forget the words that so easily left his lips like he was re-membering a birthday party or a Christmas where we were all together. A cherished memory.

Oh, God.

That's it.

That's what I can't dismiss as though he's lying.

He *cherishes* the memory.

Not for the act itself, more than likely, but for the hurt and devasta-tion he caused—he's still causing.

He eats it up like it's a steak dinner.

As a kid, the harder I cried, the meaner he'd become.

He reveled in my misery. He lived for it.

I shudder a breath. I have to stop crying. I'm going to make myself sick.

If it's possible to puke up your emotions, I'm pretty sure I'm about to find out.

When a noise at the door draws my attention, I suck in air, holding.

Waiting.

But the noise doesn't go away. It only grows.

I grab the bat, pull my feet in and pray I'm invisible.

And if I'm not. I'll fight.

No one will ever touch me again.

No one…not even—

"Kitten?"

Him.

The door clicks closed. The air thickens.

How the hell did he find me?

How the hell did he get a key to my room?

I should sue!

He can't see me. I can only shuffle back so far.

Damn, why aren't I smaller like Mom? I could hide better if I were barely five feet tall.

"Reese, baby." Rowdy's voice is so close. My heart aches to reach out to him.

"You can't be here. Please, you need to go."

My head buried in my knees, I can't see him, but I smell him—familiar and comforting.

His warmth breaches the distance when he's in front of me, his legs round mine, moving in close till his head rests on my shoulder.

A sob breaks free.

His embrace burns through my clothes as he wraps me in his arms, my knees between us, no obstacle for his big-ass 6'5" body. He strokes my hair and kisses the side of my face. "You made me promise the next time you pulled away from me, I wouldn't let you run. I'm not letting you."

"You don't know—"

"I don't need to." He picks me up, pulling the bat from my hand. "I got it from here, Slugger. I'll take care of her. I promise."

My tears fall harder. I'm helpless to resist this man.

He places me across his lap, my legs falling to his side as I hug his neck. His large arms wrap around me, his hands gripping my lower back and shoulder, melding me to his chest.

"But I know *this*, Reese. Gabriel told me."

I wail at the pain as his words pierce my heart.

"I'm sorry he did that to you—and it doesn't change how I see you. At all." He squeezes the back of my neck. "I don't care what happened before me—except that it's part of your path that led you to me... to *us*. You are mine. Always have been. Always will be."

He kisses my head and whispers in my ear, "You hear me, Kitten? You're mine. Come hell or high water, you can't scare me away with your past, with your crazy, your damage—your words, not mine. You are whole and perfect and the only one I want. As long as you love me, I'm here to stay."

CHAPTER 46

ONCE HER TEARS HAVE DRIED, I GET US OFF the floor and sitting on the bed. The room is still dark except for the bathroom light she left on when she went to blow her nose.

As devastated as she is by today's events, she didn't have all the lights on in the room. I didn't find her in a PTSD episode. She was upset, sure, but not helpless in fear, stuck in her own head. Slugger was in her hands, ready to fight.

I can't stop touching her, reassuring her I'm here, as much as reassuring myself that *she's* still here. I didn't lose her. She didn't really run away. She needed a timeout. A moment.

I'm here now. I'm not letting her push me away or lock herself inside that gorgeous head of hers. Kissing her head, I whisper across her skin, "Let me take you home, Kitten."

She sniffs and wipes at a stray tear. "Yeah, okay."

I texted Gabriel before I entered her room, letting him know I found her. I text him now to advise I'm taking her to my house and she's okay.

He replies right away:

Gabriel: *Thank you for taking care of her. Call me if you need me or need to talk. No matter the time or the topic. Don't worry about her car. I'll get it picked up. Maybe we can bring breakfast over in the morning.*

Me: *Sounds good. Talk later.*

The ride is quiet. Her fingers laced with mine on the middle console reassure me she's still with me. Her gaze out the window instead of on her hands, crying, is progress. Her rollercoaster ride of emotions is nowhere near done, but at least for the moment, she's found a modicum of peace.

In the kitchen, her eyes land on me. She looks ready to collapse. "You need sleep."

Her head hits my chest. "I do. But I want a shower more." She leans back. "Then we need to talk."

I kiss her nose and brush my fingers across her cheek. "Whatever you need, Kitten. I'm here."

While she showers, I rustle up some sandwiches. I considered grilled cheese, but decided on a classic BLT. It's fresh and light, and my girl has a thing for crunch. The toasted bread, bacon, and lettuce all have a crunch that'll hopefully hit the spot.

First, she's going to tell me she's not hungry. Then she's going to take one bite and devour the entire thing, wishing she had another. And she will. I made extra just in case. And if she doesn't... well, more for me.

With a tray of food and drinks, I find her coming out of the bathroom in one of my t-shirts. If she has on sleep shorts, I can't see them.

I pull my gaze off her legs to focus on her face. "Feel better?"

"Yes, thanks."

Situated on the couch in my room with a pillow on her lap and her plate on top of that, she smiles at the sandwich. "I love BLTs."

"I know."

"How do you know?" She takes a bite and moans her appreciation.

My chest widens, satisfied I did good. It's nothing big, but if it makes my girl happy—if it makes her smile—them I'm good.

"I pay attention." I take a bite and agree it's a darn good sandwich.

"Like I said, you're the official sandwich-maker in this relationship." Finishing off one half, she picks up the other.

"It's an honor I'll wear proudly."

Sandwiches demolished, one and a half for her and two and a half for me, we settle on the bed. She's between my legs, resting back on me as I lean against the headboard. We turned on a nature show about dolphins, but neither of us really pay it much mind.

"Do you think I need to call Gabriel?" She turns so she's sitting sideways between my legs.

"Not unless you want to. I told him you're here and that I'd talk to him later. He thought they might come over for breakfast tomorrow."

She twists her lip, her hair falling into her face as she plays with the hem of her t-shirt. "Okay."

I cup her face, tilting it until her eyes meet mine. "Do you want to talk about it?"

Her eyes mist. "I'm afraid. What if you—"

"There's nothing you can tell me to scare me away. Take your best shot, Kitten. Fire away. I promise I'll still be here. I'll keep coming back. I'll keep chasing."

"He used to come into my room..."

Oh, shit.

Fury slams into me so fast my head spins.

Okay. Time to put up or shut up.

I got this. I've got her.

I suppress my anger and disgust at him so I can be present and supportive.

"It was always dark. The house silent. Most times I was asleep and would come awake with him towering over me. His hand in his pants... Touching himself."

Fuck. I hold her hand, keeping us grounded to the here and now. Together.

"I don't remember a time when he was loving. I don't remember a kind word unless he was telling me what he thought of my looks—of my body.

"He was careful. He was quiet. I don't think anyone knew he'd visit me at night. On the nights he'd drink too much, he'd make me show him my…" Her needful eyes lock on mine, pleading.

"Body?"

She nods, not wanting to say it. "He didn't touch me. But he threatened to hurt Mom if I didn't let him look while he—"

"Masturbated?"

"Yeah. He'd say things while he touched his…"

"I got it." I'm not going to make her say his dick, and I'm sure as shit not saying it.

"He liked to talk about the things he imagined doing to me all while touching himself."

She squeezes my hand, and I cup her cheek. "You're doing good. I'm here. Not going anywhere."

"That night, when you touched yourself, and I freaked out…"

"I reminded you of him?" God, I want to throw up.

"Yeah. But I think we can work through that." Her other hand flexes on my thigh. "You're hot when you touch yourself. It's not the same. I think it was the news that Dad was dying and wanted to see us that was the culprit more than anything you did. And the optics."

I'd suspected as much. It's good to know she feels the same.

"How old were you when all this started?"

"I don't know. Maybe six? Maybe younger. It's hard to say. It seems like always. But the looking at me didn't start until I was probably eleven. When I got breasts. He liked looking and making me *see* him looking. He…" Her voice cracks, and she closes her eyes.

"I've got you. You're safe here. It's just a memory. It can't hurt you. *He* can't hurt you any longer."

259

Her eyes fly open in surprise and awe as if she just realized that. "He can't, can he?"

I draw her to my chest. "No. He can't hurt you or anyone else ever again. You telling me your story takes his power away. He doesn't control your fear. He doesn't control any aspect of your life. You're free, Kitten."

She's silent for a few minutes. Then she sits up. "It gets worse. You sure you want to hear this?"

"If you can live it, I sure as shit can hear it." No doubt. "Give me your darkness, Reese. Let me carry it for you."

She smiles. "With me. My Shadow."

"That's right. Your dark can live with mine."

"Dad rarely beat me. But he did hit Gabriel and Mom. It could get bad, but it was worse when Gabriel wasn't home. Dad would pin Mom to the kitchen counter or table. Sometimes their bed or mine. Even the couch a few times. But mostly it was the kitchen, the place my mom loved to be. She escaped into her cooking. He wanted to ruin that for her. He'd…" She bites her lip and shakes her head.

"He can't hurt you. Tell me."

"He made me watch. He'd stare at me while he…"

"Had sex with your mom?" Jesus, what a sick fuck.

No wonder she and her mom have issues. Reese is full of guilt. I'm sure her mom has to feel guilt along with some level of resentment toward her daughter. Reese caught her father's eye, but he took his aggression out on his wife. He pitted them against each other. I doubt either of them realize the level of abuse they suffered by his mind games and fucked-up sexual attraction.

"Yeah. If I tried to get away, he'd make it harder on my mom. She couldn't look at me most days. Shame, anger, I'm not really sure how she feels about me. I'm sure it's not good—how could it be? She loves Gabriel. I'm someone she had to put up with, who caused her pain and embarrassment."

"Hey, you didn't cause anything. You were the kid here. *They* were the adults. She could have left him. He could have left. She allowed you to be dragged down into their damaged relationship. This is their fault, not yours. You were kids."

She stares at me, tears looming.

It's going to take hearing *it's not her fault* many more times before she starts to believe it.

"It's not your fault, Kitten." I'll tell her as many times as she needs to hear it.

CHAPTER 47

LYING ON HIS BROAD CHEST, I FIGHT A YAWN. I thought I'd never be here again. I'm not falling asleep yet. I need to soak up as much of him as I can.

Plus, there's one more horrible detail to address. The reason I ran.

He's taken everything else in stride. Maybe this one more detail won't be the deal breaker I feared.

My Shadow says he's in for the long haul. I pray that's true. The idea of losing him is pain I don't want to face. He makes everything better. He makes me better.

I won't lose him to this…

"You're thinking entirely too hard." He tips my chin till our eyes connect. What I find is love mixed with pain but no pity or disgust. "I don't care about what you found out today. If you want to talk about it, we can. But don't think it changes anything between you and me. You're fucking mine, Kitten. I'm not letting you go."

His adamancy sends warmth through my body and a smile to my lips. "Are you mine?"

"Every inch of me inside and out. For better or worse, it's you and me."

This man.

"Your mom would be so proud of you," slips out before I consider bringing her up might make him sad.

Yet he only smiles, one dimple making a quick appearance. "You think?"

I sit up on my knees, facing him. "Absolutely. She raised a strong man with a giving heart. I'm lucky to have his eyes set on me."

"Kitten," he chokes, "so fucking on you."

I love this man so much.

One more obstacle. Laying my hand on his chest, I lean in. "I don't remember anything like my father said happened that day. I remember everything else in more detail than I care to, but that Fourth of July, he said he... Well, wouldn't I remember that? For all the horrible things he did, I wouldn't put it past him, but I'd remember it, wouldn't I?"

His hand covers mine. "You could have blocked it out because it was *too* traumatic. It's not unheard of. But you have to consider he may be lying. It could be a last-ditch effort to hurt you and Gabriel."

"I've thought of that. I wouldn't put lying past him either. Except he seemed so proud of the fact, like he couldn't wait to bring it up to get a reaction out of us. Like he knew I never would have told anyone."

He squeezes my hand and pulls me down over him. "Would you have told anyone?"

"Probably not. I never told anyone about the things he did. My mom knew only what she witnessed—him making me watch what he did to her. She never knew he came to my room. Oh, God..." I feel sick.

"What?"

"What if she did know and she didn't care? If it kept him off her. Was that my purpose?"

"Fuck, Reese." He pulls me tight against him. "Don't jump to conclusions. Give her the benefit of the doubt, but I do think you three need to talk. You need to clear the air. It's not a pleasant conversation, but it's obvious your mom has healing to do. This could be the catalyst that helps you and she heal in a way you couldn't before."

The idea seems horrible. Too much.

"I'll be there the whole time, holding your hand. You're finding your lion, Kitten. Don't let your father win by making you believe you're a mouse. You're the prettiest, bravest fucking lion I've ever seen."

"Cam," I breathe, fighting the lump in my throat.

He rolls us over, pinning me with his body and his gaze. "I'm serious, Reese. I've never met a braver woman than you. Sure, you have issues, we all do, but you face them every day. You don't hide. You don't pretend they don't exist. Sometimes you need time to come to terms with what's happening, but you do and you come out better for it." He kisses my nose, my eyes, my cheeks before facing me again. "I love you so fucking much. Please don't ever disappear on me again. I need you. I'm a better man when you're around."

"I'm your Wendy. I tacked your Shadow." I kid, but a part of me feels pride in knowing I help tame the anger he feels inside from his childhood, from the torment his brother brought on, by never feeling like he belonged in his family. Turns out he was partially right. He belongs here with Cap, right where he is.

"You're my fucking Wendy. Always have been. Always will be."

Sometime after Reese fell asleep, I slip out of bed, pull on a pair of sweatpants, track down to the kitchen, grab a water, and call Gabriel.

"Hey, man." The timbre in his voice has me searching out the clock. One a.m.

"Shit. I woke you. Sorry."

"No, I'm glad you called." He groans, sounding like he's getting up. "Just a sec."

The line is silent while I assume, like me, he's getting out of bed to find a place to talk without waking anyone else up.

I take a few gulps of water before eyeing the leftovers in the fridge. I could eat. I could always eat.

"Sorry. I didn't want to wake Frankie. Ox was up late, feeding like he can't get enough."

"He's your son. He probably can't."

He chuckles. "True."

I jump right in. "Listen. I know this is an awkward as fuck topic, but we need to talk about this."

"Yeah, no. I got it. Tell me."

"The things Reese told me, I think you, your mom, and Reese need to sit down and deal with this. I promised I'd be there. Things happened I don't think you're aware of. I'm no expert, so maybe a therapist needs to be brought in, but I feel like Reese has made great progress. I don't want yesterday's news messing with her or you more than it already has."

"Fuck, man. I hate that sonofabitch more and more every second that passes."

"I'm with ya. If he wasn't in jail and dying, I'd track his ass down and end his miserable life."

No joke.

"I'd do it with you." He sighs. "Hell, I'm only sorry I didn't choke the life out of him yesterday instead of punching him."

"I think our girls would have different opinions of us going to jail for murder."

"How is she?"

"She's sleeping. We talked. She told me everything. Here's the thing. She remembers everything that happened in detail—more detail than she wishes she did—from, like, when she was six years old until you kicked him out."

"Fuck. Six?"

Yeah, I worried he didn't know how young she was when it started.

I continue, "But she doesn't remember your dad raping her. In her memory, he never touched her in a sexual way. He masturbated in front of her, but he didn't touch her. He liked to *look*." I'm not telling him about his mom. "The rest of the details will need to come from Reese or your mom. I've already said too much, but I don't think Reese will mind. My point is, Reese remembers it all. Why would she forget the worst of it all—him raping her? Maybe he lied. One last dig before he kicks the bucket."

"It's possible. I wouldn't put anything past him."

"Do you remember anything about that Fourth of July?"

"I don't know, Rowdy. I've tried hard not to think about those times. He said it was before I kicked him out." He's silent for a second. "I pray for her sake he is."

"Me too. But if he's not, she's going to be fine. *We're* going to be fine. I don't give a shit what happened to her in the past as long as she's okay. I love her for who she is, not for what did or didn't happen to her as a kid." Everything she is, the fighter she is, is because of her childhood. I wouldn't wish it on her, but I love the woman she became despite it all.

"You really love her, don't you?" There's awe in his voice, and I don't take offense this time.

"She's my forever, and I'm hers. You have a problem with that?"

He laughs, "And if I did?"

"You'd be shit out of luck. I'd love your blessing, but I won't lose any sleep over it if you don't approve."

"Then I guess it's a good thing I approve. Frankie said you'd be good for Reese. I didn't see it at first, but you took good care of my Angel when I was an idiot. I shouldn't have doubted you'd take even better care of my sister."

"Don't think I'm the savior here, Gabriel. Your sister is saving me just as much as I'm saving her."

"Hear that."

"See ya in the morning?"

"Copy."

With a lighter heart, I climb in bed, wrapping around my girl like the protector I am. Only she's protecting me too.

She thinks my mom would be proud of me. I think she's right.

I also think my mom would have loved the hell out of Reese.

I already do, I hear Mom's voice. *Take care of your Wendy.*

I don't even second-guess if I'm crazy or not. What harm is there in believing my mom talks to me from the beyond?

"Always, Mom. Always." I kiss my girl's neck and drift away with a stillness I don't ever remember feeling and my heart full of love for Reese and Mom.

CHAPTER 48

AWAKE LONG ENOUGH TO SHOWER AND dress, I enter the kitchen to find it full of my family—well, Gabriel, Frankie, my sweet Maddox, and, of course, the man of my heart, Rowdy.

"Kitten." Rowdy spots me first and beats Gabriel to my side. "You're just in time. Your bother brought over a feast." He lands a soft kiss on my lips. "I was about to dig in, but was feeling bad about starting without you."

I pat his stomach, which is solid muscle. Hot. So Hot. "I would never keep you from food. I learned from Gabriel when a man's gotta eat, he's gotta eat."

"Damn straight." Gabriel pulls me into a hug. "Love you, baby girl."

Shit. My eyes prick. This sensitive side of Gabriel is not one I see often. "Love you too, big brother."

He leans back, his hands resting on my shoulders, his blue eyes tender and full of love. "We'll talk. But food first."

I get a tight hug from Frankie, whose face is full of emotions, but she only whispers, "I love you," in my ear.

I don't need more words than that. "I love you too."

I plant a wet kiss on Ox's cheek, making him squeal.

Love that sound. I could bottle it up and sell it for a mint.

Rowdy pulls me around the island to sit at his huge kitchen table. Most people would have this size table in their dining room. Not my man, who's got more money than I'd ever know what to do with. This table sits six with leaves that extend to accommodate ten. His dining room table can seat fourteen. Six can sit at his high breakfast bar. This house was made for entertaining.

"You okay?" he whispers in my ear when he sets a plate in front of me with more food on it than I could possibly eat.

"Yeah, I was just thinking your house is made for entertaining." I scan my food, deciding to dig into the egg casserole first.

His hand lands on mine. "You want to throw a party with me?"

My gaze flies to his. "A party?" I'm not one for social stuff. But maybe…

"An engagement party." His tone drops like twelve octaves, rough and dangerously sexy.

"Whose?"

His dimpled smile does crazy things to my girly parts, reminding me I may be broken in so many ways, but this man right here makes me feel whole in every way that matters.

"Yours and mine, Kitten." His gaze searches my eyes. "I told you to get ready. I'm going to ask you to marry me. Soon."

"B-but that was only two weeks ago."

"Two weeks too long as far as I'm concerned."

"You're crazy."

"Crazy about you, baby." He presses a warm kiss to the back of my hand. "Now eat."

Bossy. But I like it. I more than like it. I love it.

Having shoved as much food as I possibly can in my body, I push my plate away, sad I can't finish the last of my cinnamon roll.

Rowdy eyes it, asks me with a raised brow, and when I nod, he nags it off my plate and devours it in two bites.

Damn, that's hot.

"I have news," Gabriel says from the other side of the table once Frankie comes back from putting Ox to sleep on the living room floor. Gabriel pulls her into his lap. She curls into him like it's her favorite place to be.

I think it is, honestly.

Rowdy snatches my hand. "What news?"

Gabriel locks on me. "It wasn't you."

From his expression alone, I know exactly what he's talking about. My heart knocks on my chest like it's trying to run away from this conversation as much as I want to. "Explain."

He nods, glances at Rowdy before coming back to me. His hand flexes and squeezes Frankie. She pats his chest. He needs her for this conversation, just like I need Rowdy.

"Do you remember our neighbor Lola?" Gabriel asks.

"Yeah, isn't she the one who used to come over a lot, especially at night?" I snap and lean forward. "She's the one I caught you—"

Gabriel clears his throat. "Yeah, that one."

Frankie smirks at her husband. "She caught you fucking Lola, huh?"

"Stop. That's beside the point." He garners her eyes. "It's you, Angel. Always you."

She swats his chest. "I know, Big Man. Just giving you a hard time."

"I'll give you a har—"

Her hand covers his mouth. "Focus. Tell Reese what you found out."

He kisses her hand before he places it over his heart. His eyes find me again. "That Fourth of July, you and I went to watch fireworks. We snuck out because Dad was in a bad way. We didn't want to stick around, and we really wanted to see the fireworks over the strip. Do you remember?"

"Ohmygod! I do." I jump to my feet and point at him as the memories come flooding back. "We didn't go home. We stayed at..." I snap my fingers. "God, what was his name?"

"Tim or Tom. I can't remember. But yeah, we stayed at his house." Gabriel motions for me to sit.

But I can't. I'm too excited.

I wasn't home.

Rowdy steps in front of me, cupping my cheek. "What are you saying?"

Tears threaten when I see the hope in his eyes. He said he didn't mind not being my first, but I can see he really, really hopes he is, especially in this context. "I wasn't home that night. My dad didn't..."

"He raped Lola," Gabriel interjects.

Rowdy spins, pulling me around so we're both facing my brother.

"Oh, God." My elation crumbles. "She slept in my bed that night."

Gabriel's sad nod is confirmation enough, but he continues, "I called Mom this morning. Lola came over that night, asking if she could stay. Her mom was working, and she always hated to stay home alone. Mom let her in but told her to stay in your room because Dad was drunk. She wanted her out of sight. She got tired and climbed in your bed."

"No." I sway on my feet as the reality hits me. "Dad wasn't lying. He just didn't know it wasn't me."

Before I crumple to the floor, Rowdy sweeps me into his arms and sits, holding me in his lap. "It wasn't you," he murmurs into my neck.

"No. It was Lola."

My eyes meet Gabriel's. "That's why she never came over anymore. I thought her feelings got hurt because you wouldn't be her boyfriend."

The sadness in his eyes mounts. "I *was* her boyfriend. She stopped talking to me. I didn't know why. She never told me about Dad, but I do remember Mom telling me she stayed over but had left before we got home."

"We need to reach out to her," I offer. We need to make amends even if Dad never does.

"Already on it." He pats Frankie's ass before he stands, placing her on her feet. "I'm going to go see her this afternoon. She still lives in the house she grew up in with her husband and kids."

"D-do you want me to come?" Please say *no*.

"Nah, I got it. I'll let you know how it goes." He steps around the table, towering over me. "I know what you're thinking. It's bad, but don't take on *his* guilt. You're both victims of our fuck of a father. Don't make it worse by believing you had any control over what happened to Lola."

He fingers my chin, and his eyes well up. "It might be shitty of me, but I'm relieved it wasn't you. Someday, when you're ready—" His eyes skate over my head to Rowdy's and back. "We should talk to Mom. Get it out in the open, then put it in our past where it belongs." He kisses my forehead. "He's all but gone, Ree. You don't have anything to fear anymore. You're free."

CHAPTER 49

"**I**S IT WRONG THAT I FEEL HAPPY?" REESE TURNS to face me as soon as her family is out the door.

"No, baby." I link our fingers and pull her to the kitchen. "You can feel bad for Lola and feel happy for yourself at the same time. One doesn't exclude the other. It doesn't make you a bad person for being happy your father didn't rape you."

Father. Rape. Those are words I hope to never have to say again in the same sentence.

I lift her by the waist and set her on the counter, needing to be eye to eye, or closer, at least. "You okay?" I brush her hair behind her ear. "Putting the Lola guilt aside—because it's *not* your fault, are you alright?"

She swooshes her lips from side to side and then smiles softly. "Yeah, I feel lighter." Her forehead touches mine when she leans forward. "I feel like I could conquer the world with you by my side." She ghosts her lips across mine. "You make me a better me."

I love hearing that.

Pulling back, she grips the back of my neck. "Shadow?"

"Yeah, Kitten?"

"Do you think we could… You know?" As the blush creeps up her cheeks, my eyes follow.

I didn't touch her last night other than chaste kisses and holding her tight in my arms.

I need my woman, and it sounds like she needs me too. But I need her words. I graze her heated cheeks with the tips of my fingers. "Tell me what you need."

"That's the easiest question ever." She grips my shirt, pulling me flush against her. "I need you."

Her eyes match the heat in mine. "Where do you need me?"

"Get me naked, and I'll tell you." The lion has come out to play.

She squeaks in delight when I throw her over my shoulder and bound up the stairs to our room.

Our room. I like that idea of her sharing my space more and more. "Kitten, I think it's time you moved in with me."

"What?" She laughs when I unceremoniously plop her on the bed.

"You heard me."

When her mouth opens and closes without a reply, I continue, "Do you want to eat dinner together or alone?"

She frowns. "Together."

I unbutton her jean shorts and slide them down her silky legs, taking a second to admire the creature before me. Kissing the apex of her thighs over her panties, she sighs into my touch.

"Do you want to sleep with me or alone?" I continue as I pull her t-shirt over her head.

"Always with you."

That's my girl.

"Then why not live together? I want you here. Or we can live in your apartment. I don't really care. I just want to be where you are. Where you're most comfortable."

She unsnaps her bra and lets it fall down her arms before tossing it aside.

There are my beauties. My girls. I stop myself from cupping them, licking and sucking her nipples until she tells me that's what she needs.

"I love your house." She pulls me down by the hem of my shirt. But I stop, arms braced on either side of her.

"Then move in with me, baby. I know what I want, and it's you forever. If you won't marry me now, then move in with me. We can get married next month."

She giggles. "I almost think you're serious."

I edge closer, only a few inches from her face. "Never been more serious, Reese. I love you. Don't make me beg." 'Cause I'm not above it. Not when it comes to her and our future.

"Okay, I'll think about it. Then we'll address the other stuff later."

"Think hard. Think fast." She's unleashed the beast that loves her. There's no stopping me now.

I slip off her panties. I drop my sweats and shirt, leaving my boxier briefs on.

She quirks a brow, eyeing my crotch. "Nuh uh, if I'm naked, so are you."

Yes, Cocky wakes up and cheers.

Shut it. This is about her.

Of course, come here, my little kitten. Let Cocky make it all better.

He's a lost cause.

Just like me.

She points to her lips. "I need you here."

"Done." I crawl over her, pulling her up the bed to make room for me between her legs.

Slowly I skim my mouth across hers, once, twice, three times. My girl and her impatient tongue sweeps across my lips, nibbling, enticing me to take it further—to take her further.

I'm going to take her everywhere.

Locking my hand in her hair at the base of her neck, I feed her my tongue, and she sucks it like it's her dying breath.

There's no slow and easy with my lion. She's zero to nympho in a second flat.

We kiss until I'm rock hard between her sweet thighs and she's rocking against me, begging me to fill her.

"Tell me," I husk, needing her words, per permission.

"I need you here." She flexes her hips. "I need your monster cock."

Fuck. That mouth of hers.

When I slide home, her heat surrounds me, squeezing like she never wants to let me go. "Don't ever let me go, Kitten." I pull out and thrust forward again.

She arches and groans. "Never. You're stuck with me, Shadow. Today. Tomorrow. Always."

"Damn straight."

I'm gonna put a ring on that perfect hand of hers soon. Make it official.

She better get ready. It can't be soon enough for me.

For now, I swivel my hips and relish the tremor her body releases.

So fucking sexy.

My Kitten purrs and laps at my tongue like sweet milk, teasing me till I'm driving harder, deeper.

Her legs, tight around my hips, squeeze as she arches into me, taking all of me.

I'm so fucking hard, ready to blow, yet not ready for this feeling to end.

It's not only physical. When the heart and soul are involved, it's so much more.

It's everything.

I thought I saw forever in the eyes of an angel, but she wasn't mine for the keeping.

Turns out it was the lion pretending to be a mouse, who's brave enough to be my Kitten and tame my beast by tacking my darkness to my heel.

I'm her Shadow.

She's my forever Wendy.

My forever girl.

My Kitten.

My Reese.

THE END

EPILOGUE

"K ITTEN," MY SHADOW RASPS ACROSS MY neck.

"Hmm," is about all I can manage as I blink awake and groan at the sun.

He has the nerve to chuckle. I don't know how he's such a morning person. He sleeps less than I do and works his body hard.

Hard.

The thought of his *hard* body has me giving up sleep to blink up at the hunk looming over me.

"There she is." His dimpled smile gives me ideas of how I wouldn't mind him waking me up with his mouth on me—every morning—for the rest of my life. "Darlin', don't go looking at me like a lion looking for a feast. We've things to do." He kisses my brow. "Now, up."

"God, I love when you go all Texan." I rouse and roll over in silent protest.

He kneads my ass. "I promise to show you all of my *Texas* later." He sweeps me up in his arms, kissing the yelp from my lips, and carries me to the bathroom, plopping my naked ass on the counter. "But right now, I need you dressed. We have a house full of men, and I have no intention of them seeing what's mine, looking like a sex-starved Kitten."

"I wouldn't be starved if you'd feed me," I pout.

His smirk is as shameless as my begging for his attention. "Yeah?" He palms the side of my face, brushing my hair back.

I'm a mess, I'm sure.

Though the heat in his eyes says otherwise. "You need me, baby?"

"Always." I grip his t-shirt, pulling him closer and closer still.

"Fuck. I love hearing that." He parts my legs, stepping between, hands under my knees, pulling me to the edge.

"Wait. A house full of men?"

"Yeah, Kitten." His sex-graveled voice tingles along my skin seconds before his lips land on my neck, and he slips his fingers inside me. "Fuck. Love you naked in my bed, but love finding you wet for me in the morning even more."

Damn, my dirty man. His mouth, his gaze, and his wicked fingers rile me up as if he's been at it for hours, but it's only been seconds, and I could come with just a little more...

He pushes down his track pants, his monster cock popping free, hard and beautiful. "Fuck, love your eyes on me too." He pulls his shirt off, and before I can get my fill, he latches his mouth to mine, sinking inside me in one long thrust.

Gripping the back of my neck, he leans in, eyes locked on me. His other hand grips my hip as he grinds against me, then pulls out to sink back in. Slow and steady. "We've got company, Kitten. I promise to take my time next time."

His tempo increases.

I can hardly focus on his words for all the talking his body is doing.

"Company?" I manage between moaning pants.

His head falls back. He pumps faster. "Jesus, I could live here."

Ohmygod. I want that. The sight of him filling me, his cock coated in my arousal. I buck, arching. I'm done, and we just got started.

"Fuck. I feel you." He releases my neck and grabs my hips, thrusting harder, his eyes back on mine. "You're gonna come for me, aren't you, Kitten?"

Yes. Yes, I am. But I can't speak. My head thrown back, my palms hit the mirror and countertop. "Ohmygod," I scream in my head, but my ears ring on a guttural moan that mixes with his praise.

"So, fucking beautiful."

D-O-N-E. Call for the check. I'm ready to pay up. "Cam," I whimper, so frigging needy.

My man eats it up. "Squeeze me, Lion. Make me come, baby. Make me yours."

"Ohmygod!" I roar as my body trembles, waves of pleasure exploding in all directions, shattering me into a million shards of hopeless love and insatiable desire for My Shadow. My Pussy Whisperer.

"Fuuuuuck!" he slams into me on a growl and bathes my insides with his Texas-sized cum, pulsing and pulsing until he's spent, his eyes never leaving mine.

"Love you, Kitten."

"Hmmlufyoutoo," I mumble, panting to catch my breath.

He chuckles and kisses my nose, still buried deep and holding tight. "The guys and me packed your apartment up. They're here with all your stuff." He smirks at my surprise. "Need you dressed so you can tell me where you want everything."

Oh my God. This man. "You didn't?"

"I did. You said *yes*." Not a hint of remorse to be found.

I laugh and swat at his chest. "That was *yesterday*." Like, not even twelve hours ago.

"Told ya I'm not one for waiting. You said you'd move in with me. It's nearly done. You just need to come give directions."

"You're insane."

All humor disappears as he cups my cheek. "I'm crazy about you, Kitten. I need you here. Want you here." He kisses my forehead before pressing his to mine. "Don't pretend you don't love that I made it happen."

I can't. Nor can I hide my body's reaction to his dominance and strength.

"Fuck, you keep squeezing me. I'm gonna have to fuck my thanks into you until you can't walk. I don't think your brother would appreciate that."

Gabriel's here? Fuck, all the guys are here.

I groan and push on his chest. "You're going to have to release me if you want me to get dressed."

He slow pumps a few times, taking both our breaths away. "I don't want to, but—" He pulls out. We both groan at the separation.

He cleans us up before helping me to my feet, kisses my head, and softly pats my butt. "See you downstairs. Your bother made breakfast." Pulling his shirt back on, he stops at the door before turning back. "Cinnamon rolls." He smirks knowingly.

"I'll hurry!" I'm nearly giddy at the thought of Gabriel's cinnamon rolls.

But nothing can compare to Rowdy taking charge and moving my ass into his home. I hate packing. I grumbled about it for a week before I agreed to move in.

My step has a new bounce to it as I dress and take in the sight of his home with new eyes as I make my way downstairs. This is now mine too.

Two sets of blue eyes hit me as I enter the kitchen. One is blue like mine—Gabriel's. The other is lighter in shade but no less intense—my Shadow's.

"Hey, Reese." Landry's smiling face greets me before I can take another step, offering a glass of orange juice. "Mimosa?"

"Oh, yeah. Sure." I take a drink and cough, nearly choking on the ratio of champagne to juice. "Jesus," I bite once I catch my breath. "Like a little orange juice with your champagne, do you?" Not that it's horrible. I just wasn't prepared.

His cheeks pinken adorably, which I'm sure he'd hate for me to mention. "Bad?" He thrusts a new one in my hand. "Try this one. I'm pretty sure it's a better mix."

Cautiously taking another sip, I smile and force it down. "Yep, better." I pat his arm and move toward Rowdy, who's been watching me like a hawk.

"Note to self, don't put Landry in charge of drinks," I whisper into my man's chest as he pulls me in.

Chuckling, Rowdy sets my drink on the counter. "Yeah, he's a little heavy-handed."

I turn in his arms, taking in all the guys coming to help move me in. Murmured conversations fill the room, punctuated with bouts of laughter between stuffing their faces.

"You okay, Kitten?" His warm breath teases my neck before his lips find their destination below my ear.

Sinking into his embrace, I nuzzle his chest, closing my eyes. "Never better."

He nuzzles me right back, another kiss and a squeeze. "Let's get you some food."

Side by side, we fill our plates with more food than I can possibly eat, knowing he'll gladly finish off what I can't.

First things first, a bite of cinnamon roll sprinkled with bits of crispy bacon. I moan so loud, too many eyes land on me as Rowdy squeezes my knee. "Jesus, Kitten. It's food, not sex."

My eyes, impossibly wide, zoom in on him and his smirking lips as chew the sexy food in my mouth, taking extra time to lick my lips slow nough to make him moan. I lean in, whispering. "You were saying?"

His warm lips land on mine before he mumbles, "Don't make me laim you in front of all these Neanderthals." His brow quirks. "I'm not bove it. Keep that in mind."

I still the full-body shudder with another bite, keeping my

enjoyment to myself, my head down, avoiding any uncomfortable looks in our direction.

Crazy alphaholes.

When Landry sits across from me, he hands me another glass. "It's just orange juice this time." He sheepishly smiles, his head turned to the side, like he's hiding his face. But I notice the welt on his cheek and the cut next to his eye I somehow missed before.

"Cowboy, what happened?" My eyes dart to Rowdy and back to Landry.

Did they have another sparring incident? Rowdy didn't mention it.

Landry shrugs. "My roommate," is all he says, clearly annoyed and maybe a little embarrassed.

"His roommate thinks because Cowboy's a fighter, it's okay to sneak up on him and hit him, try to catch him off guard."

Heat simmers in my blood. "That's... ohmygod! Are you serious?"

Landry shrugs again. "It's no biggie."

"You need to move," Jess pipes up.

"Told you my couch is always open," Jonah throws out.

"You can have my place," I offer.

Cowboy's head pops up, his pale green eyes hopeful and unsure. "Really?"

Rowdy's arm dips around my back, his lips pressing to my temple. "My Lion," he whispers.

I tingle everywhere at his praise but ignore my body's response. This is important. "Of course." I fork my scrambled eggs. "When we finish here, we're all going to your place, pack you up." I point my fork at him. "I'm going to have some words with your *roommate*. Then you're moving into my place. My rent is paid up for three more months. It's yours." I glance around for boxes but can't see around the guys. "You can have all my furniture and kitchen stuff too. There's nothing special, but it's yours if you want it."

Landry's eyes widen, and he sits up, looking between Rowdy and me. "Is she serious?" he asks Rowdy.

My Shadow leans closer, the side of his body pressed to mine. "Damn straight." Rowdy looks to Gabriel and the rest of the guys. "Eat up, we've a bit more moving to do today."

"Damn. Th-thanks." Cowboy nods, his eyes on his plate. He wasn't expecting an outpouring of support.

I reach across the table, stretching to touch his hand. "That's what you do for family." I wink and yelp when Rowdy hauls my butt back in my chair, mumbling, "No touching."

That gets a laugh from everyone, and Landry's shoulders relax. He's here to help me. He thinks I wouldn't do the same for him?

As I climb in Rowdy's truck to head to Landry's place, Rowdy squeezes my ass. "Gonna fuck you so good when we get home." His lips press to mine. "You giving him your place..." he trails off. "Means so much, Kitten."

I capture his face when he pulls back. "Ride or die, Shadow."

He smiles and tortures my lips for a quick minute with his. "Ride, Kitten. Always ride."

ONE MONTH LATER

"What are we doing here?" We park at the private airfield I've been to once before when we flew home from his mom's funeral. "Are we going to Texas?"

Is he looking to make peace with his dad and brother?

The last month with Rowdy has been heavenly. Dad died a few days after I moved in. As much as I feared the man in life, his death was nothing more than a blip in my day. Rowdy and Gabriel keep asking if I'm okay. Yet, no matter how often I reassure them that I am, they keep asking.

I'm fine. Seriously. Fine.

My Shadow set me free with his love and protectiveness that makes me weak in the knees but also gives me room to spread my wings I thought had been clipped by my dad. Turns out, I've got beautiful wings.

I'm more lion than mouse nowadays. A fact that seems to turn my man on more times than not.

But *he* still hasn't spoken to his dad more than a few short conversations, avoiding all things about Cap and his mom making *him*. He's not ready. I've no doubt he'll tackle it when he is. Or maybe he is…

My eyes follow him as he rounds the front of the car, opens my door, and unbuckles my seatbelt like I can't do it for myself. It's an alpha thing, to be sure.

"Kitten." He clasps my hands, emotions dancing in his shining blue eyes. "I warned you in Texas that you'd unleashed the beast. I'm not a patient man when it comes to you. I want it all—yesterday."

He's not lying. We got together. He started talking about babies, warning me I needed to get ready for his proposal, moving me in with no notice after I said *yes*. His will is as big as the state he comes from, but not nearly as big as his love.

I press my hand over his beating chest. "I love your beast, your monster cock. You're my dark Shadow, my pussy whisperer, my demon slayer—"

"Kitten." His forehead falls to mine. "I'm trying to do something here. You're killing me with your words. I might have to fuck you right here."

284

Yes, please.

He chuckles, seeing the answer in my eyes. He glances at the plane. His *family's* private plane sitting a few car lengths away. He's nervous.

"What is it?"

"I'm not..." he pauses, licking his lips, and starts again, "I love you, Reese. I want forever with you. I want babies. I want grandbabies. I want to get a dog and a cat. I want to snuggle on the couch with you. I want to hold you in my arms as we watch the sun set and cuddle you close when the sun rises. I want you in my every *tomorrow*. And when my time comes, I want to be deep inside you when I die. You're my ride or die, Kitten. Marry me. Put me out of my misery and let me lock this dream down."

"Holy..." I gasp for air. "Did you? Are you?"

"Yes, dammit, baby. Marry me. Let me whisk you away." He looks at the plane over his shoulder and back. "It's ready to go. *We're* ready to go. All you have to do is say *yes*."

"That's all?" My shock morphs into excitement. Saying *yes* to Rowdy, in all things, whether he asked or not, has never been that hard.

Yes, to him being my first kiss.

Yes, to him being my first intimate connection, physically, mentally, soulfully.

Yes, to giving him my heart.

Yes, to giving him my darkness to mix with his, amazingly making us both lighter and the world around us brighter.

Yes, to giving him all my tomorrows.

The concern on his face softens. He caresses my cheek. "Yeah, Kitten, just promise to be mine. Let me be yours. Love my dark ass. Be my Wendy. Together, we'll pin our shadows and live in the light. Ride with me, baby. Say *yes*."

"You've always been my *ride*, Rowdy. Always my dark slayer. You saw a lion when I was only a mouse. This lion needs her beast." I nearly topple us when I launch at him. "Ride."

He chuffs and nudges my nose. "Say it."

"Yes, Cameron. I'll marry you."

"Fuck, yes." He extracts me from the cab, spinning us around in circles. "She said yes!" he yells, punching the air.

Whoops and hollers ring out of nowhere.

His arms tighten as he turns, bringing me face to face with all the people I love—he loves—sticking their heads through the open door of the plane. Still cheering.

"Ring, dumbass," comes from my lovable brother.

"Shit." Rowdy drops me to my feet and kneels, puppy-dog eyes focused on me as he digs in his pocket. "I guess I should have done this in the first place."

I brush my fingers over his hair. "You did just fine, Shadow." I motion to the box in his hand. "That for me?"

"Everything I have is for you, Kitten." He pops open the box, taking out the ring before I can see it. "I love you, baby. Tell me again. Will you marry me?"

If crying is for suckers, I'm pure sucker. Tears pool and spill over as I nod. "Yes. Always yes."

"Love hearing that." He stands and slips a sparkling diamond ring on my finger. "I may ask you again when I'm deep inside you." The heat in his eyes promises he intends to do just that.

My girly parts scream *yes, please*. Best plan ever. "Promise."

"Promise." His mouth crashes over mine, making even more promises I can't wait for him to fulfill.

Feet stamping draws a rumble from his chest. "I should have thought this through." His head presses to mine. "Soon."

"Let me see!" Frankie pulls me from his grasp. "It's huge!" she screams, then nearly tackles me in a hug. "I'm so happy for you both."

Me too. "Thank you."

More hugs from my mom, who's surprisingly misty-eyed, Cap, Landry, Jonah, AJ, Jess, Walker, and finally Gabriel, who passes Ox off to Frankie.

He hugs me tight, murmuring, "I'm so happy for you, baby girl. You've come so far. I'm so fucking proud of you."

Yeah, if I wasn't already crying, I would be now. Praise from Gabriel is high on my list of life goals. "Same," is all I can manage. He's come far, too, from his gruff asshole ways to loving the woman who made him a better man, an amazing father, and by the love in Frankie's eyes, a worthy husband.

"Alright. Alright. Enough." Rowdy pulls me into his side. "Get back onboard. We'll be there in a minute."

The guys grab our bags from his truck. Apparently, my man does have everything taken care of.

My eyes fall to the solitaire on my left ring finger. It's sparkling bright like my future. And it is huge. A large round diamond sits on top of a pavé diamond platinum band. "It's beautiful," I whisper in awe something so breathtaking is mine.

"You like it?" He tips my chin, swipes at my cheeks.

"What's not to love? It's incredible. You did good, Shadow."

His eyes flash with heat. "I'll do whatever it takes to get praise from my girl." He settles his hands on my lower back, holding me close. "We're having a destination wedding, Kitten. You up for it?"

"I'm up for anything if I'm with you."

"Damn." His smile pops his sexy-as-hell dimples. "Love that. It's you and me, Reese."

"Where are we going?"

"It's a surprise."

I never cared much for surprises.

Too much anxiety.

Too many unknowns.

But, like most things concerning my Shadow, he makes me want what I never thought I would or could have.

"Ride or die, Kitten." He links our hands as we start for the airstairs of the jet.

"Ride, Shadow. Always ride."

WHAT'S NEXT?

CAPTAIN's story is next.

Captain Jimmy Durant will be challenged in ways he never saw coming. Can he conquer his past and hers in order to secure the love of the woman he shouldn't want but can't seem to resist?

Add CAPTAIN to your TBR.
dmckdavis.com/all-books/series/black-ops-mma-series/cap

Join my mailing list to stay up to date on CAPTAIN's release details, other book news, promotions, and all the happenings.

BONUS SCENE

Want more?

Join my mailing list to receive exclusive BONUS Scenes for Rowdy and Reese.

There might even be a little Gabriel bonus!

Get Bonus Scenes here: dl.bookfunnel.com/b2klnmvxbi

DID YOU ENJOY THIS BOOK?

This is a dream for me to be able to share my love of writing with you. If you liked my story, please consider leaving a review on the retailer's site where you purchased this book and on Goodreads.

Personal recommendations to your friends and loved ones are a great compliment too. Please share, follow, join my newsletter, and help spread the word—let everyone know how much you loved Rowdy and Reese's story.

AUTHOR'S NOTE

I fell in love with Rowdy in No Mercy. I knew there was more to him than the good ole Texas boy with a dark streak. I couldn't wait to find out. I also knew I needed to see Reese's story through, to help her find her HEA. I had no idea where Rowdy and Reese would take me when I started writing their story. I had an inkling, but they opened up and took me further than I thought possible. I pray you love their story and will continue to read more about them and the other amazing guys—and women—I have planned for the Black Ops MMA series.

Subscribe to my newsletter to stay up to date!

On a serious note, Like Rowdy lost his mom, I lost my sister to ovarian cancer. Though the story in this book is different from my sister's, the struggle is the same. Many times ovarian cancer goes undiagnosed until it's too late to survive. Please listen to your body. If you feel you aren't being heard, find a doctor that will take your symptoms seriously. Insist on further testing. Your yearly PAP will not find ovarian cancer; it's only for cervical cancer.

Stay healthy. Love yourself enough to fight for your health. *hugs*

ACKNOWLEDGMENTS

Thank you to my husband and kids who support me endlessly. They are the first to see my teasers and book covers, both good and bad before they are finalized. They support me in my struggle to stay focused on writing instead of reading (cause a good book is just too hard to resist!). They are the encouragement I need when I fear I totally suck at this writing thing.

A mommy-special hug for my kids who tell everyone they can that their mommy is an author. They are so proud, it's hard not to accept that this is my calling. I pray they find theirs way sooner than I did.

Thank you to all the amazing authors and their books that serve as an endless distraction and source of inspiration. If I didn't love to read, I never would have found the courage to write my own stories.

To the authoring community, bloggers, bookstagrammers, and readers who support me and my books—thank you, thank you, thank you.

To my editors, Tamara and Krista, thank you for making me look like I know what I'm doing—you know the truth.

To my Divas (Facebook Reading Group), thank you for waiting patiently for ROWDY. I hope he's so much more than you thought. I love our group, thank you for being a part of it. Now, go shout your love for ROWDY from the rooftops!

Keep reading. I'll keep writing.

Thank you for taking this journey with me.
XOXO, Dana

ABOUT THE AUTHOR

D.M. Davis is a Contemporary and New Adult Romance Author.

She is a Texas native, wife, and mother. Her background is Project Management, technical writing, and application development. D.M. has been a lifelong reader and wrote poetry in her early life, but has found her true passion in writing about love and the intricate relationships between men and women.

She writes of broken hearts and second chances, of dreamers looking for more than they have and daring to reach for it.

D.M. believes it is never too late to make a change in your own life, to become the person you always wanted to be, but were afraid you were not worth the effort.

You are worth it. Take a chance on you. You never know what's possible if you don't try. Believe in yourself as you believe in others, and see what life has to offer.

Please visit her website, dmckdavis.com, for more details, and keep in touch by signing up for her newsletter, and joining her on Facebook Reader Group, Twitter, and Instagram.

JOIN MY READER GROUP

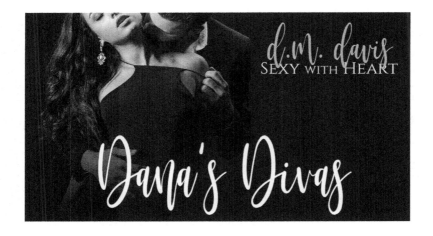

www.facebook.com/groups/dmdavisreadergroup

STALK ME

Visit www.dmckdavis.com for more details about my books.

Keep in touch by signing up for my Newsletter.

Connect on social media:
Facebook: www.facebook.com/dmdavisauthor
Instagram: www.instagram.com/dmdavisauthor
Twitter: twitter.com/dmdavisauthor
Reader's Group: www.facebook.com/groups/dmdavisreadergroup

Follow me:
BookBub: www.bookbub.com/authors/d-m-davis
Goodreads: www.goodreads.com/dmckdavis

d.m. davis
SEXY WITH HEART
CONTEMPORARY & NEW ADULT ROMANCE AUTHOR

ADDITIONAL BOOKS BY
D.M. DAVIS

Until You Series
Book 1 - Until You Set Me Free
Book 2 - Until You Are Mine
Book 3 - Until You Say I Do
Book 4 - Until You Believe

Finding Grace Series
Book 1 - The Road to Redemption
Book 2 - The Price of Atonement

Black Ops MMA Series
Book 1 - No Mercy
Book 2 - Rowdy
Book 3 - Captain

Standalones
Warm Me Softly

www.dmckdavis.com

Printed in Great Britain
by Amazon

30633249R00179